A DARK AND STORMY NIGHT

The new 'Dorothy Martin' mystery

When Dorothy Martin and her husband, retired Chief Constable Alan Nesbitt, are invited to a country house weekend, they expect nothing more explosive than the Guy Fawkes fireworks. Having read every Agatha Christie ever written, Dorothy should have known better. Rendered isolated and incommunicado by the storm, Dorothy and Alan nevertheless manage to work out what in the world has been happening at ancient Branston Abbey

A DARK AND STORMY NIGHT

A Dorothy Martin Mystery

Jeanne M. Dams

Severn House Large Print
London & New York

This first large print edition published 2012
in Great Britain and the USA by
SEVERN HOUSE PUBLISHERS LTD of
9-15 High Street, Sutton, Surrey, SM1 1DF.
First world regular print edition published 2010 by
Severn House Publishers Ltd., London and New York.

British Library Cataloguing in Publication Data

Dams, Jeanne M.
  A dark and stormy night. -- (The Dorothy Martin mysteries)
  1. Martin, Dorothy (Fictitious character)--Fiction.
  2. Women private investigators--England--Fiction.
  3. Americans--England--Fiction. 4. Detective and mystery
  stories. 5. Large type books.
  I. Title II. Series
  813.5'4-dc23

  ISBN-13: 978-0-7278-9827-2

Severn House Publishers support The Forest Stewardship
Council [FSC], the leading international forest certification
organisation. All our titles that are printed on Greenpeace-
approved FSC-certified paper carry the FSC logo.

MIX
Paper from
responsible sources
FSC® C018575

Printed and bound in Great Britain by the
MPG Books Group, Bodmin, Cornwall.

The photographer in this book, Ed Walinski, walked in more-or-less uninvited when I thought my cast of characters was complete. He quickly took on many of the endearing traits of the real photographer in my life, my husband (also Polish, also, oddly enough, named Ed).

My husband died, most unexpectedly, while this book was being written. I never had the chance to tell him I was 'putting him in it'. I trust he knows now. So – Ed, my dearest love, this one's for you.

CAST OF CHARACTERS

Dorothy Martin, American, sixty-some-thing, once widowed, now living in England and married to:

Alan Nesbit, English, retired chief constable for county of Belleshire

Lynn and Tom Anderson, American expats living in London, good friends of Dorothy and Alan

Jim and Joyce Moynihan, American expats living in converted thirteenth-century abbey, which is still called Branston Abbey

Mr and Mrs Bates, English, servants to the Moynihans

Ed Walinski, American photographer and writer

Julie and Dave Harris, American. Julie is Joyce Moynihan's sister

Michael Leonev (Mike Leonard), English, dancer

Laurence Upshawe, English, former owner of Branston Abbey, retired physician

Paul Leatherbury, English, the vicar of Branston village

Pat Heseltine, English, female, a solicitor from Branston village

ONE

Anyone who has ever read a Traditional English Mystery ought to remember that a country house weekend can be, as Pogo used to say, fraught. I think I've read every TEM ever written, so I should have known better, but obviously my memory was taking a holiday that afternoon when Lynn called. And even weeks later, when we were nearly at our destination, my doubts were of another nature. 'I don't know, Alan. I'm not so sure this was a good idea.'

My husband, fully occupied with negotiating the narrow, winding lanes of rural Kent, quirked an eyebrow without taking his eyes off the road.

'I can't think what possessed me to say we'd go. We don't even *know* these people. And an old house is bound to be freezing cold in this awful weather, and there'll be stairs everywhere, and my knees aren't really healed yet, and anything could happen to the cats while we're gone, and...' Running out of objections, I heaved a histrionic sigh.

Alan is used to my moods. 'We're committed now. And you'll enjoy yourself. You know you love old houses. Not to mention the fireworks for Bonfire Night – Guy Fawkes and all that, you know. Lynn wouldn't have wangled the invitation for us if she hadn't thought the people, *and* the house, were reliable.'

Our good friend Lynn Anderson, an American expat like me, had called from London a month or so ago. 'Dorothy, my *dear*! Tom and I have been travelling and just heard about your operation. How *are* you! How are the knees?'

I'd flexed them cautiously, one at a time. 'Better every day, and they'd be better still if the blasted rain would only stop. I wouldn't say I'd want to run a marathon just yet, but then I never did.' My titanium knees were three months old, and functioning better than I'd dared hope. 'You wouldn't believe how spry I am, compared to when you saw me last. Speaking of which, when are we going to see the two of you again?'

'That's why I called, actually. Tom and I have an Idea.'

I could hear the capital letter, even on the phone. 'What sort of idea?' I asked cautiously. The last time I'd involved myself in one of the Andersons' Ideas, before Alan and I were married, I'd ended up in Scotland with a lot of quarrelsome people and a dead body.

'How would you and Alan like to come with us for a country house weekend?'

I chuckled. 'As in huntin' and shootin' and musical beds? I thought all that went out with P.G. Wodehouse. And haven't all the traditional country houses been turned into

10

B-and-Bs these days, or given to the National Trust, or something?'

'A lot of them have been, what with death duties and the cost of living and the impossibility of staffing those enormous places. But a few are still in private hands, mostly rich foreigners, and one of them happens to belong to some Americans we know, business associates of Tom's. We ran into them in Antibes last week. They bought this huge old pile from someone who had moved to Australia or some place like that, and they invited us to come for a weekend next month. It's to be over Bonfire Night, and they'll have fireworks and all. It's a good-sized house party, I gather, with some other people staying over, so the minute I heard about your surgery I thought you'd be needing some R and R and called the Moynihans to ask if I could bring two more. They said "the more the merrier".'

I'd hemmed and hawed, but after Lynn assured me the house, Branston Abbey, was old and interesting, and that the present owners had installed central heating and an elevator, I'd said that Alan and I would go. But the rain, which had kept up for a solid month, had kept my knees aching and my spirits at low ebb.

The road straightened and widened a bit. Alan looked over at me and grinned. 'This *was* your idea, you know.'

'Actually it was Lynn's. I should have known better. How do we know we'll even

11

like these people?'

'Knees still hurting?' said Alan, responding to the real cause of my ill temper.

'Oh, not much, just stiff and a bit cranky. Like me. Sorry, Alan. I know I pushed you into this, and I expect I'll have a wonderful time once we— great God in heaven, can that possibly be the house?' I pushed back the broad brim of my hat so I could see better.

Through a stand of trees that had lost some of their leaves, I could see, on a small rise, a remarkable building. From where we were it looked like a miniature castle combined with the Houses of Parliament and a touch of Her Majesty's Prison at Wormwood Scrubs.

Alan pulled the car over as far as he could to the side of the narrow lane and leaned over me, knocking my hat off, to look out my window. 'Well,' he said at last. 'Well.'

'Lynn said it was interesting,' I said faintly.

Alan just shook his head and put the car in gear.

There was another fifteen minutes of twisting lane before we turned into the private drive. It wound for about a mile through a lovely autumn-shaded wood and across a pretty stone bridge, and finally ended up on the gravel forecourt of the house. Up close it wasn't quite so intimidating. For one thing, a lot of the details were hidden around the many odd angles.

Alan took our luggage out of the boot and stood frankly staring at the house. 'I would say,' he said, 'that this is a genuine abbey, late

1400s, that has been treated in rather cavalier fashion over the centuries. Looks like an encyclopedia of architectural styles, from the Late Perpendicular of the original abbey, to Tudor, through Georgian to a few bits of Victorian Gothick, with a hint of Brighton Pavilion thrown in for good measure.'

'A bad case of architectural indigestion, in fact,' I replied rather sourly. 'Reminds me of Brocklesby Hall.' The Hall, a big house near Sherebury, was built in early Victorian times in imitation of a number of styles. It is undeniably impressive, in a nightmarish sort of way.

'Oh, no, no comparison at all. That monstrosity was built all of a piece. It was meant to look like that, God help us. This is organic – it grew, as the needs of the owners changed over the centuries. Good taste here, terrible taste there, but it's genuine. Do you know, Dorothy, I think I'm going to enjoy this weekend. If other amusements pall, we can always go on a treasure hunt for the best and worst bits. I'd swear that gargoyle up there is original fourteenth century, for example.'

'You're showing off. Ten to one you looked it up before we started.' I craned my neck, but my interest in gargoyles is limited, and the wind was picking up. 'I'm sure it's everything you say, but I'm cold and my hat's going to blow off. Can we admire the house from inside, do you think?'

At that moment a door opened and Lynn, effervescent as always, burst out with another woman, middle-aged and running a little, comfortably, to fat. She was dressed in a tweed skirt, a cashmere sweater, and pearls, and the fact that they were a little too new and a little too flawless marked her instantly as our American hostess.

Lynn performed introductions. 'Dorothy, this is Joyce Moynihan. Joyce, Dorothy Martin and Alan Nesbitt.'

'*So* glad to meet you,' said Joyce with a warm smile. 'Lynn's told me all about you both. Dorothy, I love your hat. I wish I looked good in them. Now, dear, you mustn't try the front steps. They're one of our big-deal show pieces, but I'll bet this weather is playing hell with your knees. I had one of mine done a while back, so I know. Anyway, you must be freezing in this awful wind, so if you'll just come with me, there's an entrance to what used to be the servants' hall, and an elevator a few steps beyond. Not exactly the most elegant way to enter the house, but once you've had a nice hot bath you'll be better able to tackle stairs and we'll give you the grand tour. OK?'

Her accent was pure Midwest, speech I hadn't heard in quite a while, and her welcome glowed with that all-embracing cordiality that you get from the nicest Americans. 'OK!' I said, my good spirits restored. I followed her and Lynn into the house, Alan bringing up the rear with our suitcases.

Joyce left us at the elevator. 'I've been running around today like the proverbial chicken, and right now there's a crisis in the kitchen I have to deal with, so I hope you don't mind – Lynn knows the way. As soon as you're rested, come down and have some tea. No special time, just whenever you're ready. See you later.' With a cheerful wave, she was off at a trot in the direction of what I supposed was the kitchen.

'OK, Lynn, you've been here a day already. Clue us in to the set-up,' I said the instant the elevator door closed. 'Why is Madame dealing with kitchen crises? Don't tell me the cook has left in some sort of a huff.'

'My dear, you're *still* fixated back in 1930s novels. Cooks don't leave in huffs nowadays. They're paid enormous salaries and demand exactly the equipment they want, and cook exactly what they please. Most of them are caterers, actually, just coming in for special events. This one is a permanent fixture, lives here with her husband, who's a sort of general factotum – butler cum chauffeur cum handyman. And she's not old and fat and comfortable. Quite the contrary, in fact. Young, *très chic*, cooks divine nouvelle cuisine. Her husband is a hunk – tall, fair, great bones, classic good looks.' Lynn rolled her eyes in a mock swoon as the elevator came to a stop on the second floor, or in English terminology the first floor, the one above the ground floor. She led us down the hall, up a step, to the right, then down a step and around a corner.

'We shall need a trail of breadcrumbs,' said

Alan mildly. 'Do you mean to tell me one man looks after this entire sprawling house? Because I won't believe you.'

'Mr Bates – note the *Mister*, please, he doesn't like to be called Bates or whatever his first name is. And he doesn't look after the house at all, except for maintenance jobs, plumbing and electric and so on. There's a cleaning service that comes in for the dusting and scrubbing and all that, and a lawn and garden service for the grounds. Mr Bates supervises – in grand fashion, I might add.'

'And voilà, the servant problem is solved,' I commented, slightly out of breath. 'It must cost a small fortune.'

'Probably, but Jim Moynihan still has a biggish fortune, so it's all right. And here we are, finally. I had Joyce put you in one of the Tudor bedrooms. I thought you'd like sleeping where Queen Elizabeth might very well have slept, once upon a very long time ago.' She opened the door.

'QE One, that would be— oh!' My first sight of the room took my breath away.

This wasn't fake Tudor, 'stockbroker Tudor' as the English sneeringly used to call it. This was the real thing, a room created or at least redecorated when the first Elizabeth sat on the throne. The walls were panelled in carved oak, the linenfold panelling so often seen in the stately homes I had visited. Everything else was carved, too – the fireplace in stone, the ceiling in elaborate plasterwork. The casement windows had tiny diamond panes, and

16

the floor was made of wide oak planks darkened to near-black over the centuries.

'Wow!' I said brilliantly.

Lynn grinned. 'There are no words, are there? And this,' she said, opening a concealed door in one corner, 'is not the priest's hole or the powder closet – though it certainly may once have been one or the other – but your very own bathroom. Joyce and Jim remodelled them all – after *months* of delays getting planning permission, I might add – and all done in the very latest American-style plumbing. Yours has a whirlpool bath, *with* steps to get into it.'

I sank into a chair by the fire, which was blazing away. 'I've fallen into a dream of paradise. Don't anybody wake me up.'

'Told you you'd like it,' said Lynn triumphantly, and left us to get settled.

I walked over to the window. Alan came to stand beside me, and we looked out on to one of the most beautiful landscapes I've ever seen. A broad stone terrace next to the house gave way to a sloping lawn, the kind of lawn I'd never seen anywhere but in England – lush, green, and perfectly smooth. I remembered reading, somewhere, someone's recipe for the perfect lawn: You plant grass, and then mow and roll it for four hundred years.

The rain had stopped for a bit, mercifully, and the clouds had thinned enough to let colours assert themselves. To one side, flower gardens were still brilliant with chrysanthemums and asters, though the roses were getting sparse. In the middle distance, perhaps a hundred yards from the house, shrubs and a pond gave way to taller trees, oak and ash and some I didn't recognize. A path wound through the plantings down to a silver river on which a few swans floated, pale and graceful, their feathers ruffled now and then by the rising wind.

'"This scepter'd isle",' my husband quoted softly, '"...this other Eden, demi-paradise ... this precious stone set in the silver sea..."'

'Mmm. Or, as we crass Americans have been known to put it, this is what God would do if He had money. No wonder the Moynihans love it here. The view alone is worth however many million pounds they paid for the place. And Joyce is a perfect dear. You were right, Alan – as is your irritating habit. I'm going to have a good time here.'

I took a long, luxurious bath in the wonderful tub. I hadn't been able to get in and out of a regular tub in ages, what with the bad knees, so I was especially grateful for the steps.

'You're going to turn to a prune, love,' Alan said finally. 'Besides, tea awaits, and I'm feeling rather peckish.'

So I reluctantly got out, dressed, and found my cane, and we set out in search of a staircase to take us down to tea.

Alan has an excellent bump of direction, which is a good thing, because I have virtually none. Give me a map and I can find anything. Without it I'm hopeless. I paused in the hallway. 'This way?' I said tentatively, point-ing to the left.

'No, to the right, I'd think. We didn't pass any stairs on our way from the lift, so it must be on down the corridor.' And of course he was right – again. The next little jog brought us to a somewhat more modern part of the house and a grand staircase down to the entrance hall. 'Georgian?' I ventured, looking at pillars and pilasters, marble and polished stone.

'Well done, my dear! Basically Georgian, modified a trifle so as to blend in with the rest of the house. I imagine this part was redone when a particularly prosperous owner began to entertain largely, and wanted to show off. The place must have an interesting history, though the Internet didn't mention much.'

'Aha! You *did* look it up! Well, I'll just bet our hosts are dying to give us all the details. I tell everybody about our house, and it's not at all in the same league.' Monkswell Lodge, the house where Alan and I live in Shurebury, was built in the early 1600s as a gatehouse for the man who bought what used to be Shurebury Abbey before Henry VIII dissolved the mon-asteries. It's a wonderful house and we love it, but it's always been a modest dwelling. Bran-ston Abbey was a showplace.

The stairs were broad and shallow, easy even for my not-quite-perfect knees. They were feeling better, anyway, after my bath. The house was, true to Lynn's word, filled with a gentle warmth that spoke of efficient central heating, and when we followed the sound of voices to what was probably called the drawing room, we found the fire lit and the temperature almost too warm. Several people were gathered in the room, chatting and drinking various beverages.

'There you are,' called Joyce. 'Found your way, I see. I keep meaning to have maps of the house printed up, but I keep forgetting. It really isn't complicated, anyway, once you figure out the basic plan. So sit and have some tea – or whatever you'd prefer – and let me introduce everybody.'

Evidently the kitchen crisis had been solved. The meal laid out on several trays was an elaborate, Ritz-style spread of the kind I didn't know anyone ever did in private homes these days. Alan and I sat down next to Lynn and Tom, and I looked dubiously at the array of sandwiches and scones and cakes. 'It's all right, D.,' said Tom, *sotto voce*. 'Dinner isn't till eight. Eat all you want.'

Well, I wasn't going to do that. I engage in a perpetual struggle with my love of carbo-hydrates. Besides, I'd lost some weight after my surgery, and I didn't want to gain it all back. But I accepted a cup of tea from my hostess – 'Yes, milk and two lumps, please' – and took a couple of tiny sandwiches and a scone. Lunch was a distant memory, and I was truly hungry.

'Now, let me introduce you to everyone,' said Joyce, when we'd eaten and drunk our fill. 'You know Tom and Lynn. And this is my

20

husband, Jim. Jim, this is Dorothy Martin and her husband Alan Nesbitt. We'll all have to behave ourselves this weekend; Alan's a retired police VIP.'

My husband, who was a chief constable for many years, was used to this kind of remark and took it with equanimity. Jim Moynihan smiled and hoisted a teacup in salute, as another, very graceful and good-looking man approached.

'And I, my dear lady, can*not* wait another moment to meet you. Michael Leonev, at your service.' He pronounced it Mee-kha-ail, but his accent reminded me of the Beatles and his hair was blond. I must have looked sceptical, because he took my hand, kissed it, and grinned. 'Between you and me, luv, Mike Leonard from Liverpool, but all the best dancers are Russian, so—'

'Royal Ballet,' I said, a faint memory surfacing. '*Swan Lake*. I saw the reviews, though I didn't get to town to see a performance.'

'Yes, well, next time I hope to do Siegfried, but Von Rothbart isn't a bad role. More acting than dancing, actually, and usually done by someone *much* older.' Mike, or Michael, frowned, which was unwise. Lines appeared that made me wonder if he was really too young to play the evil sorcerer, but then he gave me a winsome smile and looked like a boy again.

Joyce deftly disengaged us and led us to the two men sitting in front of the fire, who rose as we approached. The smaller one extended his hand. 'Ed Walinski. Glad to meet you.'

'You're American!' I said, pleased. He looked the part, too. He was dressed like most of the men in slacks and a sweater, but the clothes looked more Brooks Brothers than Savile Row. Of modest height, he nevertheless looked as if he could hold his own against most challengers. At the moment, though, his round face was creased in a smile.

'Of Polish descent, with a touch of Irish and some German somewhere. And that's about as American as they come!'

'Ed's going to do a book about this house,' said Joyce with obvious pride. 'We're very excited, because no one's ever done a proper history of the place, and certainly not an illustrated one.'

'Oh, how stupid of me!' I slapped my forehead. 'You're *that* Walinski – the photographer! I've admired your work for years, and your narratives are just as good as your pictures. Are you going to take pictures of the fireworks?'

'Sure! Fireworks over that roofline – wow! And I can afford to waste shots – I brought tons of film.'

'You're not a convert to digital, then?'

'Yeah, for some things. Snapshots, Bertha-in-front-of-the-Parthenon, that kind of junk. And I use it for test shots, to make absolutely sure the picture's set up right. I'll use it for the preliminary house shots a lot, because that's going to be tricky, particularly those gargoyles. I may have to spend the whole weekend just figuring out how to get up there for a good shot.'

'No, you won't,' said Joyce firmly. 'Aside from the pyrotechnics, you're going to spend the weekend having a good time and getting to know the house a little. And Mr Upshawe, here, is going to help. Dorothy and Alan, meet Laurence Upshawe, the former owner of Branston Abbey.'

Upshawe, tall, thin, graying at the temples and looking almost too much like an English landowner, gravely shook our hands.

'Oh, my, how could you ever bear to sell such a wonderful place?' I gushed, and then could have kicked myself. If the man had had to part with his ancestral home to pay death duties or something awful like that...

But he smiled. 'You mustn't think it was a frightful sacrifice, or anything of that sort. Actually, you know, I didn't grow up here, and I was never terribly fond of the house. Branston Abbey belonged to my father's cousin. My father inherited it because his cousin's son died quite young, and Father was the next in line. The estate was entailed then, you see, and Father was thrilled when it came to him. He had visited the place often as a child, and he loved every gable and gargoyle with quite an unreasonable passion. But entail's been done away with, so when my father left the house to me, I was free to do with it as I liked.'

'And what you liked was to sell it to the Moynihans and go to – Australia, was it?'

'New Zealand,' he said with the patient air of one who grows tired of explaining the differences between two widely separated countries. 'But in point of fact, I sold Branston Abbey—'

He was interrupted when the door to the room was flung open and a couple marched in, puffing and stamping and complaining noisily.

The woman wore several layers of sweaters. The top one looked expensive, as did her wool slacks, but the net effect was lumpy and shapeless. The man was dressed in a red plaid flannel shirt over a rather dirty yellow sweatshirt, over a black turtleneck, with goodness knows what underneath that. His pants were liberally splashed with mud, as were his L.L. Bean boots. He had in one corner of his mouth a large cigar from which issued a cloud of foul smoke.

'Holy shit, tea you're drinking!' he roared, removing the cigar for a moment. 'That stuff's for old grannies and pansies. Gimme some Scotch, Jim. It's cold enough out there to freeze the balls off a brass monkey. Why anybody lives in this godforsaken country's beyond me, let alone in a draughty old wreck like this. Cheers, everybody.' He drank down at a gulp half the stiff drink Jim had silently handed him, while the rest of us sat dumb.

Joyce cleared her throat. 'Dorothy and Alan, my sister Julie Harrison and her husband Dave.'

TWO

The party broke up quickly after that. Alan left with the photographer, after getting my assurance that I'd much rather the two of them toured the house without me. The dancer, whose eyebrows had risen nearly into his hair, did an elaborate stage shrug and performed a neat series of pirouettes out the door. Upshawe murmured something in-audible and drifted away, and I had only a moment to wish I'd gone with Alan and the photographer, after all, when Tom took me on one arm and Lynn by the other. 'The ladies are tired, Joyce. I'm sure you'll excuse us.'

'I'm not in the least tired,' I said when we were out of there. 'But thanks for rescuing me. I couldn't figure out how to escape tact-fully.'

Lynn sighed. 'Tact isn't really necessary anymore. Joyce is used to Dave and the effect he has on civilized people.'

'And she's thoroughly fed up with him,' added Tom. 'Are you up to the stairs, D., or do you want to use the lift? I warn you, you have to go back through the drawing room to get there.'

'The stairs, by all means. They're not at all steep, and up is always easier than down, and I wouldn't go back in there if the alternative was climbing to the top of the Statue of Liberty. Is he always like that, or is he drunk?'

'Not drunk yet, probably, but he soon will be,' said Tom. 'And yes, he's always like that, drunk or sober. I met him something over twenty-four hours ago, and the acquaintance has already been about a week too long. And his wife is just as bad.'

'Oh?' I said. 'She didn't say a word in there.'

'She will,' said Lynn, and I had seldom heard her sound so cool. 'She's a whiner, not a blowhard. She'll be launched by now on a steady trickle of complaint about weak tea, dry sandwiches, the wrong kind of jam tarts, and hard chairs. I'm sure she'll throw in a few jabs about the village, too. The essential message will be, if it's English, it's inferior. Dave agrees, but louder.'

'So why did they come to visit, if they hate it so much?' I had reached the top of the stairs and could stop concentrating on making my knees do what they were supposed to.

'We haven't figured that out yet,' said Tom. 'You still need an arm?'

I shook my head.

'We thought at first,' said Lynn, 'that they came to sponge on Joyce and Jim. But Dave keeps telling everyone how rich he is, how he could afford to retire young because he was smarter in business than everybody else. So either he's lying or there's some other reason

they're here. I don't know how Joyce and Jim
put up with them.'

'Jim isn't going to, much longer,' said Tom.
'I overheard him—' he looked around and
lowered his voice, 'talking to Joyce earlier this
afternoon, and he's about had it. Says they
can stay through the weekend, because of the
big doings on the fifth, but after that he's
kicking them out. I think he'll do it, too. I got
the idea, from the tone of the conversation,
that the two sisters have never hit it off, and
one reason the Moynihans moved to England
was to get away from the Harrisons. So I
suspect he'll happily give them their walking
papers.'

We had reached our bedroom. 'Let's go in
and have some privacy,' I suggested. 'I guess
there aren't servants listening in every corner,
like in the old books, but I'd feel more comfortable behind a good solid door.'

We settled in front of the fire and Tom
found some sherry in a cupboard. 'Good
hosts,' he said, pouring us each a glass. 'They
think of everything for a guest's comfort.'

'Dorothy, it's pathetic,' said Lynn. 'Joyce
and Jim are so proud of their house. They've
put so much time and effort into fixing it up
– and money, my word, tons of money. Everything was to look authentic, but at the same
time be modern and labour-saving. They
went so far as to take out a perfectly good
Aga, because it was an old solid-fuel one
Joyce wasn't sure she could make work right,
and put in a state-of-the-art electric one – but

specially designed to look just like the old ones. They wanted this first big party to be perfect. I gather they've been planning every detail for weeks. And then a couple of days ago sister Julie barged in with her impossible husband and went about alienating everybody in the house. Joyce was in a rage this morning over Dave's criticisms of the house. He doesn't know a thing about the subject, but that doesn't keep him from holding forth. And Julie saw Mike yesterday making eyes at Laurence—'

'I forget who Laurence is.'

'Upshawe, who used to own the place. Such a nice, easy-going man, and absolutely brilliant – he's a retired surgeon. And good-looking, even if he's not very young. Anyway, Julie saw them, and made the most awful remarks. I won't even repeat them, they're so foul, but let's just say they represented her views about gays, foreigners, dancers, and the English in general. And Laurence, poor dear, isn't in the least interested, but he's kind, and didn't tell Mike to go peddle his papers. But Julie went straight to Joyce to tell her all about it.'

'I'll bet she just laughed. She looks like the unflappable sort.'

'Well, she didn't take it seriously – not in one sense. But she was upset all the same, because of Julie's sheer malice. Julie actually tried to get Joyce to kick Mike out of the house for "flagrantly immoral behaviour".'

'When all he did was look at the man?'

'That's all. And half of that might have been

28

acting. Mike's a trifle ... dramatic.'

Some of my sherry went down the wrong way. 'Yes, I'd noticed,' I said when I could speak again. 'A necessity in his profession, I'd have thought. And anyway, who cares, nowadays? Well, it's all going to make for an uncomfortable weekend. I wonder if we—'

'Oh, Dorothy, *don't* think of leaving! For one thing, Tom and I need someone to talk to if everyone else stops speaking to anyone. For another, Joyce is almost at her wits' end, and you and Alan can be counted on to behave yourselves. Besides, everyone is interesting except the Horrible Harrisons.'

'I'd say Dave Harrison was interesting,' said Tom thoughtfully. 'In the sense of the old Chinese curse.'

'It's a strange mixture, certainly,' I said, relaxing as the sherry took hold. 'For an English country-house weekend, there's a remarkable shortage of Brits. Let's see.' I began counting on my fingers. 'Two, four, six, seven Americans – no, eight, I forgot Walinski, the famous photographer – and just three Englishmen, the dancer – Mike – and Laurence Upshawe, and Alan. Oh, and the Bateses.'

Alan came in just then. 'Someone taking my name in vain? I'll have one of those, Tom, if you're pouring.'

Tom poured Alan's sherry and then went to put more wood on the fire, and I stretched my legs out to unkink my knees. 'So did you enjoy your tour of the house, love? You

29

weren't very long about it.'

Alan took a sip of his sherry. 'The tour was curtailed by Mr Harrison, whom we encountered in the oldest part of the house, the only remaining part of the original Abbey. He imparted a great deal of misinformation about the building materials, style, and construction methods of the period, contrasting them unfavourably to the ... er ... dwellings he was responsible for building before he retired from business. I believe he called them "manufactured homes". It seems an odd term.'

I shook my head in disbelief. 'They're houses built in trailer factories, using many of the same materials and methods. They aren't bad-looking, some of them, but they tend to crumple like paper in bad storms like tornadoes and hurricanes. The mind boggles at the idea of comparing them with a building that's stood for – what? – seven hundred years.'

'That, in rather more colourful language, was what Walinski said. The disagreement became rather heated, whereupon Walinski called Harrison a damned idiot and punched him in the nose.' Alan tossed a handful of cashews into his mouth.

'He *hit* him?' I said in disbelief. 'What did you do?'

'The man didn't seem to be in need of medical attention. So I shook Walinski's hand – gently, in case he had injured it on the idiot's face – and found my way back here.'

Lynn broke into song. '"Hooray and hal-

lelujah, you had it comin' to ya",' she carol-
led. 'I mean he had it coming, but it doesn't
rhyme that way. Anyway–' she raised her glass
– 'here's to Ed Walinski and his strong right
hand.'

Alan grinned. 'I might have done it myself if
Walinski hadn't got his licks in first. More
sherry, anyone?'

After Lynn and Tom left, I put my feet up for
a few minutes with ice-packs on the knees,
which were protesting a little about recent
activity. But I was restless, and it still wasn't
anywhere near time to get ready for dinner.
'Do you suppose,' I said to Alan, who was
absorbed in *The Times* crossword puzzle, 'that
it's safe to wander around and explore a little?
I really, really don't want to run into either of
the Horrible Harrisons.'

'He's probably retired with aspirin and a
case of the sulks. That blow to the nose was
painful, and when he fell he hit his head
against an oak door jamb. As to his wife, I
couldn't say.'

'I think I'll chance it. Coming with me?'

'Thanks, I'll finish this, if you can cope on
your own. What on earth can they mean by
"He touches with a pot, pleadingly"?'

I thought a minute. 'How many letters?'

'Ten, beginning with a P., I think.'

'Eureka! I finally got one. Panhandler.'

'Hmm. It fits, but what's a panhandler
when it's at home?'

'A beggar. An American term. Pot equals

pan. Touch equals handle, and also ask for money, and the whole thing means pleading. Ta-da!'

I'm no good at the English 'cryptic' crosswords, so I was ridiculously pleased to have solved a clue Alan couldn't. He grinned and saluted as I picked up my cane and left the room.

I walked, carefully, down the beautiful Georgian staircase and turned right, since I had seen nothing of that side of the house, the oldest part, if my vague idea of the layout was correct. Leading out of the entrance hall was a lovely panelled door, with an elaborate cornice over it and a massive bronze door knob. I turned it, pushed the door back, and stepped into a different world.

This had surely been part of the cloister of the old abbey. It was now an enclosed hallway, dimly lit. Arched windows on my left looked out on the gloomy November afternoon. Darkness had fallen early, as it is wont to do in the autumn in these northern latitudes. (The coming of short days still catches me by surprise in my adopted country. Because of England's mild climate, Americans tend to forget that all of the UK lies farther north than any point of the Lower Forty-Eight.)

By the light of a lamp outside, I could see through the diamond panes the shadows of trees and bushes, tossed fitfully back and forth by the increasing wind. Above me, the fan-vaulted roof stretched ahead perhaps forty feet to another doorway, this one pure Gothic, with a pointed arch.

On my right, small but sturdy buttresses supported a wall pierced by two similar arched doorways. The door in the nearer one was slightly ajar, and through it I heard voices.

The male voice was loud and bombastic. I would have recognized Dave Harrison anywhere. I hadn't heard Julie speak, but I assumed the petulant female voice was hers. Alan had guessed wrong. They were up and about, and in foul moods, and their bitter quarrel was getting closer to the door.

I loathe embarrassing encounters, but all the escape routes were too far away for a person with healing knees, so I took the coward's way out. Sliding behind one of the buttresses to wait in the shadows until they had left, I hoped devoutly that they wouldn't glance my way.

'...why we had to come to this pile of garbage in the first place! There isn't even a TV in our room. And the food!'

They were in the doorway now, their shadows bulking large in the light from the room.

'Well, we didn't come to watch TV,' said Dave, 'so just shut up about it. And you could stand to lose a few pounds, babe.'

'Me!' Julie's voice rose to nearly a shriek. 'What about that beer belly of yours? And you put away Jim's Scotch just fine. With no ice, yet. God, I hate this place.'

'Keep your voice down! Do you want your

sister to hear? You came, sweet cakes, for a loving family visit, and don't you forget it. And we're staying till we get what we want. And till I get even with that dumb Polack!' The last came out in a vicious whisper, as they moved past me up the hallway toward the main house.

Once I heard the connecting door open and close, I breathed again and moved on down the corridor. But as I explored the old abbey rooms, I wondered mightily. The Harrisons could have bickered and complained anywhere. Why had they chosen Branston Abbey?

THREE

I had been unsure about the clothes I would need for the weekend. 'Are we going to have to dress for dinner?' I had asked Alan, and he'd been mildly amused.

'Only as formally as you'd dress for a meal at a good restaurant. I shall certainly not take my dress suit.'

So it was a 'little black dress' I wore that first night, with a pair of small diamond earrings Alan had given me one Christmas, and a string of pearls. I regretfully left my frivolous black cocktail hat in its box. I may be the last hat wearer in the UK, barring the Queen, but there are limits to what one can get by with in a private house.

We gathered in the drawing room for a predinner drink, and my hopes that the Harrisons would absent themselves were immediately dashed. There they were, standing by the fireplace. Julie's dress was of gorgeous dark green satin, well-cut, but not quite concealing those extra pounds Dave had mentioned. Still, she looked quite nice, and would have looked nicer if her face had not been set in a scowl. Dave, with a large Band-Aid across his nose and two black eyes beginning to develop, was waving a glass of Scotch around as he lectured Jim Moynihan on something or other. Plainly the drink was not his first since he left the cloister. His speech was slurred and his discourse rambling enough to be incomprehensible.

'You said he hit his head,' I said to Alan in an undertone. 'Should he be drinking?'

'Probably not. Are you going to tell him so?'

I rolled my eyes. 'Someone should. But no, I'm not brave enough. Besides, if he passes out he'll be a lot less trouble for everybody.'

'The sentiment does not do you credit, love. I agree with it wholeheartedly.' He handed me a glass of sherry from a tray, and took one himself.

The slurred voice rose higher. 'Be damned if I will! Came to this fuckin' place and I'm not goin' home till I get—'

His wife's shrill voice rose over his. 'Shut

up, Dave! You're drunk and sounding like an ass!' She removed the glass from his hand and threw its contents into his face.

He turned to her, his face alarmingly red, his mouth opening and closing rather like a fish. Jim took a large handkerchief from his pocket and handed it to Dave. 'You'd better mop up, pal. Then we'll send a tray up to your room. Julie, you'll look after him, I'm sure.'

Julie looked rebellious for a moment, then shrugged. 'He'll pass out in a minute or two, anyway. And be better company, at that, than this mouldy bunch.' She stalked out of the room.

'Mr Bates, would you help Mr Harrison to his room, please?' Joyce took over smoothly. 'I'm afraid he's not feeling very well. And if Mrs Bates could prepare a dinner tray for them?'

It seemed as if the entire room breathed a collective sigh of relief as the butler seized Dave in a firm grip and 'helped' him out of the room. Certainly Joyce took a deep breath before she smiled and addressed us all.

'Sorry about that,' she said. 'Dave drinks a little more than he should, from time to time, but I'm sure he'll be fine. Now some of you haven't met our other dinner guests. Dorothy, Alan, this is the vicar, Paul Leatherbury. And this lovely lady is, believe it or not, our village solicitor, Pat Heseltine. Pat, meet Dorothy Martin and her husband Alan Nesbitt.'

Pat Heseltine resembled my idea of an English solicitor approximately as a peacock resembles a mouse. Perhaps fifty, she still had a perfect figure and smooth, creamy skin. She was poured into a little gold number that must have set her back hundreds and hundreds of pounds. It set off her flaming red hair beautifully. She wore no jewellery, and didn't need it.

My dear husband's eyes widened. He took her hand and held it, in my opinion, just a moment too long.

'Good evening,' I said, with a smile that, despite my best efforts, was a little stiff. I trust my husband completely, but this woman could tempt a celibate saint.

'Don't worry, luv,' said the vision in a voice of whiskey and honey, winking at me. 'They all do it – doesn't mean a thing.'

I responded with a meaningless smile and turned with some polite remark to the vicar. We were interrupted by a strident, discordant clamour from outside the room. I nearly dropped my sherry glass, and all conversation stopped.

Joyce looked mischievous. 'The dinner gong, ladies and gentlemen. I believe dinner is served!'

There were no empty places at the table. Evidently the efficient Mr Bates had removed those assigned to the Horrible Harrisons. I did a quick count as we walked into the room and nudged Alan. 'Eleven of us at table,' I whispered. 'There would have been thirteen with the Harrisons. Isn't there some kind of

English superstition about that?'

'Then it's a good thing they're not here. For more than one reason.' He grinned at me before we were separated by our hostess.

In the old days husbands and wives were never allowed to sit together at table. The Moynihans were sticking to tradition, so I found myself, quite happily, between Ed Walinski and Mr Upshawe, with Lynn, the vicar, and Mike Leonard across from us, and the Andersons, Pat Heseltine, and Alan scattered about on either side. I wasn't altogether happy that Pat and Alan were seated next to each other, but the woman had to sit somewhere, I supposed. Given our uneven numbers, there were too many men sitting next to each other. Jim Moynihan sat at the head of the table and Joyce at the foot.

For a little while I had no attention to spare for anything except my dinner. If I'd thought about it at all, I had expected decent food, but not like this. We started with a consommé julienne, none of whose ingredients had ever seen a tin. The fish was a morsel of perfectly cooked sole Bonne Femme, followed by chicken in some sort of creamy cheese sauce, accompanied by perfectly cooked vegetables. I had got to the salad course before I became interested in any conversation that didn't involve passing the butter or accepting a little more wine.

'I know almost nothing about the history of this amazing house,' I said to Mr Upshawe, 'except that it was obviously once an abbey.

Did your family live in it for a long time?'

'Well, my father was the first one in my immediate family to live here,' he said, 'and his cousin's family not for very long, in relative terms. They bought the house in ... 1843, I think it was – when the Branston line ran out. Now the Branstons *had* lived here for centuries, literally. Henry VIII gave the original Lord Branston the Abbey property, and incidentally the title, for "services rendered to the crown". Nobody knows exactly what those services were, but I gather tradition tended to believe they were of a salacious nature. Old Henry was a bit of a Jack the Lad, as I expect you know.'

'What's a "Jack the Lad"?' asked the photographer.

'Oh, sorry. Let's see ... a rip, a roué, a rogue.'

'A Royal Rascal,' Ed contributed.

'In short,' I said, 'a man who does exactly as he pleases. Which would fit Henry, all right. Although all I really know about him, come to think of it, is that he had six wives and murdered two of them.'

'Please! Beheaded them. *Judicial* murder.'

'Oh, yes. I stand corrected. It does make a tremendous difference. Especially to the victim.'

'Who should have tried to keep her head,' Ed put in. I was beginning to warm to this man.

Laurence Upshawe laughed and held up his hands. 'I'm not here to defend Henry. He would need far better counsel for the defence than I. And how did we get started on him anyway?'

'The house,' I prompted. 'He gave it to Lord Branston for services rendered.'

'Oh, yes. In fifteen-something. And it remained in Branston hands for three-hundred-odd years, until there were no Branstons left and my great-great – I forget how many greats – uncle bought it. By that time it was pretty much the hodgepodge you see now, except for the Gothick and Regency touches, which were added by the first couple of Upshawe generations.'

'For which,' put in Joyce Moynihan, 'they are either blessed or cursed, depending on whether you prefer your architecture pure or fun.'

'"Pure" was past praying for at that point,' said Upshawe with a chuckle. 'The old chaps who built the place wouldn't have known it by the time my family took possession.'

'The monks didn't approve of such monkey shines?' That was Ed. We all groaned appreciatively.

'The resident ghosts apparently took it in their stride,' said Upshawe amiably. 'If ghosts can be said to have a stride.'

'In their glide,' suggested Ed.

'Exactly. But the County didn't like us, ghosts to the contrary notwithstanding. We were called the "Upstarts" for years, my father told me, and even now I think there's some feeling in the village that we're incomers. In any case, the Vicar could probably tell you a great deal more about the history of the house than I can.'

'Then the vicar's the man I need,' said Ed. He looked across the table, but the vicar was deep in conversation with Jim Moynihan. 'Tomorrow,' said Ed.

'I want to know about the ghosts.' I turned back to Upshawe.

'Well, again, I don't actually know much about them. No one's ever seen them, so far as I know. Certainly I never have. I will admit there's an odd feeling about some of the rooms occasionally, especially in the cloisters and on the second floor. That is, the third floor to you Americans. We never used those bedrooms much, for some reason. And there used to be a story in the village about strange noises, but I don't know that I give much credence to it. I'm something of an agnostic when it comes to ghosts.'

'But surely, in a house this old, where people have given birth, and died, and lived happily and unhappily for centuries, there would be plenty of reasons for restless spirits, or at least an atmosphere,' I argued. 'I'm inclined to believe in ghosts. In England, anyway. Not in America so much. We're too young a country to have really old houses. Partly because we tear them down before they have a chance to turn into something amazing like this place.'

'"Amazing" is the word, certainly. Some would call the whole place a travesty,' said

Upshawe apologetically.

'Interesting, though. You gotta admit there's nothing boring about this heap,' said Ed, serious for a change. 'I can't wait to get started with the pictures tomorrow. Something different, everywhere you look.'

Alan left off his conversation with the delectable Pat to say, 'Dorothy and I may go with you, if you've no objection. We thought of going on a sort of treasure hunt for architectural oddities. I agree with you about the house, Ed, but it wouldn't appeal to a purist.'

'Nor,' said Mike, the dancer, with a malicious smile, 'to our American visitors the Hor— the Harrisons. One does hope their views do not prevail. I heard Mr Harrison say, this afternoon, that the entire structure – "the whole damned place" was the charming way he put it – should be levelled, and a modern resort hotel built on the site. The better, one gathers, to attract tourists, despoil the countryside, ruin the village, and make millions.'

'My brother-in-law's opinions,' said Joyce calmly, 'are often somewhat ... peculiar. Jim and I usually pay no attention. This is, in any case, a listed building, and therefore untouchable. You cannot imagine the hoops we had to jump through just to get planning permission to modernize the bathrooms, and add a few. More wine, anyone?'

We were nearly all suppressing yawns by the time we'd finished an amazing orange soufflé and refused (most of us) Stilton and biscuits. Those who cared for after-dinner coffee had it in front of the drawing room fire, with drinks available for those who wanted a nightcap.

The miserable weather had returned, with rain falling in torrents. I turned to the vicar, who sipped his pale whiskey and soda in the armchair next to me. 'You're going to get terribly wet going home, if this keeps up.'

'I've accepted Mrs Moynihan's kind invitation to stay the night,' he said placidly, 'as, I believe, has Miss Heseltine. In the words of the immortal W.C. Fields, "It ain't a fit night out for man nor beast".' His English-accented version of the famous line set me into such a fit of laughter that I developed hiccups and had to be slapped on the back.

No one lingered long. It was a night for snuggling down under the covers, and besides, 'We're all afraid the Horrible Harrisons will show up again,' said Lynn in an undertone as she and Tom left the drawing room with Alan and me.

I yawned. 'I think Dave's out for the count, but you're right. The mere possibility casts a pall. Let's just hope his hangover is bad enough to keep him in bed late tomorrow.'

'Amen,' said Alan piously, and we trooped upstairs to bed.

FOUR

I woke much later, feeling far too warm. The fire in the fireplace had died out long ago, but the duvet felt stifling.

Drat it all, I hadn't had this bad a hot flash in years! This was unexpected, and unpleasant. I didn't want to freeze Alan, but I had to have some relief. I crept out of bed, went to the window, and pushed it open.

The wind rushed in, billowing the curtains and knocking over a small lamp on the table by the window. No wonder it was hot in the room! It wasn't me – the rain had stopped, and the outside temperature must have risen twenty degrees since we'd gone to bed.

Odd.

I got back into bed, pushed the duvet away, and curled up covered only by the sheet.

Sleep wouldn't come. The wind seemed to strengthen every minute. It howled around the corners of the old house, battered against the walls, flung itself down the chimney. The house creaked and cracked, and so did the trees outside.

I have never liked wind storms. I can enjoy a good thunderstorm, but high winds make me nervous. I put the pillow over my head, but I could still hear the wind, could still feel it, too, blowing against the sheet, chilly, chillier...

For heaven's sake! Now it was cold again – and raining again. Impatiently, I got out of bed again and forced the window closed.

'Can't sleep, love?' Alan sounded pretty wide awake, too.

'It's the wind. You know I hate wind. And I was too warm, but now I'm cold. The weather is behaving very oddly. It's ... unsettling.'

'Put in your ear plugs and come back to bed. This is a strong old house. It can withstand the wind. There, now, isn't that better?' He pulled me close, as if to shut out the wind and the storm. I relaxed and after a time I slept.

What was that?' I sat straight up in bed, my heart pounding furiously. My dream of gunshots was still clinging to my consciousness. The loudest dream-shot had wakened me. In my dream it had been a cannon. But the bangs and booms continued into wakefulness, sounding loudly over the howls of the wind.

I didn't know what time it was, though it felt like the middle of the night. The room was pitch dark, but I could hear that Alan was awake, too, and getting out of bed.

'Alan, what's happening? What's all the noise?'

'It's the wind, blowing things about. Devil of a wind, I've never known one like it. That last crash was something hitting the house, something big. I'm going down to see.'

'Not and leave me here by myself, you're not!' I fumbled for my slippers as I reached for the bedside lamp.

Nothing happened. The switch clicked uselessly.

I have a recurring nightmare about waking in the middle of the night and trying, frantically, to turn on a light. I try every lamp, every wall switch. There is no light.

My nightmare had just come true. 'Alan, wait!' I shouted in panic. 'Alan!'

'I'm here.' His voice, raised over the tumult, was calm, and calming. 'I'm looking for the torch. Do you remember where you put it?'

I tried to remember what I'd done with the flashlight we always take along when we travel. 'I think it's on the table on your side of the bed. Or in the drawer, maybe.'

An interval. The wind howled, and when it let up for a second or two, we could hear voices.

Light, blessed light. Alan pointed the flashlight at me and nearly blinded me. 'Sorry, love. I wasn't sure where you were. Let's go down.'

I put on my robe and followed him out the door.

Other lights were dancing in the corridor. Ed Walinski and Mike Leonard came out of their rooms. Tom and Lynn followed closely in their wake, with Alan behind them while I brought up the rear.

46

Our host and hostess, sketchily clothed, were already in the hall. 'It's the oak!' Joyce screamed over the wind. 'We think it fell on the house!'

They rushed to the door into the old abbey, and we followed, while other guests arrived in various states of undress, carrying flashlights or candles.

The Moynihans were having trouble pushing open the door to the old cloister. Tom and Alan helped them shove and kick and shoulder it part-way open, and then shone their lights on what lay beyond.

Branches and leaves. Broken glass, splintered wood, dust, water.

The wind rushed through the open door, bringing rain and debris with it, extinguishing the candles. Jim Moynihan withstood it for a moment, then moved away and let the door slam shut. He took his wife in his arms. Tears were streaming down her face.

'It's OK, sweetie,' Jim said gently. 'Lucky it happened there and not in the main house. Nobody's sleeping in the cloister. Nobody's hurt, just the house, and we want to keep it that way. It's dangerous to go out there until the storm lets up. Come away, hon. Nothing we can do till morning.' He stroked her hair. 'We'll see what the damage is then, and start doing something about it.'

Joyce was still crying. Well, I'd cry, too, if something awful happened to our house. An old house is more than a pile of bricks. It has a soul, a life of its own, echoes of the lives of all the people who have lived there over the centuries, the master craftsmen who built it and put into it their pride of work.

I wished I could say something to make Joyce feel better, but I didn't know her well enough, and all she needed right now was her husband.

Who was treating her with great kindness and understanding. He kept his arm around her shoulder, looked up to the rest of us, and raised his voice. 'Meanwhile, I don't suppose anybody can sleep. How about some coffee?'

The word fell on my ears like a blessing. Coffee! I suddenly realized how cold I was. I took Alan's arm and snuggled close to him for warmth, and we all trooped to the kitchen.

The kitchen walls were thick; the noise of the storm was less terrifying there. A gentle light pervaded the vast room, and warmth, and the heavenly smell of coffee. Mr and Mrs Bates were up, dressed, and busy. A fire blazed away in the fireplace. The Bateses had lit kerosene lamps and set out cups, sugar, cream.

'The Aga is out,' said Mrs Bates, 'but the water was still nearly hot. We boiled it over the fire. There's tea, as well, and toast is coming, and I can make cocoa if anyone wants some.'

The scene took on a festive air, rather like an illicit midnight feast at some boarding school for superannuated children. We chattered eagerly about the storm. 'Well, I could not sleep anyway, and when I heard that awful crash...', 'I hope the house isn't badly damaged. Irreplaceable...', '...and I swear to you I positively *leapt* out of bed, a *grand jeté* if you will...'

'If the power is out for very long, I'm afraid we'll have to put you all up at the White Horse in the village,' said Jim. 'We have plenty of lamps, but the Aga is electric, and so is the central heating. We wouldn't be able to make you very comfortable.'

'Oh, but this is so exciting!' Now that I was warm and no longer frightened, I was beginning to enjoy myself. The kitchen cat lay purring in my lap, having devoured the saucer of cream I'd slipped her under the table. 'Lynn, you'll laugh at me, but I do feel exactly as if I've walked into an Agatha Christie. Any minute now, we'll find the body.'

'I certainly hope not,' said Jim dryly. 'But that reminds me. Are we sure nobody's been hurt? There's a lot of debris flying out there, and something could have come through a window someplace.'

'Perhaps a head count is in order,' said Alan. He stood. 'Joyce, remind me. There ought to be fifteen of us, am I right?'

'Right. Jim and me, Mr and Mrs Bates, and eleven guests. So let's see – Jim and me and two, four ... I only find nine more. Am I missing someone in the shadows?'

'No,' said Alan. 'I believe your sister and brother-in-law are missing.'

I could have sworn I heard someone mutter, 'No great loss,' but it might have been

49

only my own uncharitable thoughts. The party atmosphere of a moment before was certainly gone, though, and that *wasn't* my imagination.

There was an uncomfortable pause before Tom Anderson rose from a kitchen chair. 'I'll go and look for them, if you like. They may still be ... asleep.'

Well, they would have had to be the world's best sleepers to slumber through the uproar of the storm. But Dave had been drinking heavily, and for all I knew Julie might have joined him after they went upstairs. Maybe they had just passed out.

'I'll go with you.' Jim and Laurence spoke at the same time. Each stopped, hesitated. Finally Laurence spread his hands in a deprecating gesture. 'Jim, it's your house, and they're your family. I should—'

'My wife's family,' Jim corrected in a voice with no expression whatever. 'And let's have none of this "After you, my dear Alphonse" stuff. You know the house a whole lot better than I do. If they're not in their rooms, they could be anywhere, and you're qualified to search. You go ahead, and thanks. They're in the back wing, at the end – the Palladian suite overlooking the river.'

'Yes, of course. Shall we, Mr Anderson?'

'If I take my flashlight, I'll leave Lynn without one. Jim, is there another somewhere?'

'Excuse me, sir.' Mr Bates materialized with a lantern. 'This will provide brighter light, and will be more dependable. Mind you carry it by the handle – it can get quite hot.'

'I should go,' murmured Joyce.

'You're not going,' said Jim flatly. 'The storm is getting worse, if anything. This is the solidest part of the house, and the safest. You're staying here, and I strongly suggest the rest of you do the same. The damned wind can't last forever.'

We stayed. Nobody wanted to go back to bed. In moments of stress, humans crave company. But our cozy mood was gone. The cat, sensitive to atmosphere like all her kind, had jumped down and vanished, and my coffee was cold. We sat in silence, watching the flicker of firelight on ancient stone walls and listening to the roar of wind down the chimney.

I was beginning to feel sleepy again by the time the search party returned half an hour later. They were alone.

Joyce, who had been nodding on a bench next to Jim, sprang up. 'You didn't find them?'

'We found them.' It was Tom who spoke. 'They're not hurt, just a little ... er...'

'It seems they've both drunk a bit too much, Mrs Moynihan,' said Laurence, being very formal. 'We found Mrs Harrison asleep in a bathtub three bedrooms away from her own, and Mr Harrison on the floor of the small sitting room next to the Blue Room. We did attempt to rouse them, but it proved easier to leave them where they were, so we found blankets and covered them. I fear there'll be ... er ... some cleaning up to do in the morning.'

'Oh. Well.' Joyce bit her lip and then visibly pulled herself together. 'Thank you so much for checking on them. In the morning I'll ... do what I can.'

'The morning, hon, is now,' said Jim. It was still dark as the pit outside, but the kitchen clock chimed six. In less than an hour the sun would rise behind those lowering clouds and the day would, officially, have begun.

I was suddenly unutterably weary.

FIVE

'What time is it? Why did I wake up?'

'Getting on toward eleven,' said Alan, 'and I have no idea why you woke. I was trying to be quiet.'

'Quiet. That's it. The quiet woke me. That awful wind has stopped. Well, died down, anyway. How long have you been up?'

We'd all gone back up to bed to get what sleep we could for what little remained of the night, and I'd conked out as though I'd been hit on the head. I still felt muzzy.

'About an hour,' said Alan. 'I went down in

search of breakfast, but the pickings are a trifle slim. The electricity is still out, and from the look of things – well, see for yourself.'

He pulled open the draperies, letting in light. The rain had apparently stopped. I staggered to the window.

'Dear God.'

I had seen such devastation before. On television. In the newspapers. The aftermath of tornadoes, floods, hurricanes. Of war. I'd never seen it outside my window.

The little wood we had driven through yesterday when we arrived was gone. Just ... gone. As far as the eye could see, no big trees were left standing. They'd been torn out of the ground, their twisted roots pointing distorted fingers at the sky. Among them, saplings looked forlorn, bereft. Nearer the house, what had been the garden was a sea of mud with a few twigs shivering, naked, in cold, unforgiving sunshine. What must once have been a greenhouse lay in a heap of glass shards, and broken slates and bits of carved stone were strewn everywhere.

'But, Alan, this is ... what *happened*?'

'Hurricane-force winds. That, coupled with the saturated ground, and the trees went down like so many wisps of straw. I listened to the car radio for a few minutes. A storm the like of which we haven't seen since 1987. And even that one wasn't as bad as this, not in this part of the country at least.' He shook his head and held up his hands in a despondent gesture. 'Joyce and Jim are beyond distraught.

The house can be repaired, but the land-scaping! The famous Capability Brown land-scaping was one of the things they loved best about the house. They keep talking about it. It's a bit depressing.'

'Alan, let's go home! They don't need company at a time like this. And I want to see what's happened to our house, to Sherebury.'

Alan is a lovely man. He was patient with me. 'My dear woman, how precisely do you think we might get home? Remember the drive, that picturesque mile-long drive from the road to the house? With trees on either side?'

'Oh. I suppose they're all down.'

'One good big one would be enough to block the drive. Not to mention the state of the roads once one got to them.'

'Trains?' I asked hopelessly.

'Not running. Nothing's running. The entire south-east of England is shut down.'

'We'll go to the pub, then. The White Horse. We can walk there if we have to. Jim said last night...'

Alan just looked at me pityingly. 'It's nearly five miles, and your knees aren't up to that yet awhile. *If* they're open, which I doubt.'

'We could call and find out.'

'Love, get a grip. The phone lines are out of service and the mobile masts are down, which between the two of them also puts paid to the Internet and email. Let's just hope Jim and Joyce laid in plenty of food, because until crews can get the thousands of trees cleared away, we are well and truly isolated.'

I sat down hard on the bed. It was sounding more and more like an old mystery novel, but I wasn't having fun. 'Satellite phone?' I suggested – one last, feeble attempt to pretend there was some kind of normality within our grasp.

Alan smiled wearily. 'Joyce and Jim might have one, I suppose. But not many people do, so whom could we phone?'

'Oh, but ... other people will be trying to reach us, and when they can't—'

'They'll try to reach the authorities, and be told the situation. It's no use, really, love.'

I gave it up. In this age of instant communication, it was hard to believe we really couldn't communicate with anyone, but I would accept the idea for now. At least Alan was here with me. Isolation from the rest of the world was bad enough, but I didn't think I could manage if I were isolated from him.

When hunger and cold finally drove us downstairs, there was little cheer. Oh, it was warmish. A big fire in the kitchen fireplace heated the place a bit, but not enough. Lynn was the only person there. She came over to us when we entered.

'Fry your face and freeze your backside – or the other way around? Your choice. Have you ever used a toasting fork?'

'Um ... maybe for marshmallows, a long, long time ago.'

'It works the same way for bread. If you have patience enough, the bread will toast. If

55

not, or if you get too close, it burns.'

'I used to like burnt marshmallows.'

'I *don't* think you'd care for burnt toast. Anyway, it falls in the fire. There's cold ham, or the pot over there' – she pointed to a spot in the corner of the hearth – 'has boiling water for eggs or tea.'

I ladled some of the boiling water into a teapot. 'Where is everybody?'

'The Bateses are helping Jim and Joyce clear away the tree that fell in the cloisters. So is Tom, and I think some of the other men. I don't know where the women are. Joyce said we were just to help ourselves to anything we could find. Dorothy, I'm *so* sorry I let you in for this.'

'You didn't conjure up the storm. And we're lucky, really. We can keep sort of warm, and I'm sure there's plenty to eat – if we can figure out how to cook it. Lord knows there's enough firewood for ten years – and most of it's already in the house.'

'It's green wood, Dorothy,' said Alan, a little grumpy now that I had someone else to help me cope. 'Won't burn for months.'

'You're hungry,' I replied. 'You always get cross when you're hungry. How about a nice ham sandwich? And I just made a pot of tea.'

We both felt slightly better when we had some food inside us, and Lynn came up with an idea. 'Look, Dorothy, why don't we see if we can put together a meal? Everyone will be starved when they come in. Surely we can concoct something besides boiled eggs and ham sandwiches.'

'Do you think Mrs Bates would mind us invading her domain?'

'I doubt it. She seems like a sensible woman. Anyway, she's busy elsewhere, and somebody has to think about food.'

So we foraged. 'Make sure there's an inside latch on that door,' said Alan as Lynn and I walked into the cooler. 'I'm going out to help with the clean-up effort, and I don't want the two of you getting stuck in there and turning into ice sculptures. Yes, I do know the power's out, but it's going to be very cold in there for a long time.' He gave us a dubious look and then left the room.

'There's a lot of round steak we could cut up into stew meat,' said Lynn after a moment or two.

'That might do for supper, if it thaws fast. Can't have it ready in time for lunch. Oh, here's five pounds or so of hamburger!'

'We could make that into a soup with canned vegetables, and heat it in a big pot in the fireplace. I knew all those years in Camp Fire Girls would come in handy some day.'

There were obstacles. We had no way to brown the hamburger, so we just chopped it up into the smallest chunks we could manage and put it into the biggest pot we could find. Then the can opener was electric, but I had my Swiss Army knife with me. Slowly, laboriously, we opened tins of tomatoes and corn and green beans. I chopped onions and found herbs. 'Potatoes, do you think?'

'Not sure they'd cook in time. Better cook some macaroni in the boiling water, if we can find any macaroni, and add it at the last minute.'

The pot had no bail handle, which didn't really matter, because the fireplace hadn't had hanging hooks for generations, probably. We used other pans to improvise a platform for the big pot, thrust it into the fire, and hoped for the best.

'And that's enough of that,' I said, dusting ashes off my fingers. 'I wish we could bake some cornbread, but even if we had the ingredients, I do *not* know how to bake on an open fire, and I don't intend to try to find out. What do we do now?'

'Why don't we see what we can do outside? We might find roof slates that are reusable, and some of the plants might be salvaged.'

I had serious doubts about the plants, but it was worth a try. I'm no gardener, but I do love flowers, and the sight of the ruined garden was painful. 'I didn't bring my wellies. Do you suppose there are some I can borrow?'

'Bound to be. Shall I go ask Jim?'

'No, don't bother him. We'll manage.'

We found our coats and hats and a variety of footwear. Lynn slipped into somebody's garden clogs and I found a pair of wellies so big I could wear them over my shoes, and we went out into the hard, bright sunshine and the devastation.

The wind was still blowing steadily, a cold,

insinuating wind, but by comparison to the storm winds it was as a gentle zephyr. We wandered more or less aimlessly, and soon stopped trying to pick up slates. They were heavy, and so many of them were chipped or broken that I doubted they would be of any use. As for the garden, it was heartbreaking.

'Still,' said Lynn after we had looked in silence at the stripped rose bushes and the flattened annuals, 'the perennials will come up again in the spring, and the bulbs. Small plants are sturdier than trees, in a way.'

'The bigger they are, the harder they fall,' I said glumly. 'Look at that oak, with its roots in the air.' I pointed to one on the edge of the wood. 'It's fascinating, in a macabre sort of way. Do you suppose they ever save trees that are uprooted that way?'

'I wouldn't think so.'

We walked in that direction, squishing through the mud. 'Well, but they wouldn't have to dig a new hole,' I argued. 'The hole is there, see? Darn it all, if they could just get to it with a crane or something, before it dries out, I'll bet— *what's that?*'

We were at the edge of the deep cavity left by the fallen giant. Tangled in its roots was ... something...

'Dorothy Martin, if you faint I'll never speak to you again! You've got to stay sensible, because *somebody* has to, and I don't know if I can.'

Lynn's voice seemed to come from far away, but her hand gripped mine painfully.

I cleared my throat and gave my head a shake. 'Tell me that isn't what I think it is.'

'Oh, yes, it is.' Her voice rose higher and higher, and she began to laugh. 'You can't really mistake a skeleton, can you?'

SIX

I have seen a few dead bodies in my life. I didn't enjoy it. If I had ever thought about it, I suppose I would have expected a skeleton to be less disturbing. A body, after all, looks like a person. A skeleton is just bones.

Or so I would have thought. It isn't so. There was something so absolutely final about that skeleton, so utterly and irretrievably dead, that it turned my own bones to water.

Once when I was a teenager I went into a 'fun house'. For me it wasn't fun. I've always been claustrophobic and a little afraid of the dark, and I didn't, even at that age, like things that jumped out at me and made loud noises. But the worst thing, the absolutely worst, was the skeleton that dropped down an inch from my nose with a horrific shriek. The word 'blood-curdling' is overused, but I felt exactly as if my blood had turned solid and stopped my heart. I had nightmares for weeks afterwards, that grinning skull looming closer, closer...

That skull had been plastic, or something. This one was real. I turned away from it and sank down on the nearest fallen branch.

My friend was still giggling. 'Lynn!' I said sharply. 'Pull yourself together and go get Alan. You can run. I can't. Don't tell him what's happened yet, just bring him out. I'll stay here.'

'Why?' said Lynn, still in that high voice, near hysteria. 'He–she–it isn't going anywhere.'

'I don't want anyone else seeing it yet, if I can prevent them. Lynn, *go*!'

She went. I took a deep breath, and then another, and tried hard to think.

The skeleton was not intact. The ligaments that had held the bones together had gone the way of all flesh. But the smaller roots of the tree had intertwined with the bones, creating a kind of net that held them in some semblance of their original alignment. I shuddered at that thought. Roots, weaving their tough, mindless, inexorable fingers through muscle, through heart and brain and...

I shook myself, nearly dislodging my hat, which was being teased by the wind. I replaced it more firmly and gave myself a lecture. Dead tissue feels no pain, knows no indignity. What happens to our bodies after we're dead doesn't matter a hoot. It's what happens when we're alive that counts.

That skeleton had once belonged to a

living, breathing human being. If its owner had met a natural death, he or she would have been buried in the usual way in a churchyard. The implication was obvious.

On the whole, I came down on the side of 'she'. The sad fact is that it has never been uncommon for a young lord of the manor – or an old one, for that matter – to seduce a serving maid or village girl. If the girl, discovering herself pregnant, or humiliated past endurance by her 'ruin', killed herself, she might well have been buried to prevent talk. Some story would have been put about that she had left for greener pastures. Or, if the seducer was someone whose reputation would have suffered, he might have killed the girl. Murder in either case, according to my way of thinking.

I wondered how long ago the murder had taken place. I had no idea how long it took for flesh to decay and leave clean bones.

My stomach was getting queasier and queasier. Better stop thinking about that sort of thing. There was no point, anyway. The place would soon be swarming with Scene of Crime Officers, some of them with enough knowledge of forensics to make a very good guess about the age of the skeleton.

And then, with sinking heart, I remembered. No, there would be no SOCOs. There would be no one to help, no one to study the scene and then take away that pathetic evidence of murder, no one to set in motion the efficient machinery of homicide investigation.

We couldn't call the police. We couldn't get to a police station. Or if someone managed to walk to the village, the constable there would have no way to summon the nearest homicide team.

We were cut off, alone here with a group of people who barely knew each other and the skeleton of a murdered person. I wrapped my coat more closely around me and wished Alan would come.

It seemed a long time, but was probably only a few minutes before I saw him striding across the muddy, littered lawn. He was alone. Lynn had undoubtedly sought the comforting presence of her own husband. I could understand that.

When Alan was close enough, I simply pointed.

My husband, bless him, can meet almost any occasion with aplomb, and he'd seen lots of corpses and probably a few skeletons in his long and distinguished police career. He studied the bones, then took my hand and grinned. 'I can't take you anyplace, can I?'

I was able to smile back. 'Now really! I know I've managed to get involved in a few crimes over the years, but you can't blame me for a body that's been there for ... how long, would you say?'

'Probably years, but I don't know how many. It would take some time for the roots to entwine themselves around the bones like that. As for the decay of the body, there are so many variables – type of soil, temperature, whether the body was naked or clothed, what insects are in the soil – sorry, love. Not pleasant, I know. But only an expert would be able to say with any certainty, and even then, it will be an estimate.'

'And we can't get an expert here,' I wailed. 'Alan, what on earth are we going to do?'

'First we tell our host. It's on his property, after all. Then we're going to have to try to get through to the authorities.'

'How? Smoke signals?'

'A satellite phone, if someone here has one and I can find someone at the other end. Or I'll walk to the police station in the village and see what, if anything, they can do. At the very least, a constable might be sent to guard the remains, though given the storm emergency, I'm not sure if that will be possible. The village probably has only the one constable.'

'Shall I stay here and keep watch?' I asked. 'I don't mind, now.' Alan has a marvellous gift for steadying me in a crisis.

'That would be a help, love. I'll send someone to relieve you. I can trust Tom. Then I'll talk to our hosts and see what can be done, given the circumstances.'

'Jim and Joyce will be shattered.'

'They already are. Blast this storm! There are times when I'm tempted to move to some place with dependable weather.'

'If there is any such place, which I doubt, you'd be bored to tears.'

'I've heard parts of Australia— ah.' His

64

voice took on a speculative tone.

'What?' I asked apprehensively.

'I believe I remember someone saying Laurence Upshawe lives now in Australia.'

'New Zealand,' I murmured, but Alan wasn't listening.

'Do you have any idea when he sold Branston Abbey and moved away?'

'Not a clue.' I was getting impatient. 'Alan, shouldn't we—?'

'Because,' Alan went on with maddening calm, 'depending on how long the body's been there...'

'Oh! Oh, obviously. My head's getting soft in my old age. But Alan, I *like* Mr Upshawe!'

'So do I.' But he said it grimly, and strode off toward the house.

I sat back down on the uncomfortable branch, left alone once more to listen to the wind and commune with a pile of bones.

In the few minutes before Tom Anderson came to take over the vigil, I was able to notice a few things in that huge cavity left when the tree toppled. I dared not approach too closely. The ground was soft and unstable, and I shuddered at the thought of falling into the embrace of that grinning horror. But from where I sat I could see some dark fragments of something hanging from the tree roots, moving in the wind as if alive. They could almost have been leaves. Oak leaves are tough, and decay very slowly. But how would leaves have made their way deep into the earth?

No, I was pretty sure they were rags of cloth, the sorry remnants of what the person had been wearing when he, or she, was buried. And if they were identifiable...

'What a hell of a thing!'

I jumped. Tom had come up behind me while I was brooding.

'Sorry, D., didn't mean to scare you. Honestly, I don't know how you manage to get into these messes.'

'Alan said something like that, too. I refuse to take any responsibility for this particular mess! That pile of bones has been down there since before I even moved to England, probably. And may I remind you who is responsible for Alan and me being here this weekend? How's Lynn holding up, by the way?'

'She's fine. She's pretty resilient, you know. She was just a little perturbed by the bones. You don't expect to find a skeleton when you're out for a walk in the pleasant English countryside.'

'You don't expect hurricanes in the pleasant English countryside, either. I've never seen destruction like this, and I've lived through a couple of tornadoes, years ago in Indiana. I *wish* I knew what was going on at home. In this age of instant communication, it's incredible that we have none.'

'Well, D., you'll get your wish as soon as Alan manages to get in touch with the outside world.'

'*If* he manages to get in touch with them.

Anyway, even if the police get here, they won't be wanting to waste time putting me in touch with our Sherebury neighbours.'

'Not the police, sweetie. The media.' He jerked his head toward our grisly companion. 'This is *news*. As soon as they hear, they'll be here in force, if they have to use a helicopter.'

'Oh, Lord. I hadn't thought of that. Talk about your mixed blessings! They could be a big help – but they'll also be a major nuisance. I've changed my mind. I don't need news from home that badly. I hope the TV crews and all the rest don't learn about this for a while. Especially for the Moynihans' sake.' A thought occurred to me. 'Tom, when you first talked to them about this house, back in Cannes or wherever it was, did they say how long they've owned it?'

'So you've thought about that, too. It was Antibes, and no, I don't believe they said. I got the impression it'd been a couple of years, because they talked about how much work had needed to be done, and their frustration over the usual delays. So...' He held up his hands and shrugged.

'So they could maybe be involved. Or some of the workmen could. Tom, we need to get this ... this thing identified as soon as possible, and find out how long it's been dead. Because until we do...'

We didn't need to spell out the unpleasant possibilities.

I was glad to leave Tom on guard duty and get back to the house. I met Alan on the way.

He was carrying a tall walking stick.

'What luck?' I thought I knew the answer.

'No satellite phone. Jim and Joyce have been thinking about getting one, but haven't got around to it yet. So it's Branston village and any help I can find there.' He sounded tired.

'Alan, it's five miles! And I hate to mention it, but you're going to be seventy in May. Should you walk all that way?'

His discouraged expression changed to one of amusement. 'My dear pampered American, I'm English. We still remember what feet are for. Five miles is nothing, at least on clear roads. These will be littered with debris, so it may take a bit longer. That's why I borrowed the staff.'

I know a lost battle when I meet one. 'Have you at least had something to eat? And do the others know? Besides the Moynihans, I mean.'

'I told Upshawe. And obviously Tom and Lynn know. I haven't broadcast it yet. I made a casual remark to the effect that I needed a stroll, and would come back to report on what damage I found. And yes, I had some of your excellent soup. Go in and have some yourself, love. I'll be back well before nightfall.'

'But you have a flashlight, just in case?'

'I do. Stop fretting. A brisk walk will do me good.'

He gave me a peck on the cheek and strode off. I went inside to fret.

SEVEN

The entire party was gathered in the kitchen. The moment I opened the door I could hear Julie Harrison, who was, predictably, taking the disaster as a personal affront.

'...slates came right through our window. We could have been killed!'

Which window, I wondered. The sitting room where she'd slept it off, or the bathroom her husband stumbled into?

She whined on. 'And I think one of them hit me on the head. I have the most god-awful headache. I need to get to a doctor!'

Joyce said, 'Sis, I've told you.' She was near tears. 'No one can go anywhere. All the roads are blocked by fallen trees. And we can't call a doctor or a pharmacy, or anyone. We're cut off.'

'Yeah, well, I'll tell you right now, I intend to sue.' The other Horrible Harrison spoke up. 'Bringin' us out here in the middle of nowhere to a rickety old house that's fallin' apart—'

'I will remind you,' said our host through clenched teeth, 'that we did not "bring you out here". You came for reasons of your own, and without invitation. I'm not sure whether you plan to sue God for the storm, or the long-dead builders of the house for the flying slates, but I think your lawyers will advise against either course. And I'm not exactly astonished, Julie, that you have a headache. You drank enough to fell an ox. As soon as the roads are clear and the trains are running again, I will escort you to the station in Shepherdsford.'

The shrill voice and the hoarse one rose in united protest.

'That's enough!' Jim didn't shout, but the Harrisons stopped in mid-tirade. 'I've put up with a lot, but I'm not going to subject Joyce, or our guests, to any more. You have a choice. Pack up now and set out on foot if you think you can get a train quicker that way. It's something like ten miles to the station at Shepherdsford. Or stay in your room until the roads are clear.' He held up a hand as Dave started to bluster. 'There is no third option.'

'Dave! Do something!' shrieked Julie.

'Oh, I'll do somethin', all right,' he growled. 'I'll sue the pants off both of 'em when we get back to civilization. Right now we're getting out of where we're not wanted.'

He grabbed Julie's arm and towed her out of the kitchen.

I was beginning to get used to the sort of silences left behind by the Harrisons. This time it was broken by Mike, the dancer. 'Ooh, do you suppose he *could* have meant what one hopes he meant? That they're actually leaving?'

'I doubt it,' said Lynn. 'He had a bottle

70

under his arm. I saw him filch it from the liquor tray a few minutes ago.'

'Then perhaps they will anaesthetize themselves again,' said the vicar, mildly, 'and we will hear no more from them for a while.'

I sighed and sat down to the bowl of soup Mrs Bates offered me. Conversation resumed, in bits and snatches. The gorgeous Pat was trading witticisms with Ed, but neither was being especially brilliant. Mike and the vicar were discussing emergency steps to secure the house against further damage by rain or wind until a repair crew could get through. Lynn and I tried to find something to say to each other that had nothing to do with storms or skeletons, but without much success.

The Moynihans were huddled in a corner of the vast room with Laurence Upshawe. Their voices were inaudible, but for those three, who knew about the grisly discovery under the tree, there was only one likely topic of conversation.

Mrs Bates was going about preparations for supper, a set look on her face. These were not, her expression said, the conditions under which she was accustomed to working. I didn't know where Mr Bates was. Probably repairing something. There was certainly no shortage of work to be done.

I finished my soup, ate an apple from a bowl on the table, and was trying to decide what to do next when the kitchen door opened and Alan walked in.

I stood, startled, but he ignored me, went

straight to Jim Moynihan, and spoke to him in an undertone. Jim grimaced and nodded, and Alan moved to the centre of the room.

'May I have your attention for a moment, please?' He sounded perfectly courteous, perfectly relaxed, but there was something in his manner that stopped all conversation. I drew in a quick breath. This was a man I scarcely knew, the chief constable in person.

'I'm afraid I have two pieces of unpleasant news. The first is that evidence of what appears to be a crime has turned up quite unexpectedly. A human skeleton, apparently buried under one of the oak trees at the edge of the wood, has been unearthed, literally, when the tree was uprooted by the storm. My walk was intended to take me to the village, where I meant to try to find some help in dealing with what will soon become a crime-scene investigation.'

There was a shocked murmur from those in the party who didn't already know about the discovery under the tree. Alan waited for it to subside before he continued. 'And that brings me to my second piece of bad news. I will not be able to walk to the village. Nor can anyone come to us, for quite some time. The river is in flood, and I'm sorry to say that the bridge has been destroyed by falling timber. Until it can be replaced, we are marooned.'

'Oh, no!'

'But, surely—'

'That's impossible! A boat—'

'But I have to be in London—'

72

Everyone was shouting at once. A resurrected skeleton was distressing, but disruption to one's own schedule was outrageous.

'What's in the other direction?' Ed, the photographer, asked.

It was Laurence Upshawe who answered. 'No joy there, I'm afraid. I don't know how much chance anyone has had to explore the grounds. The river makes a loop around the estate, making us very nearly an island. Branston village is to the north of us, on the other side of the bridge at what one might call the top of the loop. There are no bridges to east or west. To the south lies a particularly deserted stretch of country, without so much as a farmhouse for probably ten miles. In any case, the bottom of the loop, where the river nearly bends back upon itself, is low-lying ground, marshy at the best of times. In flood, it, too, is impassable, making the estate a true island.'

Tom Anderson began to tick items off on his fingers. 'No way to get out. No electricity. No phone. I don't suppose anybody's cell phone works?'

'Almost all the masts in the south-east are down,' said Alan. 'I heard the news on the car radio earlier this morning.'

'No cell phone,' Tom continued. 'Nobody has a satellite phone?' The lack of answer was answer enough. 'What about wireless Internet?'

'The card's on order,' said Jim glumly. 'Should have been here last week.'

This time no one spoke, no one protested. It's sinking in, I thought. They're realizing. We're all stuck here with no communication till heaven knows when. I cleared my throat. 'Alan, how long did it take for everybody to get their power back after the storm in 1987 – and phones, and so on?'

'Two weeks, as I recall, for the most remote areas.'

'And the roads?' Joyce asked tremulously. 'How long before...'

'The Army cleared the main roads quite quickly. Secondary roads took longer, and private drives...' He shrugged. 'It was a few days before all the railway lines were cleared, as well.'

'Well, then,' said Jim, 'we need to get to work. Thank God the chainsaws don't need electricity, and we've got plenty of gas.'

'No, we don't, Jim.' It was Joyce's disconsolate voice. 'We're nearly out. You were going to drive into the village today for that, and some nails and things. Remember?'

'Oh.' Jim looked blank. 'You're right. Still, there's some left. Maybe ... well, who's game to help me try to cut up some trees and build a bridge?'

The men, and most of the women, rose in a body, but Alan had more to say. 'Is there anyone here who has any medical experience?' Well, at least it wasn't 'Is there a doctor in the house?' but it still sounded ominous.

Surprisingly, Laurence Upshawe spoke. 'I am a doctor. Retired. How can I help?'

I was sure I knew. Upshawe, a very likely suspect in the crime, was not the ideal person to examine the skeleton, but someone had to, and the sooner the better.

Alan hesitated, though, and Joyce saw what he was thinking. She buried her head in her hands and began to sob.

As Alan and Upshawe moved off, I went to Joyce. Whether she was mourning her beautiful house, or worrying about an old crime, or despairing over the now-compulsory continued presence of the Harrisons, she needed comfort.

'It's all a bit much, isn't it?' I murmured. 'One thing on top of another. Would you like a cup of tea?' Good grief, I thought with exasperation. I've lived in England too long. A cup of tea, indeed. 'Or some brandy?'

'I'm sorry,' she said, sniffling and trying to control her sobs. 'I'm just ... it's just...'

'I know. But at least you have lots of workers, and lots of company. I'll bet the guys will get some kind of a bridge rigged in no time, even if it's just a tree or two across the river. And then there'll be professional help. It'll be all right.' I could hear the false brightness in my voice.

'My trees! My beautiful trees!' she wailed. 'And the gardens! They won't be all right.'

Lynn joined us and handed Joyce a glass of something amber that looked a lot more like brandy than tea. 'Drink it,' she said. 'You'll feel better. And no,' she went on, 'the old oaks won't be all right. They're gone forever. But

75

not the young ones. Just think what an opportunity you have now to redo the gardens. You can plant all sorts of interesting trees and shrubs, plants you really love, and watch them take shape.'

The outcome hung in the balance for a moment, and then Joyce took a sip of brandy, sniffed, and reached in her pocket for a tissue. 'It's true there were some changes I wanted to make. The rhododendrons are terribly overgrown. And I've never much liked white roses ... but the trees! The landscaping was by Capability Brown, you know, and it was famous!' Tears threatened again.

I was nearly in tears myself. If I'd owned one of the famous gardens of England and seen it destroyed in a night, I would have been devastated. But Lynn is made of sterner stuff.

'Now, Joyce,' she said bracingly. 'That was two hundred and fifty years ago. Brown himself would have wanted to get rid of some of those trees. They were too tall. Out of proportion. The saplings are OK, a lot of them, and they'll grow much better without the shade of the old ones. Stop fussing over what you can't change and start planning what you can.'

Joyce mopped up her eyes, blew her nose, and sipped some more. 'You're right. I'm in England now. Soldier on, keep a straight bat, and all that.'

'*And*,' said Lynn practically, 'as soon as the front drive and the bridge are negotiable, you can get your sister and brother-in-law out of your hair. I don't mean to be rude about your family, but surely their absence is something to look forward to.'

'Yes ... well ... you've gathered we don't exactly get along. To tell the truth, Julie and I never did.' The brandy, or something, was loosening her tongue. She became confidential. 'I'm the eldest, and Julie was the middle child. We had a kid brother. He died when he was a teenager – hit by a car – but he was the pet child before that. And I was the one who was given responsibility. Julie, the middle kid, had nothing special. I think she thought it would be better after Stevie died, but my parents never got over him. Well, naturally they wouldn't. I mean, you don't get over the death of a child, but somehow they resented Julie for still being alive when Stevie was dead. They had always compared the two of them. You know, "Why can't you do as you're told? Stevie does, and he's only a baby." That sort of thing.' She polished off the brandy.

'Sounds like an unwise way to raise a child,' I commented.

'Oh, it was, but they couldn't see it. Anyway, I didn't mean to tell you my life story. The point is, Julie has always resented me, and when—' She broke off, suddenly cautious. 'Good heavens, I think I've had too much to drink ... I'd better go see what everyone's doing about the bridge.'

Lynn and I exchanged glances, then followed her out the door.

EIGHT

We could hear the snarl of the chainsaws, even over the rising wind, the minute we stepped outside the house. Jim had two of them, in different sizes, and both were going full blast. It's a sound I've always hated, a sound that nearly always means the destruction of some living thing. In this case the trees were already destroyed. That didn't make the sound any more pleasant.

No progress had yet been made in bridge-building. They had to get to the river first, and the drive was impassable. Everyone was working hard to clear it. Even Pat, to the imminent ruin of her manicure, was helping the vicar tug and roll logs out of the drive as the other men positioned them and cut them apart.

It was a heartbreaking job. The drive was a mile long, and there must have been fifteen or twenty big trees lying across it, in some cases one atop another. Mike, slender though he was, was working like a lumberjack. I saw him single-handedly nudge one oak tree off another, nimbly skipping aside so as to protect his feet. I must have been staring, because he caught my eye and grinned. 'Nothing at all, compared to lifting a hefty ballerina forty or fifty times a night.'

Well, most of the ballerinas I'd seen were the reverse of hefty – anorexic, one might have said. But I took his point. Dancers were athletes, first of all.

They'd dealt with one tree so far. Jim and Mr Bates had used the chainsaws to cut off the portion actually lying on the drive, while the others used handsaws and loppers and axes to remove protruding branches. At this rate it would take days even to get to the river, much less bridge it. And how long could they work at this pace? Most of them weren't young, and none except Mike had any genuine physical strength.

And how long would the gas hold out?

Lynn and Joyce moved into the work area and picked up tools. I found a pair of loppers and looked half-heartedly for some branches to cut. It all just seemed so pointless – emptying the ocean with a teaspoon.

I had created a small pile of brush and a couple of large blisters when Alan and Laurence hove into sight. I laid down my loppers with relief and went to meet them.

'Well? Have you figured out anything about her?'

Alan looked confused.

'The skeleton,' I said impatiently. 'Weren't you trying to identify her, or at least fix an approximate time and cause of death?'

'Where did you get the idea it was female?' asked Alan. 'The doctor says quite definitely not, and you know that's one of the easiest things to determine.'

'Oh! I thought— but never mind. A man, then. Anything else? Age, maybe?'

'I can't be certain,' said Upshawe. He looked tired and distressed. 'This isn't my field – I'm a surgeon – but one learned a certain amount in anatomy classes. The man was past adolescence and not yet senescent – not yet old. There is no obvious arthritic degeneration. The femurs are relatively long; I think we can assume a man of above average height. Beyond that...' He spread his hands. 'An expert in these things would be able to tell you a great deal more.'

'Gideon Oliver,' I murmured. 'Where are you when we need you?'

'Who?' said Upshawe and my husband simultaneously.

'Sorry. A fictional detective. A physical anthropologist. Never mind. Is there any way to tell about how long he'd been there?'

'Not for non-experts like us,' said Alan. 'There were some fragments of cloth, probably clothing, but as I don't know how long it takes clothing to rot, that takes us no forrarder.'

'Nothing else, then? No billfold? Leather surely doesn't rot as soon as cloth.'

'No, it doesn't, usually. We did find bits of his shoes, but nothing that told us much – except that he went to his grave shod. It wasn't easy to look, love. You understand we were actually down in the hole with the tree roots, very insecure footing and none too safe, if the tree had shifted. When we can get the proper equipment and personnel here, we'll institute a search. Until then, we're pretty well stuck.'

Laurence Upshawe was looking a bit green. I glanced at him and said brightly, 'Well, then, we'd better get to work on that drive.' We moved back to join the work party, but before we could even pick up tools, Jim Moynihan stepped up, sounding irritated.

'What did you think? Who died? What's going on?'

'We don't know,' said Alan. 'A man, aged anywhere from the late teens to perhaps the forties. Tallish, probably. No identification.'

Jim rolled his eyes. 'Then what the hell do we do now?'

'If we were in any position to do so, we – you – would call in the police. They would bring equipment to get the skeleton up and out to a forensics laboratory, where every effort would be made to solve a number of questions – how the man died, how long ago, and naturally who he was.'

'Yeah, well, we can't do any of that, can we?' He gazed bitterly down the disaster area that used to be his drive.

'Not at present,' said Alan with a sigh. 'But as this is plainly a crime scene, we must do what we can. I will put a guard on the – one hesitates to call it a body – on the remains, and ask whatever questions I can think of. None of it is likely to be useful, but it has to be done.'

'And by what authority,' asked Laurence, 'do you take it upon yourself to ask these questions?' He tightened his grip on the axe he had picked up.

'No authority at all,' said Alan calmly. 'But as we are isolated on our island, and I am the only representative of the law present, I considered that some questions were in order. Anyone may certainly refuse to answer.'

Upshawe put the axe down, carefully. 'Representative of the law?'

'Perhaps our host didn't mention to you that I am the retired chief constable of Belleshire. I'm off my turf, this being Kent, but once a policeman, always a policeman. If I can gather any facts to lay before the real authorities when they can get here, it may make an investigation a bit easier. Don't you think?'

Upshawe swallowed. 'Yes, you're right. I'm sorry. I didn't mean to be rude. It's just a bit ... difficult ... the idea of a murder here. This was my home for many years, and although ... well, yes, naturally we must all do what we can.'

'Then if you agree, Jim, when we take a break from work here, perhaps we could gather in the house and pool our ideas.'

Jim looked at his small crew, who were beginning to flag. The irritating whine had diminished. I could see only one chainsaw working. Had the other run out of gas?

The vicar stood at one end of a log, arching

82

a back that was obviously hurting him, while Pat had sat down on the other end of it and was rubbing one shoulder. We were all cold. Jim shook his head helplessly. 'We might as well go now. This is getting us nowhere. I was an idiot to suggest it. We can't even get to the river, much less fell a tree to bridge it. It'll take bulldozers to clear away this mess. God, we'll be cut off for weeks!'

'Or until phone service and electricity are restored.' Alan was trying valiantly to look on the bright side. 'That will take days, probably, but not weeks. May I suggest that in the meantime we leave two people to keep watch at the oak tree, and the rest of us go in out of the chill?'

Tom and Lynn volunteered to take the first watch. 'Because,' said Lynn sensibly, 'we never heard of this place until a few weeks ago, so we can't possibly have anything to do with old Boney there.'

'And apart from Dorothy and me,' Alan replied *sotto voce*, 'you are very nearly the only people who can make that claim.'

'Let me make my position quite clear,' said my husband, when he and the others had seated themselves in a group around the cold hearth of the drawing room. The wind was still blowing, not as it had, but steadily, strongly. Now and then the curtains swayed a little. I was glad to be inside, even if the room was cold.

The Harrisons were nowhere to be seen. I

thought about asking Alan if someone should look for them, and then thought better of it. If Alan wanted them he was perfectly capable of saying so, and meanwhile this was going to be unpleasant enough without them. I took a chair a little distance away and tried to fade into the woodwork.

'As I said outside,' Alan began, 'I have no authority whatsoever in this matter. No one is under any obligation to answer any of my questions, or even to remain while I ask them. In a certain sense, Mr Moynihan, I am abusing your hospitality if I carry out any investigation. However, having said that, I must also say that in this situation, with all indications that a serious crime has been committed, an investigation *will* have to be launched. We are in the peculiar position of having, for the present, no one to call upon who does have authority. With your permission, then, Mr Moynihan, I'd like to do what I can to get at some of the truth.'

Jim set his chin pugnaciously. 'OK, let's clear the air. In the first place, my name is Jim. Second, this is my house, and it used to be Laurence's here. Now I don't know about you, Laurence, but when a human skeleton's found on my property I want to know how the hell it got there, and I guess you feel pretty much the same way.'

'Certainly. I merely— no matter. Proceed, Mr Nesbitt.'

'Splendid!' Alan sounded composed, as though there were no tension in the air. 'Now

I think you'll all agree, our first task is to learn who the unfortunate fellow under the tree is, or rather, was in life. In a week or so, when we can get a forensics team here, we will be in a position to know much more. For now, we simply have to muddle through.'

An English specialty, I thought with a private grin.

'At the moment,' Alan went on, propping one ankle on his knee in an attitude of total relaxation, 'we know two things about the chap. First, that he *is* a chap, not a woman. Even I know enough about skeletal anatomy to make that guess, and Mr Upshawe – Dr Upshawe – confirmed it. Second, that he's been buried there for some time. I wish I could be more definite than that, but it's simply not possible at this stage. Still, I can make an educated guess that the roots of an oak tree grow fairly slowly, as does the part of the tree above ground. And the bones were well entangled with the roots, so provisionally – *very* provisionally, I must say – I think it's fair to assume the body's spent several years where we found it.'

Alan reached into his pants pocket, made a grimace, and withdrew his hand. I knew he'd been feeling for the pipe he gave up some years ago, on doctor's orders. Old habits die hard.

'Now you and your wife, Mr— Jim, took possession of this house some time ago. When, exactly?'

'Two years ago last May,' said Joyce. 'It was

85

the most beautiful place. The gardens were...'
Her voice broke.

Alan looked at her with sympathy, but he went on. 'And did you notice any evidence of digging around that particular oak tree?'

Jim snorted. 'We didn't do a detailed inspection of each tree, man!'

'I'm sure. But that one was quite near the house, and an impressive specimen.'

'The grass ran right up to it, Alan,' said Joyce. 'I did notice that. It wasn't in the wood, proper – more a part of the lawn. Sort of reminded me of the old oaks in people's yards back home.'

'Splendid. That helps. It would surprise me very much to learn that our friend was put there in the past two years, and you've strengthened my opinion. Now, Ms Heseltine.'

The femme fatale cocked her head to one side with a half-smile. 'Yes, luv?'

I refrained from gritting my teeth.

'You have lived in the village for some time?'

'All my life – except for Oxford, and my time at Lincoln's Inn, eating my dinners.'

Ed Walinski, sitting next to me, looked bewildered, and I whispered, 'Part of getting admitted to the Bar. I'll explain later.' I hoped I could. The process confused me, too.

Alan went on. 'Under normal circumstances I would never ask a lady her age, but may I ask just how long "all my life" implies?'

'You may,' she cooed in that devastating

voice of hers. 'But as you pointed out, I am under no obligation to answer.' She gave him a brilliant smile.

'Yes, indeed. I will simply ask, then, if in your years in Branston village – however few or many they may be – you remember anyone going missing.'

He had put just the slightest stress on 'many', and given me the briefest of sidelong glances. I don't think Miss Glamourpuss of Kent noticed, but I grinned.

'Not a soul. Except for Harry Upshawe, of course.'

NINE

That caused a stir. Everyone looked at Laurence, who held his hands up in a gesture of annoyance.

Alan frowned. 'Can you tell me about that, sir? Harry Upshawe is...?'

Upshawe sighed. 'Was. Harry Upshawe was my second cousin. And he died in a plane crash when I was about ten. There was no question of his "going missing".'

'This happened when you were ten, you said. That's rather a long time ago. Can you tell me any of the details?'

'One remembers the pivotal events of one's

life, Mr Nesbitt, even the ones that happened fifty years ago. I remember that Harry was going away, going to America. I wasn't sorry, I recall. We were of the same generation, but Harry was too much older than I to have ever been a playmate. In fact he ignored me as much as possible. I was simply the poor relation, the son of his father's no-account cousin.'

'You disliked him?'

'I had no attitude toward him at all, really. We almost never saw each other.'

'But you remember his attitude toward you.'

'No. I'm sorry if I've conveyed the wrong impression. I remember what my father told me, later, about his attitude. About Harry I remember, from my own memory, only an impression of tallness and a hint that I shouldn't cross him.'

'And he was killed in a plane crash,' said Alan. 'You were ten when this happened, you say. That is, when your cousin went away.'

'Just ten. I remember because it was only a few days after my birthday that we heard he was missing in the crash.'

'"Heard he was missing"?' Alan's tone made it a question.

'Yes. It was a private plane, you see, piloted by a friend of Harry's. When it didn't arrive in New York, the authorities launched an investigation. The last radio contact was a message to São Miguel, in the Azores, where the pilot had planned to land for refuelling.

He never got there. By the time anyone got out to search there was no sign of the plane, and as far as I know, nothing has ever been found of the wreckage.'

'Ah. So no bodies were ever recovered.'

'No, obviously not.' Upshawe sounded impatient.

'So in actual fact you do not know that the plane crashed, only that it disappeared.'

'The plane disappeared. Neither the pilot nor my cousin has been heard from in the intervening fifty years. The inference that the plane crashed would seem to be justified.'

Upshawe sounded very stiff. Jim Moynihan cleared his throat.

'You're thinking me ridiculously precise,' said Alan, smiling. 'I quite agree with your inference – about the plane. Apparently flight plans were filed, the plane took off with your cousin's friend piloting it, it never reached São Miguel. It is reasonable to assume it crashed. My point is that, so far, I can find no justification for the inference that your cousin was aboard.'

'But ... he was going! He told everyone. He left the morning when he said he did, with his luggage.'

'Who saw him leave?'

'His father, naturally. No, I'm wrong. His father was away at the time. In London, if I remember correctly. But the servants...'

'Are any of the servants still living, sir?'

Upshawe sagged in his chair. 'No. My father kept them on, after he inherited the place, and after my father died I could hardly sack them. They'd lived on the estate forever. I pensioned them off when they got too old for the work, but I didn't replace them as they left or died. I couldn't afford to run the place on those lines. That's why I sold it – that, and the fact that I'd never really liked living here. I prefer a simpler way of life.' He ran a hand through his hair. 'Look, Nesbitt, I do see what you're getting at. My cousin "disappears". Years later we find bones on his property, bones that could, by a wild stretch of one's imagination, be identified as his. But it's impossible. My cousin's body, or what little must remain of it, lies under two or three thousand metres of cold water, somewhere in the Atlantic Ocean.'

A polite cough interrupted what threatened to become an awkward silence. 'Excuse me, sir. Mrs Bates and I have assembled a rudimentary tea in the kitchen, where it is warmer. It is ready when any of you care to partake. It is not all I could wish, but under the circumstances, perhaps it will suffice.' Mr Bates bowed and withdrew, and we followed him gratefully to the warm kitchen.

Mrs Bates was a true wonder. She had transformed store-bought petit-beurre biscuits into a treat by dipping them into melted bittersweet chocolate. She had prepared hot buttered toast over the fire, turning some of it into cinnamon toast and leaving the rest to be spread with homemade marmalade or strawberry jam. She had even, somehow, made scones, plump with currants, and brought out clotted cream for them. I bit into one and looked at her with amazement. 'You baked? However did you manage?'

She smiled. 'It's John's doing, really. He's a genius with anything mechanical. He managed to rig a wood fire in the Aga. It isn't terribly reliable, and almost impossible to control, but it made enough heat in the one oven for scones, and I *think* I can brown the steak for supper – and heat some water for washing. There won't be enough for baths, unless he can find time after tea to split a lot more wood.'

Oh, dear. I hadn't thought of that. And we all needed baths, after working outside. Well, we'd just have to make do. Smelling like lumberjacks was going to be the least of our troubles.

'Speaking of troubles,' I said in an undertone to Alan, who could almost always follow my thoughts, 'has anyone checked on the Harrisons? I do hate the idea of those two loose cannons rattling around unsupervised.'

'I don't know, but it's a thought. Jim?'

Our host came over and Alan spoke to him. He nodded and left the room. I'd finished my tea by the time he returned, looking disturbed.

'They're not in their room,' he reported to Alan in a low tone. 'I did a pretty thorough tour of the house, including their ... um ... lairs of last night. I can't find them anywhere, and their coats and things are gone.'

'The fools!' Alan smacked the table. 'You don't suppose they've decided to try to get away? It's quite impossible, and they're very likely to come to grief trying. We'd better organize a search party.'

Jim shook his head. 'Not yet. I don't want Joyce to know about this, if she doesn't have to. She and Julie dislike each other heartily, but they are sisters, and I know Joyce would get upset. Anyway, if I know Harrison, he'll come back the minute he gets cold, or hungry … or thirsty.'

Alan relaxed a little, I saw. 'You may be right. He isn't a terribly hardy sort, is he? But the thirst could take a while to set in, if he took that bottle with him.'

'I didn't see it in their room.'

'So,' I put in, 'it'll keep them warm and reasonably content for a few hours, at least. I'm with Jim, Alan. Let them wear themselves out. They'll come home like Bo-Peep's sheep, wagging their tails behind them.'

That, as it turned out, was one of my less fortunate remarks.

There didn't seem much to do the rest of the afternoon. The vicar half-heartedly suggested work on the drive, but when no one took him up on it, he seemed relieved and disappeared. Alan called Tom and Lynn in from their vigil with the skeleton; there seemed little point, since a guard couldn't very well be kept up for the next several days. La Heseltine found a copy of *Bleak House* in the library and sat down in front of the kitchen fire to read, with every evidence of enjoyment, about greedy Dickensian lawyers. (I was nastily pleased to see that she required reading glasses.) The Moynihans, with murmured apologies, went upstairs for naps, and Tom and Lynn followed suit. Mike Leonard wandered about restlessly for a while, then disappeared, and Ed Walinski established himself in a sunny corner of the kitchen with a book of Steichen photographs.

I was tired, but too keyed up to sleep, or to read. Scrounging in library drawers, I found a gigantic jigsaw puzzle, one of those virtually impossible ones with irregular edges and a few extra pieces. Alan helped me spread it out on a reading table, and we set to work. I didn't know what had happened to Upshawe and the vicar, but they were also probably napping.

The wind had died down, gradually, sometime after tea. The hard, brilliant sunshine of the day faded into an early twilight, and then quickly to full dark. Mr Bates brought a kerosene lamp into the library, but we had lost whatever interest we'd ever had in the puzzle, and were growing increasingly cold.

'Let's give it up, shall we, love?' said Alan, and I gladly followed him back to the kitchen, where most of the rest had gathered, and Mrs Bates was trying her best to cook dinner with house guests under foot. I debated offering my help, but a look at her face changed my mind. The best thing I could do was try to stay out of her way.

'It's going to be really cold tonight,' Alan said.

'Mmm. Maybe we'd better find another blanket? I'm not going to bother Joyce about it.'

'That wasn't what I was thinking. The Harrisons haven't come back. Nor does Laurence appear to be around anywhere.'

'Oh. Oh, dear! Dark out, and cold. Do you think...?'

'I do. Reluctantly, but I do. Laurence ought to know his way around, but the storm has changed the landscape so much that even he might have got lost. I think we'd better organize search parties to go and look for them. Bloody idiots!'

My husband seldom swears. He was genuinely worried, then.

Three parties were organized: Alan, Mr Bates and Joyce; Jim, Tom and me; and Mike, Ed, Lynn and Pat. The vicar would have been excused on account of age, but he insisted on being included, so he joined Alan and his party. Only Mrs Bates was persuaded to stay in her kitchen, as we would all need something hot when we came back. Pat admitted openly that she was happy to search for Laurence, but had no real desire to hunt for the Harrisons. 'I hope they got away safely – just so long as they got away,' she remarked, and no one, not even Joyce, could disagree with her.

We all went off with flashlights and lanterns, having set up a communications system by means of the lights and three whistles Mr Bates had produced from somewhere. Alan, who had organized a good many search parties before, handed out ties and scarves and belts and pieces of rope Mr Bates had also found. 'Hold hands as you leave the house, and then form gradually longer chains as you fan out. Those of you who are heading into the wood will have to drop the links to get through the trees, but keep in contact with each other. Shout. Whistle. We don't want to have to search for the searchers.' He indicated directions for each of the three groups, and we set off.

It was like a gruesome children's game. Jim held the lantern and Tom had a flashlight. I, in the middle between the two men, had no hands free to carry a light, but I was grateful for their support as we walked over the debris-littered lawn, making for the wood to the north-east.

'Aren't we headed for the tree?' I asked suddenly. We had been silent until then.

Nobody had to ask which tree. 'We'll need to be careful,' said Jim. 'That's a hell of a big hole, and the ground is muddy and slippery.'

'And everything looks different by lantern-light,' Tom added. I shivered, not entirely from the cold, and moved on.

'I think we'd better spread out now,' said Tom presently. We dropped hands. 'D., if you tie this scarf around your wrist you can hold this flashlight. Just give a shout or a tug when you need me to drop the other end, to get around a tree.'

I did as he suggested. Jim, on my other side, knotted a couple of neckties around his wrist. We moved forward, more slowly now that we were separated.

I moved very slowly indeed. The flashlight Tom had given me was a powerful one, but no flashlight deals well with shadows. We had to drop our tethers almost immediately; the wood was too dense. I was terrified of falling. I was terrified of what I might find – or not find. The downed trees, which had looked unpleasant enough by day, were now monsters, reaching huge gnarled, arthritic fingers up to trap the unwary. As I moved my flashlight the trees seemed to move, shadowy shapes stopping just the instant before I looked directly at them.

It took every bit of self-discipline I possessed to keep moving forward, keep on shining my torch into every gaping hole, under every fallen trunk, around every upright tree – not that there were many of those. Once I stepped on something, a branch or a round stone, that rolled under my foot and nearly brought me down. I stifled my cry, but it brought an immediate response from the men on either side. 'All right, D.?' Tom called, while Jim said, 'Wait there, I'm coming.'

'No, don't. I'm fine. Just ... banged my elbow.' No need to make them feel they needed to protect me. I'm not a fragile person, and I've never thought of myself as elderly, though I suppose I am. If I fell, I'd do my best to be quiet about it.

I've never known how long we kept on putting one foot in front of the other, flashing our lights here and there, hoping and fearing to find someone – or some*thing*. I had reached the point where almost any discovery would have been welcome, if only to put an end to the nightmare.

It was Alan and his party who found them. We heard shrill whistles blown in the agreed-upon pattern, and when we turned to look, lights were flashing into the air. Jim called to me. 'Dorothy, stand still and shout, and point your light in the direction of my voice. I'll find you.' When he had reached me, and had tied his tether to my wrist, Tom had found both of us, and did the same. In single file, with agonizing slowness now that we longed to rush, we made our way to the designated meeting point at the back of the house.

Alan did a quick head count, and then said soberly, 'There is no easy way to say this. We have found Mr Harrison. I'm afraid he has drowned. Mr Upshawe was nearby, badly hurt. We're rigging up a stretcher for him and will bring him back to the house. He needs medical attention, but as he is the only doctor present...' Alan made a helpless gesture.

'And Julie?' asked Joyce in a whisper. 'No one has found Julie?'

'We found no trace of her. I'm sorry.'

TEN

'We'll go out again as soon as it's light,' Alan said to me. 'For now, Upshawe is our chief concern.'

We were all huddled in the library. None of us had had much appetite for Mrs Bates's excellent boeuf bourguignon, a fact she had accepted philosophically. Mr Bates had collected some dry wood and built a big fire, but we couldn't seem to get warm, despite the blankets and afghans that Joyce had dispensed. There was no general conversation. We sat about in groups of two or three, talking quietly. All of us, I think, had the same passionate wish: that somehow we could get out of here and pretend this weekend had never happened.

The vicar, Mr Leatherbury, had remained to pray over the body of Dave Harrison before the men used their makeshift stretcher a second time and brought him back to the stables. They were occupied now only by cars. Joyce and Jim didn't ride, and planned, when they could, to turn part of the building into a workshop, with heat and electricity. For now it was simply a large space. The cars could be turned out, and it was the coldest place on the property that could be properly secured. Harrison was now definitely a secondary concern; there were too many other critical issues to face.

'How is Laurence?' I asked.

Alan shrugged and waggled a hand. 'Holding his own, I presume. Bates has some first-aid training, and naturally I do. Bates was, fortunately, the one who found him, and had the sense to get me there before moving him at all. Then the vicar came, and the three of us we did what we could. We kept Joyce away, though of course we told her a little. The vicar is sitting with him, but he needs a doctor.'

'What actually happened to him?'

'When he comes out of his coma – if he does – we'll know more. From what little we could see at the scene, there had been some kind of a struggle on the riverbank. We found Upshawe lying with his head on a stone; that, presumably, is what knocked him out, although he also has a bad bruise on the left side of his jaw. Harrison's case looks like simple drowning. We could just make out tracks where he apparently lost his footing in the mud and simply slid off. Jim says the bank is undercut just there. You can't see it now, with the river in flood and over its banks, but apparently once Harrison was in the water, he would have had a hard time pulling himself out, even if he was conscious and could swim.'

'He couldn't swim?'

'We don't know, love.'

And if we can't find Julie, we may never know, I thought. 'So Dave and Laurence had a fight.'

'It looks that way, certainly.'

'But *why*? What would those two have to fight about?'

'That's the question, isn't it? But let's defer it till morning, my dear. This day has been a thousand years long, and I'm for my bed.'

One of the supremely competent Bateses had found extra blankets for everyone, so we slept warmly enough. Alan woke once in the middle of the night to go check on Laurence Upshawe, but when I asked him about the man's condition, he just shook his head and went back to sleep.

He was awake at first light. 'Don't get up, love,' he told me. 'It's absolutely freezing in here; you might as well stay in bed where it's warm. I need to get back to searching for Julie.'

But the bed cooled rapidly without Alan's comforting presence, and I couldn't sleep anyway, so I dressed in my warmest clothes and went downstairs in search of coffee.

Mrs Bates, as usual, was efficiency itself. Coffee and tea were standing ready, along with ham (cold) and eggs (boiled), toast, and a steaming pot of oatmeal at one corner of the fireplace.

'I'm sorry I can't give you proper eggs and bacon, Mrs Martin,' she said when I walked in, 'but the fire in the Aga's just about cold, and John's out with the search party. There's porridge if you fancy it, just for something hot.'

'We used to call it oatmeal back where I come from, and it's always been my ultimate comfort food. And I think you're marvellously inventive, coping as you have with a non-functional kitchen.'

'I enjoy a challenge,' she said as she ladled out a generous portion of oatmeal. 'I must thank you, by the way, for dealing with lunch yesterday. John and I were both needed elsewhere, as you could see.'

'Was it only yesterday? It seems like an eternity ago. I hated to invade your kitchen. It's good of you to take it so well.'

Having thus completed the civilities, I asked her to sit and have some coffee with me. 'Is no one else up yet? Except for the searchers, I mean.'

'Joyce went out with them. And the vicar was down a bit ago. He took some coffee and toast back up to Mr Upshawe's room. I think he doesn't like to leave him.'

'Did he say anything about how the poor man's doing?'

'Only that he's still unconscious.'

We sat in companionable silence while I demolished my bowl of oatmeal and poured myself another cup of coffee.

'Mrs Bates – what is your first name, by the way? If you don't mind my asking.'

'Rose. No, I don't mind. It's John who's so stubborn about being called Mister.'

101

'Well, then, I'm Dorothy. Are you from these parts, Rose?'

'Born in Branston village, but they closed the village school before I was old enough to start, so I had to go to the comprehensive in Shepherdsford. My father had flown the coop by that time, so mum moved us to Shepherdsford to be closer to the school. There were three of us kids. She had to take a job as a cashier at Tesco.'

Rose sipped her coffee.

'Not an easy life,' I said.

'Not easy, no. That's why I worked so hard in school. I was determined I was going to have marketable skills. I got four A-levels – you know what those are?'

I nodded. 'Advanced examinations for the college-bound. University, I mean.'

'Yes, well, I actually won a scholarship to uni, but by that time I knew I could cook. Really cook, you know. So I went to the Cordon Bleu school in London instead, and once I got out I could take my pick of jobs.'

'I admit I was a little surprised to find a cook of your calibre in a private home. I'd have thought someone with your incredible skills would be at the Ivy or somewhere like that – some posh London restaurant.'

'I don't care for London. Oh, I could make more money there, but believe me, I do all right here, and I prefer the country. I suppose you could say my roots are here.'

'Is your mother still living?'

Rose's face lit up. 'She lives in Branston, in

a lovely new house we bought her, John and I. Fresh as new paint, all the latest labour-saving devices, and a beautiful garden. Mum always loved her flowers, but she didn't have time for them when we lived in Shepherdsford. Nor the space, either. Our front garden in that nasty little house was about three feet square, and wouldn't grow anything but weeds.'

'And your husband, is he—'

A commotion at the back kitchen door interrupted me. Rose ran to see what was the matter, and opened the door to Alan and the other men, two of them bearing between them a blanket-wrapped bundle.

'Julie?' I cried.

'Julie,' Alan answered.

'Is she—'

'She's all right, except for being nearly frozen to death. Mrs Bates, can you heat some water, please? We're going to need lots of warm compresses.'

The next hour or so passed in a blur. John brought in enough wood for several fires and kindled one, first, in the Aga, and then in all the downstairs fireplaces and Julie's bedroom. Meanwhile Julie was tucked into bed with lots of blankets, with Rose spooning hot, sweet tea into her a teaspoon at a time.

When she was finally warm she was left to sleep, with Joyce at her side, and I was able to question Alan in the privacy of our room.

'Where was she?'

'In an old shed, or hut of some sort, a

couple of miles away. I suppose it must have belonged to a farm on the estate years ago, or maybe it was a shepherd's hut, but it's obviously been derelict for a very long time. There was nothing in it but a few rusted pieces of iron, bits of ancient tools, probably.'

'So what on earth was she doing *there*?'

'Hiding,' said my husband laconically.

Julie had, he said, been too cold and confused when they found her to say much. But from the way she had shrunk against the wall of her shelter when they entered, Alan could tell that she saw them as pursuers rather than rescuers. She had, in fact, tried to run from them, but she was too weak to get out of the hut.

'Does she know about Dave?'

'Nobody's told her.'

The answer was ambiguous. My eyes met Alan's. 'So you think...' I said slowly.

'Love, I don't think anything yet. Too much has happened too fast. First the body under the tree—'

'Sounds like the title for a mystery novel,' I interrupted, flippantly. 'There was one like that, actually, some years back. *My Foe Outstretch'd Beneath the Tree*. V. C. Clinton-Baddeley.'

'Yes, dear,' said my husband patiently. 'Stolen from William Blake, I believe. Then Harrison after the skeleton – and Upshawe – and now Julie. There has to be a connection, but I'm blest if I can see it.'

'It was the skeleton that started it all.

Finding him, I mean. Somebody buried that man and never wanted, or expected, him to be found.'

'And let's face it, Dorothy. The most logical person to be upset by the man's premature resurrection is Upshawe.'

'But he was attacked himself! He's a victim, not the villain.'

'Yes? Or did he simply slip and fall while fighting with Harrison?'

'Alan, none of it makes any sense. Why Harrison, of all people? Just because he's – he was, I mean – a boor and a thug and all the rest of it? His character, or lack of it, was a good reason to dislike him, to heartily wish him elsewhere, but surely it wasn't enough reason to kill him.'

'You'd be surprised at how little motive murder sometimes requires. But if you don't like that scenario, turn it around. Harrison started the fight; Upshawe was defending himself.'

'But why, Alan, why? What could Harrison have against a man he'd barely met?'

'Harrison was drunk, remember. Well, we won't know that for certain until the autopsy, but it seems a reasonable conclusion, since he was last seen with a full bottle of whiskey in hand.'

'The bottle, Alan! Jim said it wasn't in their room. You haven't found it, have you?'

'I've been a bit too busy searching for Julie.'

'Oh, I know, and I didn't mean to sound ... anyway, if you could find it, it would tell you something about where Dave went, and probably Julie, too. It could be a clue!'

'Yes, Nancy.' He grinned at me and ruffled my hair.

'OK, make fun. But I'm far too old for Nancy Drew. Jessica, if you must. Now look, my dearest love. We're cut off from any of your normal resources. No medical examiners, pathologists, crime lab people. All we have to work with is our minds. And— oh, wait! We do have one essential scene-of-crime man.'

The light dawned for both of us at the same moment. 'Oh, good grief! Dorothy, I've been an idiot. Why didn't I think sooner – we have a photographer!'

'Yes, and a really, really good one. I don't suppose he's trained to do police work, but I'll bet if you tell him exactly what you want, he'll get great pictures. He brought lots of film; he said so. And he's got a digital camera, too, if necessary.'

'He could be a godsend,' said Alan fervently. 'As soon as we've had some lunch, I'm going to sic him on the skeleton.'

'And I,' I said firmly, 'am going out in search of that bottle.'

ELEVEN

Naturally Alan tried to dissuade me. 'There could be someone very dangerous out there.'

'I thought we agreed it was either Harrison, who is dead, or Upshawe, who is unconscious. The Gingham Dog and the Calico Cat, except they didn't quite eat each other up.'

It took him a moment to get that one. 'Ah. The American version of the Kilkenny cats, I presume.'

'Probably. Anyway, I'm in no danger from either of them at this point. And if you're still worried about me for some obscure reason, I'll take someone with me. Lynn, maybe. She got me – got *us* – into this, she can jolly well help out.'

'Your English is coming along, my dear,' was his only response. I assumed silence meant consent.

I cornered Lynn while we ate our lunch (a chicken curry, which was superb), and she agreed to go for a walk with me in the afternoon. I didn't tell her why until we were on our way. Probably everyone in the house was honest. Probably. But on the off chance, I thought it was better not to broadcast my intentions.

'And what do you think it'll prove if we do find it?' Lynn asked, reasonably enough.

'Well – where one or both of the Harrisons had been yesterday after they left. Maybe no more than that. But at least the bottle is something tangible, and there isn't much else about this thing that is.'

'Yes, well, it's a lovely day for a walk.' She shivered ostentatiously as she spoke. The sun shone brightly, but the wind, which had picked up a bit again, was freezing.

'Pampered American! I thought you'd lived here long enough to become inured.'

'In London, my dear, not in the country. My walks usually consist of the four yards from my front door to a taxi. I don't mind walking a little on a beach in high summer, but this, I remind you, is November.'

I sighed. 'And tomorrow is Bonfire Night. I was so looking forward to the fireworks, but I don't suppose they'll have them now.'

'I don't think they can, even if they wanted to. They were going to have a pyrotechnics expert in, and he'd have brought his own van with a battery and a computer and all, to set off the rockets electronically. No expert, no truck ... no fireworks.'

'So that's that. Maybe they'll burn the guy, anyway. I suppose they have a guy?'

Lynn laughed. 'You bet they do! Joyce hinted that it's a really funny one. They wouldn't show it to me, though. It's supposed to be a big secret.' She sobered. 'It really is a shame. They invited the whole village to come, you know.'

'The old lord-of-the-manor bit? And would the village have come? If they were stand-offish about the Upshawes, I can't imagine they'd exactly warm to a couple of genuine foreigners in their midst.'

'I get the impression things have changed quite a lot since the middle of the nineteenth century when the Upshawes were the incomers. I believe the village has lots of non-English living there now. A Pakistani couple run the shop cum post-office, I know, because I was in there the first day we came. Not a trace of an Asian accent, either, so they're probably second- or third-generation. But I don't think Jim and Joyce are trying to be the village squires. It's just friendliness. But now nobody can get here. Look, where are we going?'

I had led Lynn through the walled kitchen garden and out the gate. We could more easily have stepped over the wall; it had collapsed in several places, and the gate hung crazily from one hinge. But to treat the wall thus cavalierly seemed, somehow, to give in to the devastation. So we had edged through the gateway.

Now we were headed downhill, southward toward the place where Harrison and Upshawe had been found. I shrugged. 'They ended up here. They might have gone this way. It wouldn't have been as dark as heading north, for one thing, or as hazardous. This part is mostly open meadow, with no trees to block the starlight or lie in one's path.'

'I can't figure why they left at all, any of

them,' said Lynn. 'The Horrible Harrisons must have understood they couldn't get very far. Jim made it plain enough. And Upshawe didn't seem to have any reason to be out here at all.'

'The Harrisons are, I think – were – I don't know what the right tense is – anyway, I don't think logic is a big part of their make-up. They were furious and wanted to get away; therefore they left. Maybe they thought they could ford the river down that way, or something.' I retied my headscarf; it was much too windy for any hat. 'Upshawe is a harder one to figure out. Alan thinks maybe he went after the Harrisons for some reason, and ended up pushing Dave into the river. But he can't come up with any compelling motive, or any motive at all, really. And neither can I.'

We fought the wind all the way down to the 'bottom of the loop', as Upshawe had described it, and stood, awestruck.

It was impossible here even to guess that there was a separation between the east and west arms of the river. An angry yellow torrent rushed past us, carrying tree limbs with it. As we watched, one limb snagged on something, rotated wildly in the current, and then broke free and sped on downstream. The wind tossed up waves, giving the illusion of rapids.

The river was still rising. Ripples spread closer and closer to us, drowning here a patch of coarse grass, there a clump of dead weeds. 'Those dead branches will have dammed up somewhere downstream,' Lynn said, shouting above the noise of the wind. 'The flood is going to get worse.'

I nodded. 'We'd better get back. I think Alan wanted Ed to take some pictures, and I'll bet the footprints on the riverbank would be something he'd want. And they'll be gone soon.'

We hurried up the hill, moving as fast as my new knees would take me, our quest for the liquor bottle forgotten. It had always been a silly idea, anyway. As Lynn had suggested, finding it wouldn't tell us anything relevant.

But we did find something. As we neared the house, we passed a clump of gorse, that thorny shrub that is so beautifully yellow in an English spring. Low, sturdy and compact, and somewhat protected by a stone bench, it had escaped the devastation of the storm. It wouldn't have many blossoms left now, but—

'Look, there's still one little gold flower clinging here,' I said, charmed. I reached out a hand to it and then pulled back.

'What's the matter, stuck by a thorn?'

'No. Look. It isn't a flower.

Hanging from an inch of broken chain that had caught on a thorn, a small gold cross shone brightly in the hard wintry sun.

'Alan needs to see this. And look at the way the wind is tugging at it. It could blow away any time. Lynn, could you find him and bring him here? And Ed should come, too, to take pictures.'

I thought I would freeze into an ice statue

before Lynn returned with the two men. 'They were taking pictures of the skeleton,' she said, panting. 'I ran all the way. Is it still there?'

I had protected the cross as well as I could without touching it. Alan and Ed approached and looked it over, and Ed pulled out his digital camera. 'Because,' Alan explained to me, 'we'll need to show this around, to see if anyone recognizes it, and we won't be able to get prints from the film shots for a while.'

'Won't be too long,' said Ed, busy all the time shooting. 'I brought chemicals with me; didn't know if the village would have a photo lab. Not many places do, nowadays. And I wanted to see prints of the house pictures before I left, to make sure they turned out.' He guffawed at that, and I joined him. I wondered just how many decades it had been since one of Ed's pictures hadn't 'turned out'.

'Any closet can be a darkroom,' Ed went on. 'I even brought a safelight. Don't know for sure how well that's gonna work, with no electric. These OK, do you think?'

He handed his camera to Alan and showed him how to page through the images.

'Splendid,' said Alan. 'We'll show these to everyone as soon as possible. Meanwhile, though, we'd better go down to the river and see if any of the footprints are still above water. Dorothy, take this up to the house and seal it in an envelope for me, will you?' He pulled the cross free, using his pen, and put it in my gloved hands. 'Handle it as little as possible, and don't touch it with your bare hands. I want to keep this very safe until we can identify it as someone's property.'

'It'll probably turn out to be Joyce's, lost months ago,' I said crossly to Lynn as I walked on up to the house. I was cold, and my knees hurt.

'You don't really think so,' said Lynn calmly. 'It's as shiny as the day it was made. It hasn't been out in the weather for more than a day or two.'

'Gold—' I began.

'Even gold gets dirty.'

It was, thank God, tea time when we got to the house. I would have headed straight for the kitchen, the fire, and some boiling-hot tea, had not Lynn reminded me. 'You need to seal that up, don't forget.'

In martyrly fashion I detoured to the library, where I found an envelope in a drawer, dropped the little gold ornament in, sealed it, and stuffed it in the pocket of my slacks.

Our ranks were sadly depleted around the tea table. With two of our number confined to their beds and two out documenting the scenes of various crimes – and one beyond the need for sustenance – we were only eight. I was glad to see that the vicar had joined us.

'How are your patients, Mr Leatherbury?' I asked when I had one cup of hot tea inside me and had poured myself another.

'Mrs Harrison is feeling much better,' he said. 'There was, I think, nothing much wrong there except exposure, and she was found before any permanent damage had been done. That is, I'm not a doctor, but her skin seems healthy, and she has no fever.'

'Has she said anything about what she was doing out there?'

The vicar looked uncomfortable. 'I don't quite know how much I am at liberty to repeat. She was rambling a bit, but she knows I am a clergyman. She may have felt I would keep her remarks confidential. In any case,' he hastened to add, 'much of what she said was unintelligible.'

Pat Heseltine, gorgeous Pat, was listening closely to this. 'I'm not at all sure the confidentiality privilege applies in this case,' she said thoughtfully. 'You're not her priest, nor were you attending her qua clergyman. If she was rambling, she might not even have known who she was talking to. In which case...'

'My dear Pat,' said the vicar with unusual firmness, 'the question is not a legal, but a moral one. It is up to me to make the decision to reveal or not to reveal her ... conversation is hardly the word ... her comments.'

'You could be required to, you know, in court. Or I think you could. It's an interesting point. I must look it up when I get back to my books.'

'The matter will scarcely arise. In any case, no one can force me to speak if my conscience forbids it. And the point is moot. I'm sure nothing she said has the slightest bearing

114

on ... on any of our worries.'

Pat looked stubborn. As she opened her mouth to continue the argument, I hastily spoke again. 'And Mr Upshawe? I gather his condition is much more serious.'

'Yes,' said the vicar. 'Excuse me, please.'

And he left the room.

'*Well!*' said Mike, who had been silently watching the action, his eyes avid. 'The good father has more nerve than one would have expected from that placid exterior.'

'The good father, as you put it, is a man of courage and integrity,' said Pat fiercely, 'and don't you ever forget it.'

'My dear!' Mike looked startled. 'I never doubted it, I do assure you.'

'Then stop sneering at him! We're in enough trouble here without your attitudes to contend with.'

Jim and Joyce started to speak at the same time, thus cancelling each other's good intentions. It was Tom who poured oil on the increasingly troubled waters. 'I'm sure Mike was just saying what we were all thinking, that Mr Leatherbury is handling a difficult situation with grace and kindness. I know we're all grateful he's here, though the poor man must be worried about his duties.'

I looked a question.

'Sunday. Tomorrow's Sunday. Who's going to take the service at St Michael's?'

Speculations about that occupied them for a few minutes, while I consumed tea and various improvised biscuits, and wished Alan would come back.

He wasn't long after that. He and Ed came in looking cold and famished, and proceeded to remedy their condition before they did anything else. The others finished their food and drink and began to push back their chairs. Alan stopped them.

'Ed took a picture I'd like you all to see. Tell me if you recognize the object.'

Ed fussed a bit with the camera until he had the best image of the cross on the small screen. He handed it around. Heads were shaken until the camera came to Pat.

'But that's the cross from Paul's prayer book! I'd recognize it anywhere – see the carving on it? At least, it's scarcely carving, just tracery, but very nice, I've always thought. He's had it for years. His daughter gave it to him, and he always uses it as a bookmark. However did it come to be caught in gorse?'

'That,' said Alan mildly, 'is what I need to find out.'

TWELVE

Alan asked me to come with him, and bring the cross. 'I'd like a witness to what he says, Dorothy, and you're the only one I can trust completely.'

'But you surely don't think he had anything to do with Dave Harrison's death!'

'Caused it, no. Had something to do with it – that's what I want to find out.'

So he tapped on Upshawe's door and went in. We found the vicar sitting at Laurence Upshawe's bedside, his prayer book open on his knee.

'Mr Leatherbury, I need to talk to you for a moment. Will we disturb Mr Upshawe if we do it here, do you think, or would another room be better?'

The priest looked up, his face unreadable. 'Some say the unconscious can hear, even when they can't respond. Perhaps it would be better to move into the corridor. I need to be within earshot, you understand, in case he speaks, or...' a helpless little shake of head '...or makes any sign of returning to consciousness.'

'It isn't good that he hasn't come out of it yet, is it?' I asked.

'Not as I understand it. No.'

We pulled chairs into the hallway and sat clustered around the door of the sick man's room. The vicar sat quietly, asking no questions. He looked unutterably weary, and far older than I had earlier judged him to be.

Alan held out his hand and I gave him the envelope containing the cross. Alan pulled a clean handkerchief out of his pocket, spread it on his hand, and tipped the cross out onto it.

'Oh, you've found it! I treasure that little cross and wondered what had become of it.' The vicar reached for it, but Alan moved his hand away.

'I'd rather you didn't touch it just yet, sir, if you don't mind. You recognize it, then?'

'How could I not? My daughter gave it to me when I officiated at her wedding. I've always used it as a bookmark.' He held up his prayer book. 'The chain has worn very thin over the years, and I noticed only last week that one of the links was weak. I should have had it repaired then. It was in its proper place last evening, but when I opened the book this morning to read the office, I saw that it was missing and was greatly distressed. May I ask where you found it?'

Alan nodded to me and I answered. 'It was caught on a gorse bush, Mr Leatherbury, just by that bench at the bottom of the garden.'

'Oh! But that was where—' He broke off, glanced through the open doorway, and sighed. 'I have been somewhat unclear in my mind, Mr Nesbitt, about what I should do. But I believe it is time for me to speak. I should not do so, please understand, if there were any question of clerical privilege.'

'No, of course not,' Alan murmured. Folding the cross in the handkerchief and putting it safely in his pocket, he looked as bewildered as I felt. Was Mr Leatherbury about, after all, to tell us what Julie Harrison had said to him? But what could that have to do with a cross missing since, presumably, before the vicar left his room this morning? I was bursting with questions, but Alan gave me an unmistakable *keep still* look, so I waited for what the vicar had to say.

'I went out just after tea yesterday to read the evening office. I was disturbed in my mind by the events of the day and needed a quiet place to pray. It was cold outside, certainly, but the wind had dropped and the sun was still shining a bit. I found the bench, the one by the gorse bush, Mrs Martin. It was far enough removed from the house that I thought I should have some privacy.

'However, I had barely begun the first psalm when Mr Upshawe approached me. It was apparent from his demeanour that he was troubled, so I asked him if I could be of help. He told me a remarkable story.'

Alan took his pen from a pocket, folded the envelope that had held the cross into a more-or-less rigid surface, and waited.

'It seems that when Mr Upshawe assisted you to examine the ... er ... remains under the tree, he found something which he concealed from you. I have it here.' From the pocket of his clerical gray shirt, he took a gold ring with a carved black stone. 'This ring, or I should say copies of this ring, have been worn by the Upshawes for generations. Mr Upshawe's father had one. So did his father's cousin, one-time owner of this estate, and so did that cousin's son, Harry.'

'Ah.' Alan pondered the implications of that for what seemed like a long time. 'And why did Laurence Upshawe not tell us about the ring?'

'For the same reason that people often lie, or conceal the truth. He was confused and afraid. The ring, you see, has an inscription inside.' The vicar turned the ring to the light and showed us. 'HU. And the date is, according to Laurence, the date of Harry's coming of age. So he realized, when he found it down there under the tree, that there could be little doubt the ring was Harry's. But how could it be? Harry died in a plane crash over the Atlantic. So Laurence took it, resolving to think out the problem before he said anything to you or anyone else.

'But when Pat brought up the story of Harry's "disappearance", and you pointed out that the fact of the crash did not necessarily prove Harry's death, Laurence was forced to acknowledge that the skeleton could very well be Harry's. And that, in turn, raised the question of who murdered him. For with the best will in the world, Laurence could not make himself believe that a man dead by natural causes would be interred secretly beneath an oak tree.'

'And of the people who stood to gain by Harry's death, one stood out,' Alan pointed out with calm logic. 'Laurence's father, who coveted the house and the estate.'

'That, obviously, was what caused Laurence such distress. He said his father loved the house with a quite unreasonable passion, and was infuriated when he learned that Harry was moving to America and leaving it behind.'

'The plane trip wasn't to be just a holiday, then?'

'Not according to Laurence's memory. He was young, but he remembers the tirade his father went into, talking about a worthless young man who didn't even care about his priceless inheritance – and so on. One gathers he tackled Harry about it, and the young man laughed at him, saying he, Harry, was going to sell "the old relic" as soon as he inherited, and that he, Laurence's father, could buy it then if it suited him. That would have meant breaking the entail, but even in those days it wasn't impossible. What was impossible was the notion of Laurence's father buying the place. That branch of the family never had much money. And Harry knew it.'

'He sounds like a really nasty person,' I put in with a shiver. 'Not a great loss to the world, however he died.'

The vicar looked at me sadly, but said

nothing. I knew what he was thinking. "Any man's death diminishes me..." et cetera. And John Donne was right, and so was Mr Leatherbury, and I was wrong. But ... it all happened a long time ago. 'Suppose, for the sake of the argument, that Laurence's father – what was his name, anyway?'

'Laurence, I believe. Confusing, I agree.'

'Oh. Well, supposing he did kill Harry in a fit of temper. He's dead now. Why is the present Upshawe so worried about it? I know, it isn't pleasant to think your father might have murdered someone, but after all these years...' I shrugged.

'You haven't thought about the question of inheritance, my dear,' said Alan. 'If Laurence senior killed Harry, the law would not allow him to profit from his crime. He could not have inherited Branston Manor, nor passed it on to Laurence junior. And if Laurence junior didn't own it, he had no right to sell it to the Moynihans.'

'Quite,' said the vicar, and we sat in a melancholy little silence for a moment. 'Laurence first asked me if my predecessor in the parish had told me anything that would clear up the matter. I suppose he thought that his father might have confessed his crime; that family was always rather High Church. I told him that if such a confession had taken place my predecessor would have been most wrong to tell me anything about it, and that in fact he had not so much as implied such a thing. So then Laurence asked if I had any advice about what he should do, and I told him he needed to make a clean breast of the whole thing to you, Mr Nesbitt. Only then can the matter be investigated properly, and the truth known. I firmly believe he intended to take my advice, and that is why I have confided his story to you.'

'Oh, but—' I stopped. It was no use pointing out that the Moynihans would be devastated if it turned out they had no legal claim to their wonderful house. Both men fully realized that. I tried to find a ray of hope somewhere. 'Isn't there some provision for a good-faith transaction?'

Alan and the vicar both nodded. 'Some,' said Alan. 'The law is complicated on the subject. Ms Heseltine could probably brief us, but I suspect what she would say is that the matter would have to go to court and could take a long time to settle.'

'And meanwhile Jim and Joyce couldn't spend money on repairs to the house or the garden, couldn't do a thing, in fact, except sit and worry.'

'Dorothy, do please remember that this is all speculation,' said Alan gently. 'It's now pretty obvious that the skeleton is what remains of Harry Upshawe, but the rest of the story stems from Laurence's fears, and is based on no evidence whatsoever. Furthermore, it does nothing to explain the rest of the things that have happened here.'

'One thing, perhaps,' said the vicar mildly. 'When Upshawe left me, he left in such a state of perturbation that I nearly went after him. I got up to do so, in fact, but I tripped over the leg of the bench, and by the time I had recovered myself he was far away. I suspect that was when I lost my cross.'

'Very likely,' said Alan, handing it back to him. 'Let me restore your property, sir. I doubt it has much more to tell us. I very much wish, however, that you had followed Upshawe. To think that we're so close to knowing what happened down at the river!'

'You can't possibly wish it more than I. I had some feeling that he was upset enough to ... to do something foolish, but I am not a young man, and he was walking too fast for me. I had planned to talk more with him as soon as he returned. That is why I went with you to search for him. I was most perturbed that he had not returned. I fear now that he went down to the river with some thought of jumping in, but Harrison tried to stop him and perished in the attempt. If Laurence doesn't recover, I shall feel I have two deaths on my conscience.'

And on that unhappy note we let him go back to praying over his patient.

THIRTEEN

Alan went back out with Ed to take some more pictures of anything they could think of that might be useful, and I wandered without direction, exploring the house more than I had taken time to do earlier.

The inside of the house was relatively un-damaged. Some ominous patches of damp were beginning to appear on some of the third-floor walls where, I assumed, roof slates were missing, and water was leaking down from the attics. Here and there Mr Bates had neatly boarded up a broken window or two, but by and large the rooms were intact. The Moynihans' excellent taste showed everywhere. I assumed that some of the furnishings were original to the house, but the rest had been found or commissioned to suit the various styles of the house perfectly. Here Jacobean windows were draped in colourful brocades; there a Georgian bedroom reflected that period's interest in *Chinoiserie*. Many of the rooms reminded me, in fact, of the exquisite miniature rooms assembled by Mrs James Ward Thorne of Chicago and on display at the Art Institute there. The same care and expertise had gone into these full-scale rooms.

It broke my heart to think Jim and Joyce might have to leave this house. They had plenty of money. They could buy another fine home. But no amount of money could make up for the lavishly expended love.

I couldn't think about it. I made my way, getting lost a couple of times, down to the kitchen, where Rose was busy with preparations for tea.

'Goodness, you must get tired of the endless succession of meals to cook and clean up after,' I commented, watching her assemble jam tarts.

She laughed. 'I told you I enjoy a challenge, and cooking for a crowd without electricity is certainly a challenge. I don't enjoy the washing-up part so much, I admit. That's not usually part of my job here; the dailies do that. But needs must.'

'Look here, can't we all help? It's ridiculous—'

She stopped me, looking positively alarmed. 'Oh, no, that would never do! You're guests.'

'But the circumstances are unusual, for Pete's sake. You can't be expected to slave away all by yourself. I know Jim and Joyce wouldn't want you—'

She interrupted me again. 'No, really. I imagine you're right about Mr and Mrs Moynihan, but John wouldn't have it. He has very high standards about service in this house – and before you say what you're thinking, yes, he does help a great deal. It isn't easy keeping this stove stoked with wood, not to mention all the repairs he's been trying to do as time permits. Don't think he's a slave driver, for he's not. He just feels strongly about this house and its traditions.'

Well, I had my own ideas about the slave-driving. It was absurd to expect Rose to do all the work that was usually done by a small army of daily workers, and under emergency conditions, at that. Bates seemed happy enough to let the men plan and probably help with repairs, after all. But it was plainly time to change the subject.

'Is Mr Bates from these parts, then?'

She smiled at that, and relaxed a little. 'You Americans do have such interesting ways of expressing yourself. "From these parts." I'll have to remember that. Yes, John was born and bred in the village. His people have always lived here, many of them actually on the estate, in the old days.'

'That would be ... when?'

'Seventeenth, eighteenth centuries. By the nineteenth the land was giving out, and agriculture didn't pay as it used to, so the Bates family mostly got work in the village. But they never lost their feeling for the estate. John's always felt it belongs to him and his kin, in a way.'

'That's why he works so hard, then. Keeping up tradition, keeping the place up to snuff.'

She smiled again at my odd English, and I

127

went away feeling hopelessly inadequate, involved with people to whom 'the old days' meant three or four hundred years ago. The English and the Americans are two peoples divided not only by a common language, as Churchill or somebody put it, but by a completely different understanding of the words 'history' and 'tradition'.

'His people have always lived here.' I wondered sadly what would happen to the Bateses if the ownership of the house were called into question. What would happen to anyone connected with the estate?

What a royal mess, I thought in another burst of pure American.

I shook myself, mentally, like a dog shaking itself free of water. This mood was non-productive. What I needed was someone to talk to, and my choices were limited. I couldn't say anything to Tom and Lynn about what Alan and I had just heard. They're my best friends in England, but Lynn, bless her, is incapable of keeping a secret. Obviously Jim and Joyce shouldn't know the latest developments until a good many maybes were settled into definites. Ed was with Alan, and Mike was an interesting person, but I couldn't see him being of much help in the present situation.

That left Pat. Plainly one of us needed to talk to her, in hypothetical terms, about the inheritance question. Plainly I would prefer doing it myself; I wasn't wild about the idea of my husband closeted with that undeniably gorgeous – and perhaps predatory – woman.

I went off in search of Pat.

She was in the library, a Dorothy Sayers novel in her hands, its garish yellow and red dust jacket looking out of place in that oak-panelled repository of wisdom. She looked up as I entered.

'Dickens palled?' I asked, pointing to where *Bleak House* lay discarded on the table by her chair.

She grinned. 'I know it by heart. A gross libel on the legal profession.'

'I thought a written work had to be untrue to be libellous.'

She laughed out loud at that. 'Touché. Not that I admit a thing, mind you.'

'I prefer Sayers, whatever the truth about Dickens. Which one is that?' I peered at the title. 'Ah, *Gaudy Night*. My favourite.'

'Mine, too. But I presume you didn't come in here to discuss literature. Looking for something to pass the time?'

'No, I was looking for you, actually.'

'Ah. There have been developments. Or are you going to warn me off your very appealing husband?'

'I might do that, if I thought there was the slightest chance he might respond to your—'

'Charms? Blandishments? It's a reflex, you know. Or protective coloration, if you will.'

I cocked my head to one side.

'You see, Dorothy – you don't mind if I call you Dorothy? You see, in my youth I had to fight off men. Literally, sometimes. It grows tiresome. I pondered my alternatives. I could, certainly, make myself as unattractive as possible, but I was too vain to do that. Quite frankly, I enjoy the way I look.'

'Yes, I can see how you might.' My tone was as dry and chill as the wind outside.

Pat only nodded. 'Yes. So I simply could not wear baggy clothes from Oxfam, eschew make-up, and take to wearing sensible shoes. My alternative was to go on the offensive.'

'Meaning?'

'Take the initiative. Most men, you know, are afraid of a woman who pursues them. The little dears want to "make the running", as my great-grandmother would have put it. So I started to flirt outrageously, and most of the time it scares them off.'

'And when it doesn't?'

'I have a mean left hook.'

I broke up at that. I couldn't help it. I didn't want to like this woman, but she had a sense of humour. And she liked Dorothy Sayers.

'OK, truce,' I said when we had both stopped laughing. 'I didn't come in to fight over Alan, anyway. I want to ask your legal opinion. Hypothetically. What if—'

'Wait.' She held up a hand. 'Do you have any money with you?'

'I might have a few pence in my pocket – yes, here's ten pence.'

'Hand it over.'

'Wha–at?'

She held out her hand and I put the coin in it.

'Now you have paid me a fee, and I am officially engaged as your solicitor. That makes anything you say a privileged communication. Go ahead.'

'Solicitors cost a lot less here than lawyers do in America,' I said, shaking my head. 'I'll have to remember that. Anyway, what if—'

'Purely hypothetically, right?'

'Right. What if the heir to a large estate were murdered, but no one knew about it at the time. And later the murderer inherited said estate, and in due time passed it on to *his* heir, his son. Time elapses – many years. The owner of the estate, the entail having been broken or dissolved or whatever, sells the place. What is the legal position of the new owners?'

'Do you read crime novels a lot?'

'Yes, as a matter of fact. Sayers is my favourite.'

'Yes, well, this *hypothetical* case you've just posed is worthy of the Golden Age – Agatha Christie at her most convoluted. Coils within coils. Are you sure there isn't going to be a long lost heir in there somewhere?'

'Not that I know of. I mean, not in this hypothesis.'

'Well, the short answer to your question is, I haven't the slightest idea how the present owners of this fictional property would stand, legally. There are too many variables. For one, how certain is the identity of the murderer?'

'Not certain at all. It isn't even certain that murder was done, though the evidence makes it extremely likely.'

'Ah. Then plainly, until murder is proven against an individual, the question of the legal ownership of the property doesn't arise, assuming all the documents related to the inheritance and the transfer of property are in order.'

'I think we can assume that.'

'Well, then, what are you worried about? This could take as long as Jarndyce vs Jarndyce, and Jim and Joyce could be dead before it all came to a head.'

'Wait a minute – we were speaking hypothetically,' I objected.

'Sure. And "Love is a thing that can never go wrong, and I am Marie of Romania". Don't fret, luv. My lips are sealed with that ten-pence piece.'

I grimaced. 'How am I going to go on resenting you when you read Sayers and quote Dorothy Parker? You are a woman of parts, Patricia Heseltine.'

'Pat. My given name, believe it or not, is Patience.'

'Oh, dear. I can see why...'

'Yes. Especially as the aforementioned virtue is not prominent in my character. I suppose my mother lived in hope, but she hoped in vain. Now look, Dorothy. Let's take the gloves off. What reason do you have for believing Laurence Upshawe's father murdered Harry? I take it there's good reason to believe it really is Harry under that tree?'

'Very good reason. Laurence found—'

Again she held up her hand. 'I don't want to know. I'll take your word for it. But what makes Alan think the senior Upshawe killed the little rotter?'

'Was he?' I asked. 'A rotter, I mean? I got the impression he wasn't a very likeable person, certainly, but that bad?'

'From what I hear. And I hear most things that circulate in the village. I never knew him, obviously. He was gone – gone away, everyone thought – before I was born. But his memory lingers on – rather like the faint aroma of skunk long after the animal has vanished. If the truth were known, I understand, there are a good many folks in the village who should rightly be named Upshawe. He wasn't liked, you know. Back in that era, a small place like this still expected a certain acknowledgement of noblesse oblige. His father had been good to his tenants and the villagers, but Harry never bothered. There were only two things about the village that interested him; the other was drinking at the White Horse.'

'A wastrel, then, as the Victorians would have called him.'

'Good word, that. Yes, he wasted his substance, like the original prodigal son. Unlike him, he never came back.'

FOURTEEN

I felt a little better after talking with Pat. It seemed that, unless or until Laurence's father was proved to be Harry's murderer, there was no question about the ownership of Branston Abbey. That was pretty much what we had thought, but it was nice to have it confirmed by an attorney.

I wasn't sure Alan would be comfortable with my telling Pat as much as I had. This business of working with Alan was tricky. He wasn't official anymore, and I'd never had any standing, but his policeman's conscience was acute. When it seemed that he needed to know all I'd said to Pat, then I'd spill the beans, but until then I was working on the assumption that I was old enough to use my own judgment. One thing I would report, though. It seemed there had been a good many people with reason to dislike Harry Upshawe, perhaps to hate him. And where there is hatred, there is motive for murder. The father, perhaps, of one of the village maidens he had seduced? Or perhaps they hadn't all been maidens. A husband or fiancé would have an equally powerful reason to wish Harry ill. Motive is the least important of the three prongs upon which criminal investigations rest. Means and opportunity are much more important, evidentially. But working in the dark of non-communication as we were, and fifty years after the fact, motive loomed larger than usual. And it was certainly good to know that others besides Upshawe senior had a motive for getting dear little Harry out of the way.

The vicar came down for tea, briefly. He asked Rose to prepare a tray for Julie, who was, he said, now fully conscious, but prostrated by the news of her husband's death. 'I had to tell her,' he said. 'She kept on asking me where he was. She is grieving, as one would expect, but she also seems afraid, terrified, even. She refuses to tell me who or what she's afraid of, but she keeps her door locked and won't allow anyone but me to come near her.'

'Not even Alan?' I asked incredulously. 'Surely a policeman...'

'Especially not Alan,' said the vicar with a sigh. 'She grew nearly hysterical when I suggested she let him know what had happened.'

'Will she tell you, then?' asked Alan.

'Not a word. I asked if I could pass on even what little she said yesterday, but she was adamant.' He sighed again. 'I have hopes that perhaps her sister might win her confidence in time.'

'I wonder,' I said. 'They're not on good terms. Never have been, I gather. Ah, well. When we have proper policemen here –

saving your presence, my dear – maybe she can be persuaded to talk. Meanwhile, how is Laurence?'

'No change.'

Well, that was as expected, but unwelcome news anyway.

The sky had grown overcast, then cloudy, then dark and heavy with impending rain. I had planned to go for a walk, there being nothing very useful for me to do in the house, but the lowering sky discouraged me. Alan suggested a nap, but I was too restless. 'Later, maybe, love. I'm getting stir-crazy. I need to get out of the house, but it's going to pour.'

Without much enthusiasm I began another tour of the house; my knees needed the exercise. I found a long gallery that occupied much of the top floor. It had few pictures in it, but a number of mirrors, and there I encountered Mike. Clad in a sweater, tights and leg warmers, and ballet slippers, he was positioned in front of a mirror, holding the back of a chair and doing *pliés*.

'Practising?'

He nodded. 'One has to, you know. Every day. The muscles have to be worked constantly.'

'Do you know what Arthur Rubinstein said about practising? "If I miss one day, I know it. If I miss two, my wife knows it. If I miss three, the audience knows it." Do you have a show coming up?'

'Alas, no. But one must keep in shape. Hope on, hope ever. And besides.' He left his improvised barre and began doing various steps in front of the mirror. 'I have had an idea.' A *grand jeté* down the long room, then another, then one of those spinning leaps that look so utterly impossible, then a *tour jeté en l'aire* and several *fouettés* brought him back at my side. 'I have been thinking, you see,' he went on, his breathing not even slightly laboured, 'about how to get out of here.'

'Not you, too. There *is* no way out of here, at least not until we get the phone and electricity service back. Then we might be able to get rescued by helicopter, or something, but until then, no. Be reasonable, Mike. Trying to get out of here cost Dave Harrison his life.'

'Dave Harrison, besides being a thoroughly objectionable git, was a lump. I am not a lump. I am a *danseur*, not quite yet *premier*, but not at all bad. Did you see those *jetés*?'

'I did. Very impressive, but what's your point? Are you proposing to entertain us while we're stuck here?'

'I am proposing to go for help. I have been to the river, not to the south where it is wide and flooded, but to the north. It is very high, deep and swift and dangerous, *but* ... it is narrow, and has not yet breached its banks. I believe I can jump it.'

I goggled for a moment, then began to rant. 'Are you out of your everlovin'? You just said yourself that the river's dangerous right now. If you missed the bank and fell in, you'd be dead in seconds. I've seen it to the south, where it's wider and slower, and it's terrifying

137

even there. Nobody could get out of that torrent alive. If you're grandstanding, Mike, cut it out. I'm not impressed.'

'My dear lady, I am unsure what "grandstanding" means, but I presume you imply that I am seeking attention. I do assure you, nothing could be further from the truth.'

'Oh, for Pete's sake, come off it. Sure you're looking for attention, and at this point, I have to tell you it's not becoming.'

'Dorothy.' He dropped the pose. 'Do you really think I'd risk my life – or worse, my career, if I broke a leg or something frightful like that – for a publicity stunt? I'm the only one who could possibly go for help, and I mean to try it.'

'But why? We'll get out of here eventually, with no death-defying heroics.'

'Laurence Upshawe could die without medical attention. He's a nice chap. I'm the only one who might be able to help.'

I simply could not speak. I had thought Mike a facile, shallow, if amusing, poseur. Now he was prepared to risk everything for someone he barely knew.

I moistened my lips. 'You're not planning on doing it now, are you? We're going to have a storm.'

'That is precisely why I need to do it now. If we get more rain, the river will rise still more and might flood to the north, too. It's very near it now. I was just warming up a bit when you came in, but I fear, dear lady, I must bid you adieu. There is no time like the present.

If it were done when 'tis done, then 'twere well it were done quickly. And other assorted clichés. Unfortunately I fear I shall have to wear shoes. Clumsy, but necessary. Where did I ... ah, yes. You will excuse me, won't you?'

He was out of the room before I could recover. 'Mike, wait! You can't ... Mike! ... I'm coming with you!'

But an ageing woman with artificial knees is no match for a young man, fit and trained as a dancer. By the time I found my way to the stairs and reached the front door, Mike was already loping across the front lawn toward the wood. I saw him leap several downed trees with careless grace before I turned drearily back to the house. I couldn't catch up with him. I couldn't deter him. That beautiful man was running with foolish gallantry to his death, and there wasn't a thing I could do about it. I went upstairs to find Alan.

He was asleep, but he woke instantly at the sound of my voice. 'Dorothy! You're crying! What's happened?'

I hadn't known I was crying. I mopped up with the handkerchief he gave me, and said, 'It's Mike. He's gone on a fool's errand, thinking he can save the world – or us, at least. Alan, he's going to drown, and I could not lift a finger to save him!'

Long before I finished Alan had swung his feet off the bed and slipped into his shoes, and was looking for his overcoat. 'Where has he gone?' he asked crisply.

'To the river. Near the bridge, I suppose.

He was taking off through the wood, the last I saw him. I couldn't catch him, Alan! He can run like a deer.'

'If he thinks he can swim that river, he is indeed going to drown, the bloody fool.'

'He isn't going to swim it. He's going to jump it.'

Alan turned on me a look of sheer astonishment, and then was out the door and racing down the stairs, calling for help as he went.

The sky grew darker still, and I heard a distant menacing rumble of thunder like the tympani in the Brahms Requiem, low, inexorable, ominous. I looked out the window to watch the storm come, the tears again running unheeded down my cheeks.

The men were all back in less than half an hour, drenched to the skin and shivering with cold – and without Mike. I went downstairs to meet them.

The admirable Mr Bates had prepared a large pitcher of hot toddies, while upstairs Mrs Bates was lighting bedroom fires and slipping hot-water bottles into beds. Hot baths were still impossible to organize, and I worried about Alan catching cold.

They all changed as quickly as they could. Everyone was running out of clean, dry clothes, but I had no doubt the Bateses would somehow manage to wash – and dry – whatever was needed. Downstairs again, in front of the roaring kitchen fire with hot cups in their hands, they told the story.

'We never saw him,' said Jim. 'It had started to rain by the time we got to the river, and the visibility was pretty bad. We found the place where he jumped, though.'

I tried to speak, to ask the question, but found I could make no sound.

Alan took up the narrative. 'It was only the place where the marks of his shoes were pressed deeply into the bank on this side. Or the mark of one shoe, rather. He tried a broad jump, evidently.'

'A *grand jeté*,' I murmured. 'And ... on the other side?'

There was a silence. Then... 'Nothing,' said Alan.

No one had any appetite for dinner. Rose had somehow contrived a pot roast. Under normal circumstances it would have smelled delicious. Now I found it nauseating.

The rain kept up all night, drumming on the roof, as menacing as the tympani/thunder. I suppose in the end I slept.

FIFTEEN

'This is beginning,' I said to my husband in the morning, 'to remind me of *And Then There Were None*. Only they were ten, to start with, and we were thirteen. Now two of us are gone, two are in bed, one is keeping a death-bed watch. Who's next, I wonder?'

'You're getting morbid, and your arithmetic is at fault. We started fifteen, if you count in the Bateses.'

'Oh, they certainly count,' I agreed reluctantly. 'But I was thinking of the ... the above-stairs crowd, if that archaic term can be allowed.'

Alan just grunted. He hates unresolved problems, and the weekend had produced nothing but. Coils within coils, as Pat had said. No wonder he was a bit testy.

The vicar conducted a simple church service that morning for anyone who wanted to attend. It would have been nice to do it in the old cloisters, but they were unsafe, as well as freezingly cold and wet. The rain had stopped, or had paused, rather. More was certainly to come. We gathered in the library instead, for Matins and an abbreviated Eucharist.

Sunday, November 5. The day I had been

so looking forward to, with fireworks and all the trimmings. No mention had been made, naturally, of the aborted festivities, but they were on everyone's mind, I was sure. When one is enmeshed in crises, the mind hunts, almost frantically, for trivialities to fret about instead. I tried to pray for a resolution to all our disastrous difficulties, but found myself wondering wistfully if the display would have been truly spectacular.

After church Jim went to the cloisters with his tools. If escape was impossible, at least he, with the other men, could keep on with repairs to the house. Alan told me to stay away. He almost never issues a command, but this time he had sense on his side. 'The roof could cave in, Dorothy. It's extremely touchy work, and I don't want you and your dodgy knees anywhere near it. See if you can keep the other women in the house, as well.'

I argued that if it was all that dangerous, he and the others shouldn't try it either, but I knew it was a lost cause. The gentleman's code of honour, the laws of hospitality, centuries of unwritten rules about the way an Englishman should behave – I could never win against those odds. So I left him to it and, in the perverse spirit of biting down on the aching tooth, started off on a walk through the wood to the river.

It was a thoroughly unpleasant day, not actually raining but threatening to at any moment. All the colours of the world seemed to have faded to gray and brown, and the most depressing shades of both. The floor of the wood was sodden and slippery with fallen leaves, which made the footing uncertain. More than once I wished I had brought my cane, but I was too stubborn to go back for it. I kept seeing Mike, yesterday, leaping through the wood like a fawn – or a faun. After one nasty near-fall, I picked up a fallen branch to use as a stick, but it was rotten and crumbled the first time I leaned on it. After that I went more carefully, picking my way and testing each step. I should have followed the drive instead. At least my knees hurt hardly at all; there was that to be thankful for.

I smelled the river before I saw it, and when I came upon it I gasped. The placid stream of three days ago was an angry, pulsing, living thing, boiling and foaming, terrifying in its mindless intensity. It had not yet risen above its banks, but it was visibly rising and would surely breach soon.

Walking toward the drive, I tried to find the place where Mike had attempted his crazy, quixotic leap, but it was hopeless. I should have realized that the rain would have washed away every trace. I had hoped, foolishly, that I might be able by daylight to see what the men last night had not, some sign that he had, however improbably, reached the far bank. There was nothing.

I said a little prayer for a lost dancer. Maybe someday someone would compose a ballet for him, along the lines of Debussy's Drowned Cathedral – *Le Danseur Englouti*. But someone else would dance the role.

There was something hypnotizing about the angry, ceaseless, rushing water. I couldn't take my eyes off it, and I could feel myself drawn to the brink. If I watched it much longer, I knew, I would go mad, or jump in, or ... something. My mind and senses numbed, I fled back to the house.

The men were still at it in the cloisters, cutting up the tree that had fallen through, clearing away broken glass, shoring up the roof where it threatened to fall in. I went close enough to take a look, though I knew I mustn't get in the way. The destruction was pitiful to behold, but I could see signs of progress. John Bates was working like a demon, everywhere at once, giving precise orders which everyone seemed to obey. I didn't know what his work had been before he came to the Moynihans, but he clearly knew what he was doing.

I went to seek out a like expert.

I found her, as usual, in the library, this time absorbed in a bound volume of *Punch*. 'Your tastes are catholic, I see.'

'"Age cannot wither her, nor custom stale the humour in these pages",' said Pat. 'Are you seeking company or reading material?'

'Neither. Pat, something has to be done. This can't go on.'

She put down her book and gave me her full attention. 'I agree, in principal. The men are working it out in sweat or prayer. What do you suggest we do?'

145

'I want you to do what you do best. You're a solicitor. Are you also a ... is it a barrister, someone who goes to court?'

'Yes, barrister, and yes, I am. In a village there isn't a lot of scope for that sort of thing, but in London, before I moved back here, I was a pretty good trial lawyer, as I believe the term is in America.'

'I thought so. Now, look. There is only one person who knows anything at all about what went on the night Dave Harrison died, and she's locked up in her room upstairs refusing to talk to anyone. I want you to make her talk.'

Pat said nothing for a full minute. Then she rose, removed her reading glasses, and said simply, 'Yes. I think I might be able to do that.'

I followed her into the kitchen.

'Rose,' she said, 'I thought I'd take a cup of tea up to Mrs Harrison. Please don't bother about it – I'll make it – but I'll need your pass-key for her door. Let's see – third on the left after the small landing, isn't it?'

Now if I'd made that request, Rose would probably have insisted on taking the tray up herself. Pat, with her inborn self-assurance, got her own way. In a few minutes we were heading up the stairs to Julie's room.

Pat handed me the tray while she unlocked the door. She didn't bother to knock.

Julie was not in bed, as I had expected, but was sitting slumped in an armchair in the bay window. They had moved her from the isolated suite she had occupied with Dave to one nearly at the west end of the house. It faced the front, so she had a good view from the bay window of the cloister and the work going on there. She didn't look up as we entered, but pointed and said in her whiny voice, 'Look at that, Reverend. It'll cost a fortune to fix that part of the house, let alone the rest. Why, there won't be anything left by the time they get done—'

At that point she looked up and saw us, and screamed. 'What the hell are you doing in here? Out! Get out!'

'I don't think so, Mrs Harrison,' said Pat calmly. 'I've brought you some tea. We need to talk.'

'I don't want any tea! I don't want to talk to you! You had no right to come bustin' in here. I – I'll sue.'

'Well, there you are, then. You *are* talking to the right person. I'm a lawyer, and I never lose my cases.' She had moved a little table closer to the chair, and I set the tray down on it. Pat poured out the tea, then took a small flask from the pocket of her slacks. 'This is good for shock,' she said gravely. 'I think you'd better have a little. You've been through a lot these past few days.'

Julie's eyes lit up at the sight of the amber liquid Pat poured into the teacup, and she offered no more protest. I've never been sure if it was the drink or Pat's air of intelligent sympathy that opened Julie's previously sealed lips. Or maybe she was just tired of her own company. At any rate, once she started talking, the torrent flowed like the river in spate.

'Lady, you ain't just whistlin' Dixie. Let's go visit your sister, he says. Have a nice European vacation, he says. And it's turned out to be nothin' but trouble, right from the get-go. My snooty sister and her snooty husband and their run-down old house, and all too good for the likes of us.' She took a healthy swig of the heavily laced tea. 'Dave, he says we can talk 'em around. Money talks, he says, and when they find out how much money they could make, they'll be draggin' us to the lawyers for the papers. Hah!' Another swig, and the cup was empty. 'Treated us like dirt, tried to throw us out, and then changed their minds and said we had to stay here. We don't gotta put up with this, I told him. I don't care what they say, they're up to something. Stands to reason there's a way out of here, storm or not. They just don't want us to find it, damned if I know why. Dave, he says they're tryin' to put us off the place, makin' out like it's a dangerous place to live and that. So we took off, lookin' for the secret way out. Thanks very much, don't mind if I do.'

The fluid in the cup this time was neat whiskey. If this was Pat's usual technique with reluctant witnesses, I could believe her claim of never losing a case.

'So anyway, we start to look. Kinda sneaky-like, y'know? Dave, he figures there might be a tunnel or somethin' under the river, like they used for smugglers way back when.'

Way back where, too, I thought. Branston was in the heart of Kent and miles from any coast. Smugglers would have had to build an awfully long tunnel. But Julie's geography was apparently a trifle vague.

'So we figured, if the tunnel came out in the house, it'd be in the basement somewheres, so we went down to poke around. But there was nothin' much down there but a lot of wine in one part, and the furnace in the other. Nice and clean, it was, I'll have to say that for 'em. Course, if you've got tons of money like them, you can get somebody else to do all the work. Must cost a fortune to run this house. I wouldn' mind a li'l bit o' that money, myself.'

Julie held out her cup for another round. Pat and I exchanged glances. At this rate, she'd pass out before she told us anything useful. This time Pat made the mixture mostly tea. Julie didn't appear to notice.

'So where was I? Oh, yeah, we're tryin' to find the way out, but there wasn't nothin' in the house, not that we could find, anyways. So Dave says, maybe it came out in one of those other buildings, the garage or somethin'. Well, I told him, I says, dummy, I says, they didn't have garages back then. But he says, hey, brain, they had horses, didn't they? And where they kept the horses, now they keep cars. Dave could be smart sometimes, when he wasn't being dumb.' She sniffed. 'Maybe he wasn't the best husband in the world, but he had ideas, all right.' She sniffed again, and I feared she had reached the weepy stage of her rake's progress, but she took another drink, and it seemed to buck her up.

'So we headed for the garage, and when we was almost there, Dave stopped so sudden I ran into him, and he says, there's somebody out here. Then I heard 'em, too, a couple of guys talkin'. So Dave tells me to keep still.' Julie put her finger to her lips in exaggerated pantomime. 'Ooh! He told me to keep on keepin' my trap shut, and here I've been shootin' my mouth off to you.' She opened her mouth again to finish off the contents of her tea cup, and then shut it firmly, an owlish look in her somewhat bleary eyes.

Oops. Was this all we were going to get?

I had reckoned without Pat. 'Quite right,' she said, putting the flask back in her pocket with a gesture that could have been seen from the third balcony. I wondered if she had ever acted when she was at Oxford, in OUDS, perhaps? 'You wouldn't want to say anything foolish. Dave knew best, I'm sure, so if he told you to shut up, you'd better not say anything he wouldn't like.'

'Whaddya mean, Dave knew best? I'm the brains of this operation! *I* was the one told *him* he'd better do somethin' quick when that Upshawe guy was gonna blab about— never mind what. *I* was the one told *him* to follow Upshawe and tell him he'd better keep his lip buttoned, or else. *I* was the one had the sense not to go with him, in case there was trouble.'

She paused and hiccuped. 'And there was!' she said with a wail, and began to sob.

'That's all she wrote,' I whispered, and Pat nodded. She got out the flask and put it on the table, and we went downstairs, leaving Julie to her alcoholic blues.

SIXTEEN

'Frustrating,' was my comment when we were back down in the library. 'We're no closer to knowing what happened in the encounter between the two men. And I was so sure she could tell us!'

'It's still possible that she could, if she would. I think we've got all we can out of her for the moment, but I wonder if she's the sort to respond to a séance. Do you think, if the egregious Dave came back and told her to tell all, she's credulous enough to believe, and talk?' asked Pat thoughtfully.

'Hmm. She's not the brightest bulb in the chandelier, but she's shrewd in her own way. I suppose, perhaps, if we could work it out so that she could see some self-interest in the proceedings – but we're talking nonsense. I wouldn't have the slightest idea how to stage a séance, and anyway that sort of thing went out with the thirties, surely.'

'We're trapped in the thirties, hadn't you

noticed? That wasn't just a storm we experienced, it was a time warp. I expect at any moment to hear someone cranking up a gramophone to play Rudy Vallee records.'

'You've been reading too much, is what's the matter with you. What did you make of her ramblings, though? Was there anything of use?'

'Well, we know she and Dave overheard Upshawe's confession, and that it upset them. I couldn't quite follow why.'

'I think I know. When we first got here—goodness, was it only three days ago? Feels like several lifetimes. Anyway, the Andersons had been here a day or two already and had had far too much time to get acquainted with Dave and Julie. They told us, Alan and me, that Dave had some scheme to tear this house down—'

Pat uttered a horrified shriek.

'—and build some sort of resort. He seemed to want to go into partnership with Jim. Yes, I know, it was an obscene idea, and impossible with a listed building, anyway. But that would explain why Dave went off after Laurence.'

'It would? Oh, sure! What a ninny I am. Your hypothetical situation. If Laurence's father killed the heir, then he couldn't inherit, et cetera, et cetera. And if Jim didn't own the house, he couldn't sell it to Dave, and all the scheming was for naught.'

'Exactly. So Dave had a motive for silencing Laurence.'

'Not a very strong one, though.' Pat frowned. 'You and I talked this out. There are so many ifs, the threat to Jim and Joyce's claim is practically non-existent.'

'Yes, but would a Dave Harrison realize that? I would say that logical thinking was never his strong point, and he was not only drunk at the time, but in the grip of a monomania. He had convinced himself that Jim was going to buy into his plan, that this house was as good as his— oh!'

'Sudden pain?'

'Sudden idea, and ... rats! It's gone again. Something I said triggered ... it was right on the tip of my mind...'

'Stop thinking about it. Those things are like cats. They only run away and hide if you chase them, but if you ignore them, they come out and beg for attention. So you think Dave followed Laurence and tried to push him in the river, but ended up getting pushed in himself.'

'Or falling in, more likely. He was bound to have been pretty unsteady on his feet at that point.'

'I don't know. Julie was still conscious and more or less coherent when we left her, and I'd poured the best part of a pint of whiskey into her. I think Dave must have had a formidable capacity.'

'Years of practice, probably.' I shook my head. 'How on earth did a sister of Joyce's find such a useless specimen to marry?'

'Just lucky, I guess.'

* ★ ★

The vicar surprised us by coming down to lunch. He had retired to Laurence's room as soon as the church service was over, and we hadn't expected to see him the rest of the day, except perhaps to fetch a tray. We all wanted to know about his patient.

'He seems to me to be quite a bit better. He's breathing more easily and looks as if he's sleeping, rather than unconscious. At least his eyes move now and then, beneath the lids.'

'REM sleep,' someone said. 'They say that means he's dreaming.'

'I shouldn't think the dreams would be pleasant,' said Alan.

'He has made little noises today,' the vicar acknowledged. 'Sounds of discomfort, as I interpret them. Moans, I suppose one could call them if they were better defined. Actually, they sound like nothing so much as the little whines produced by a dreaming dog.'

'He hasn't tried to speak? Or open his eyes?' Alan tried to sound casual, but I could hear the sharpened awareness in his voice.

'His eyelids fluttered once, but never opened. And there's been nothing that sounded like words. Still, I am encouraged by his progress, and thought I might venture to take a few minutes away from him.'

'I should think so,' I said warmly. 'You've done nothing but look after him for days.'

'Less than two days, Mrs Martin. We found him Friday evening, remember. It seems longer, I agree. Many things have happened in those two days.'

I think we all tried not to think about Mike.

'Look here, sir,' said Alan. 'Suppose I take the duty for a few hours, and let you get some rest. I have a bit of basic medical training. I think I could serve.'

Mr Leatherbury smiled a little. 'I'm sure you know more than I about nursing. My concern is the cure of souls, not bodies. As I could be of next to no help anywhere else, I chose to sit with poor Laurence in case he took a turn for the worse and needed a priest. But I admit I'm not as young as I used to be, and trying to keep alert all this time has been a bit exhausting. If you truly don't mind...'

'Not a bit.'

Pat spoke up at that moment. 'Paul, Alan. I'm of no earthly use to anybody, just sitting around. I don't know a thing about medicine, but I know how to keep my eyes and ears open. Let me take the next shift.'

I was gaining more respect for Pat with each passing hour. It was agreed: Pat went off to sit with the victim, or the chief suspect, depending on how you looked at it, and Alan returned to his work in the cloister.

'I expect you're badly in need of a nap,' I commented to the vicar.

'No, I need fresh air more than anything, I believe. I intend to take a walk.'

'It isn't very nice out there,' I said. 'I went out this morning, to look at the river, and...' The lump in my throat stopped me.

'Yes. That poor young man. It was a gallant

gesture, no matter how ill-advised. Perhaps, Mrs Martin, you would care to walk a little way with me? The rain will keep away for another hour or so, I believe, and you can wrap up well. I'd be grateful for the company.'

What he meant, I suspected, was that he thought I needed some comfort. He was right about that, certainly. I found my coat and hat and borrowed some wellies, and we set out.

Mr Leatherbury was silent, a companionable silence, waiting for me to choose a topic. I didn't want to talk about tragedy. I was weary of disaster, frustrated by our inability to do anything about – anything. At least Jim and Alan and the other men were doing something constructive, clearing away the worst of the messes and beginning repairs. I could find nothing useful to do or say.

But the thought of repairs reminded me of what, centuries ago, I had wanted to ask the vicar. 'Mr Leatherbury, Joyce or Laurence or somebody told me you knew a lot about the history of this house. All I know is the brief outline Laurence gave us at dinner that first night. Can you tell me more?'

His face lit up. 'Ah. You've hit on my passion. I warn you, I can talk about this house until you're begging for mercy. What specifically did you want to know?'

I laughed. 'I know too little even to ask. But I suppose I'm most interested in the ghosts – if you as a clergyman concede their existence.'

He chuckled. 'Not officially, but I'll tell you

some of the stories, and you can judge for yourself. The oldest ghost who is purported to haunt these premises is, as one might expect, a monk who resented being turned out. The story has it that he fought King Henry's men, against the express orders of his abbot, who had commanded them all to go peacefully. So not only was he – Brother David – killed in the scuffle, but his abbot refused him absolution.'

'So he has no home in heaven and must walk the earth,' I finished. 'That's rather a creepy story. Would an abbot actually do such a thing?'

'That's hard to tell. It was a long time ago, and such stories are notoriously unreliable. On the other hand, Abbot Benedict – it was a Benedictine house, and he had chosen the name of the founder – was by all contemporary accounts a tough old bird, harsh with the men under his jurisdiction. And Brother David, as one would expect, was a Welshman, with the fiery temper of his race.'

'What was a Welshman doing way over here in Kent?'

'That,' said the vicar, negotiating a stretch of lawn that was especially littered with storm debris, and giving me his arm for support, 'is one of the details that make the story somewhat suspect.'

'Have you ever seen him? Brother David, I mean?'

'Certainly not.' It was said with a twinkle that left me unsure of whether he was speaking the literal truth or taking the official line that ghosts didn't exist.

'So you said he's the oldest of them. There are more, then?'

'Legions. The usual spurned lovers and bereft maidens. An early Branston, around 1650, who was said to have drowned in one of the garden ponds, is reputed to go about with a fish in his pocket, slapping it in one's face.'

'Ugh!' I shuddered. 'A real goldfish in the face would be bad enough, but a long-dead one – no, thank you! Are there no really romantic legends about the house? Alan had a temporary appointment at Bramshill once, and they had a marvellous ghost story, about a bride who was, with her guests, playing hide and seek on her wedding night. I'd have thought she'd have had better things to do, but anyway, she hid in a chest, it locked itself, and she wasn't found for years.'

The vicar laughed. 'Oh, that one's been around for a long time, at various locations. Hiding on one's wedding night appears to have been a popular pastime. But no, there aren't any like that here. The house has seen its usual share of tragedy, as one might imagine. From the time the monastery was established in 1042, people have lived here. That's a long time. Wars have taken their toll, as have diseases. The household was not immune to the Black Plague, nor to the influenza epidemic in the early twentieth century. Several of the Upshawes fell to the flu, which explains why there was no closer heir than a cousin when old Charles died.'

I sighed. There we were, back at the problem. The elephant in the room. 'Mr Leatherbury, do you think Laurence ... had anything to do with Dave Harrison's death?'

'I should think that was obvious,' he said, with a touch more acid in his voice than I expected. 'Plainly he was on the scene. However, if you're asking me if I believe he pushed the man in the river, I do not. I've been a clergyman for a good long time, Mrs Martin. One comes to know something about people. Laurence Upshawe is not a killer.'

He had a point. Still... 'You knew him before he went to New Zealand?'

'No. I've been incumbent here for only twenty years, and Laurence left in ... 1982, I believe it was. I know his family's history because I'm fanatically interested in old houses and have read everything I could about this one, but I met the man for the first time on Thursday night – when you did. You're perfectly justified in doubting my judgment.'

'It isn't that so much. As a matter of fact I agree with you, and I think Alan does, too. But the police have to go by evidence – and Laurence was the only other one on the scene.'

'That,' he said with finality, 'is their problem, not mine. It's getting rather chilly. Shall we go in?'

SEVENTEEN

'Wait. Please.' I put my hand on his arm. 'I didn't mean to offend you. It's just that this horrible business is the only thing I can think about. I wish to goodness I'd never seen that miserable skeleton. That's what started everything!'

'No, my dear. And it is I who should apologize. I should not have been so snappish with you. But your discovery did not begin this matter. It began long ago, with whoever buried the poor man under the tree. And if you had not found the evidence, someone else would have.'

'Yes, well, that would have suited me better,' I retorted. 'I was so looking forward to seeing a proper Guy Fawkes celebration. I love fireworks. I'm being childish; sorry.'

'It is a great pity, all round. Have you never celebrated the Fifth of November?'

'No. I've lived in England only a few years, and somehow Alan and I have never been in the right place on that day. He's told me all about it, of course, the Catholic plot to blow up Parliament. I'm still not quite sure why the Gunpowder Plot should be a cause for celebration.'

160

'But we celebrate not the plot, but the fact that it was foiled.'

'Isn't it just a little ... well, politically incorrect? Burning an effigy of Guy Fawkes, a Catholic? It seems a bit grisly.'

'You may not know that a celebration of the saving of the King and the House of Lords was mandated by Parliament shortly after the event. Bonfires and the ringing of church bells became traditional. The fireworks and the burning of the guy came later, having little to do with the historical occasion – any more than parades and baseball games have to do with your American Independence Day.'

'Well, it's not quite the same – but I see your point. At any rate, I'm sorry to miss all the fun, though fireworks aren't at all important compared to the issues we're dealing with here.'

'True. Whoops, here it comes!' The rain came as suddenly, and as copiously, as turning on a faucet. We were soaked to the skin in seconds.

At this rate, I thought bitterly as I squelched up to my room to change clothes yet again, I might as well just walk around all weekend in my underwear and have done with trying to keep clean and dry.

The rain also put a stop to the restoration work in the cloister. Alan came upstairs shortly after I did, nearly as wet as I and a whole lot grubbier. He washed as best he could in the limited hot water available, and grumbled. Alan isn't a grumbler, by nature, but this endless 'holiday' was trying even his patience. 'And what am I meant to wear?' he asked, standing in his shorts and undershirt when he had removed as much grime as possible. 'Everything I have here is either wet or dirty or both.'

I paused a moment to admire the view. My husband is a large man, not fat but tall and, even at his age, powerfully built. His gray hair adds authority to his commanding presence. He is, in short, a hunk.

And one of the dearest people on the planet – even when he's grumpy. I smiled at him. 'Aha! You reckoned without your brilliant wife. I thought ahead, and borrowed some clothes from Mr Bates. He's just about the same size, and he was happy to oblige. They're not quite your style, but in the circumstances, I didn't think you'd mind too much. They are at any rate both clean and dry.'

He actually looked quite nice in them, if somewhat more casual than he usually appears. I hadn't fared so well. No one in the house was my size, which rather runs to the dumpling configuration. But one of Joyce's sweaters fit not too badly with my cleanest pair of slacks. Beggars, as I carefully had not said to Alan, can't be choosers.

We went down to a badly needed cup of tea. The rain slashed at the window panes and dripped down the chimney, hissing in the kitchen fire. Nobody had much to say.

'We wouldn't have been able to do the fireworks anyway.' That was Joyce.

'No,' Jim responded listlessly. 'And we can't work on the house until this lets up.'

'But we're coming along on the ark.' Ed tried to lighten the atmosphere. He didn't succeed. I missed Mike, who would have made everyone laugh with some drawling, bitchy remark. Astonishingly, I missed Pat, who had come down when the vicar relieved her, downed a cup of tea and a biscuit or two, muttered an excuse, and gone off, presumably to the library to read something classic. She could strike sparks, but apparently wasn't in the mood. Tom and Lynn hadn't come down at all.

The house party was utterly demoralized, and Jim and Joyce didn't even seem to notice.

'Somebody has to do something,' I whispered to Alan, 'or we'll all go stir crazy.'

'You're right about that.' He rose, stretched, and addressed our host. 'Jim, I have a proposal to make. I know Mr Bates has been trying to assess the damage to the house, but he has a great many other responsibilities. Suppose you and I take a complete tour of the house and see what we can from the inside. An outside inspection is needed, too, but with this kind of rain, we'll be able to tell a good deal from where damp spots appear, where the rain is actually coming in walls and windows – that kind of thing. And anyone else who would like to come along can get the house tour we were promised and never had time for. What do you think?'

There was no wild upsurge of enthusiasm. Everyone was too dispirited for that. But eventually we recruited Ed, who hadn't yet been able to see the house thoroughly, and dragged Tom and Lynn out of their lair. Pat, who was in a strange mood, growled that she already knew as much about the house as she cared to, thank you very much. Mr Bates found several lanterns, since the rain made the house dim as well as gloomy, and we assembled what flashlights we had.

'Should have waited until morning,' Ed complained. 'Can't see worth a damn this afternoon.'

'If we had waited,' I said, *sotto voce*, 'there would have been more murders done. And I might have been one of the villains.'

In truth it was a somewhat futile exercise, but it gave us something to do besides sitting around wishing we were anywhere else on the planet. And though we couldn't see much in the way of storm damage, from the stand-point of a house tour it was perfect. Those rooms hadn't been designed for harsh electric lighting. Daylight, candles and, later, lamps would have provided the illumination for the first many hundred years that the house had been standing. Our lanterns restored the lovely proportions of the rooms, softened and mellowed the old panelling, showed the carving at its best.

They also, less fortunately, made the un-even floors and odd corners that much more hazardous. The first time I tripped on a raised floorboard I nearly fell. After that I kept my hand tucked securely in Alan's arm.

I had wandered a good bit of the house by myself, or so I thought. I soon realized I had only scratched the surface. Mr Bates, who knew the house intimately and soon became our guide, knew the history of every room, every piece of furniture, every painting. This bit of panelling was reputed to have been removed from one of Thomas More's rooms after More fell out of favour with the king. This was an Adam fireplace, this a Gainsborough painting. Here was the bed Queen Anne had slept in, bought for the purpose, her visit nearly bankrupting the family. And so on.

'Mr Bates,' I said when we were climbing to the third floor and I could get a word in edgewise, 'the Harrisons apparently had some idea there were tunnels leading from the house. I thought it unlikely, myself, because those were mostly used for smuggling, and we're too far from the sea. Right?'

'Indeed, madam. To my knowledge there is no history of smuggling or piracy connected with the house, but during the civil wars various hiding places were devised, because the Branstons were royalist, and there were pockets of Parliamentarians out to do mischief wherever they could. The family plate was locked up on several occasions, and once, if the stories are true, the family themselves had to go into hiding. Most of the secret rooms have been converted over the years into bathrooms and closets, but I can show you one of them, or I hope I can. I came across it the other day when I was repairing a bit of the panelling.'

We were in one of the unused third-floor bedrooms. He stepped to the wall near the fireplace and, carefully moving aside a chair, pushed on a piece of moulding. It moved aside to reveal a keyhole, surrounded by old brass, black as iron. Bates took from his pocket a huge old key, the kind I associated with castles and dungeons. 'I don't know that this will fit, but it's the right size and age. It was in a drawer in one of the attics, with a lot of other old keys, and I've found the locks that match most of them. Even if it fits, the lock's apt to be a bit stiff,' he said, manoeuvring the key into the lock. 'I don't imagine this has been opened for a hundred years or more.'

We were very still. The rain pounded against the house; the lanterns flickered. Our modern clothes were hidden in the gloom; only our white faces could be seen. I felt suddenly oppressed, as if back in that time of terror when King James's loyalists were hunted down by Cromwell's men, Christian against Christian, Englishman against Englishman.

And I suddenly did not, very much did not, want to see that door opened. If I had followed my instincts, I would have fled that room, run down to warmth and light and normality. But I suppose my manners were overdeveloped, so I gripped Alan's arm and waited.

The lock was indeed stiff, but Bates persevered, and suddenly, with a harsh grating sound like the gnashing of teeth, the lock gave. Bates pushed, shoved, then tugged at the door, which finally, with an eldritch shriek of hinges, opened outward. Bates took the lantern he had asked Jim to hold, held it high, and illuminated the interior of the dark hole in the wall.

And crashed to the floor in a dead faint.

EIGHTEEN

Somebody screamed. Maybe it was I. I don't know. I vaguely remember Alan pulling me close, burying my face in his shoulder so I couldn't see. Tom and Ed hustled Lynn away, while Jim tried to deal with the inert form of the butler. When I could think again, I said shakily, 'Love, you'd better see to Mr Bates. You know CPR and all that. I'll take Lynn to the next room and wait for you. Just – just be as quick as you can.'

'Sure you'll be all right?'

'Sure. But give me the flashlight. Come, Lynn.'

The flashlight didn't give us as much light as a lantern, but it was modern. It didn't flicker evocatively, didn't conjure up images of past dreadfulness.

Lynn and I just sat for a few minutes, our hands clasped together tightly, trying to stop shaking. When I thought I could speak without chattering teeth, I said feebly, 'Was that thing real?'

'I don't know.' Lynn's voice was no steadier than mine. 'I thought it was maybe a ghost. Dorothy, it moved! I swear it moved!'

'I think it just fell forward. I – at first I thought it was the guy. You know, for the bonfire. But it wasn't, was it?'

'It was a woman. I think. There was a dress...'

'It looked like ... Lynn, do you know what it reminded me of? You remember that terrifying scene in *Psycho* when they go into the room where the mother is, and she's in that rocking chair, and—'

'Don't! She looked like that, exactly like that, all dead and dried up and horrible...'

Lynn's voice was rising higher and higher, and I wasn't feeling steady enough myself to calm her down, so I was most relieved when Tom and Alan walked in. No two men ever looked more like white knights. I could feel my blood pressure drop about thirty points just at the sight of him. Lynn started to sob on Tom's shoulder.

It took me differently. I had to know. 'Alan, what *was* that thing?' I didn't at the moment even remember to be concerned about Bates.

'A body, my dear. Long dead, mummified

168

by being in there close to the fireplace for so long.'

'A woman?'

'From the clothes, yes. They're remarkably well-preserved.'

'And ... how old? How long was that poor thing walled up in there?' I was starting to shake again, to gasp. The space was so small, so airless, so dark...

'Easy, love. She was dead when she went in. Even a quick glance told me that. No abrasions to the hands. And the clothes are modern. Long hair, held back with a ribbon. It's pretty easy to guess that she was killed sometime in the middle of the twentieth century.'

'When Harry Upshawe died, in other words.'

'About then, yes.'

'It can't be a coincidence.'

'One wouldn't think so.'

Belatedly, I remembered Mr Bates and asked Alan about him. 'Is he all right, Alan?'

'He will be. It was just a faint. Jim and Ed got him down to the kitchen, where it's warm. I'm sure his wife will look after him. He'll be all right,' Alan repeated.

I sighed, a long, shuddering sigh. 'What are we going to do, Alan? Just this morning I said to Pat, this can't go on. But what options do we have?'

'Very few, but you're right, it can't go on. Somehow we must get in touch with the outside world. I have a ghost of— I have a faint idea. It may work, and it may not, but it's worth a try.'

'Anything's worth a try. You're surely not thinking of a boat, though, are you? Because the river's way too dangerous until it calms down.'

'No, not a boat. Fireworks.'

I thought I'd heard him wrong, or had gone crazy from shock. I looked at him dumbly.

'Fireworks and flares are very much the same thing, you know, and flares are always a danger signal. If we can somehow touch them off, it might attract some attention.'

'But ... the rain. And it's Guy Fawkes Night. Even if you can get them to fire, won't people just think they're part of the celebration?'

'I don't know, love. We have to try. It's the only chance we have. I cannot deal with multiple murders on my own, even with you to help.'

'Two of them are old. And Dave might not have been murdered.'

I was grasping at straws, and we both knew it. We had landed squarely in the middle of a horrible situation, a nightmare, and I wasn't sure how – or if – we were ever going to get out.

'What have you done with ... her ... it?'

Alan looked at me, considering. 'I'm not sure you want to know.'

'Oh. Walled it up again?' I gulped and push-ed the picture firmly out of my head.

Alan nodded. 'It seemed the most sensible thing to do, until we can get help. I made sure the door was firmly locked, and I have the key.' He patted his pocket and turned to Tom and Lynn. 'Shall we go down? I for one could use a good stiff drink.'

That seemed to be the general feeling. We assembled as usual in the kitchen, where Joyce was holding forth, for once.

'I'm not quite sure what we'll have for dinner, folks. Mr Bates is still feeling unwell, and Mrs Bates is, naturally, looking after him. So I'm mistress of my own kitchen again! There will be plenty to eat, but it may be rather ... peculiar. Certainly not what Mrs Bates has accustomed us to.

'Now there's something I want to say to you all. I've been a terrible hostess all weekend. OK, OK.' She held up her hand at the protests that arose. 'I'm not going to apologize for anything, because you're all friends and you all make allowances for ... um ... circumstances beyond our control. Including what the insurance companies call an Act of God. But here we are, and here we stay, perforce, until the army or somebody rescues us, or the river goes down.

'I won't suggest that we forget all that has happened in the past several days. We would not be human if we could do that. But Jim and I moved here because we love England and the English, and one of their traits we admire most is the stiff upper lip. So I intend to emulate them and suggest that we try to relegate all the unpleasantness – how's that for fine British understatement? – to the back of our minds, and spend the rest of our time here like civilized people. Shipwrecked on an island, if you will, but civilized. And to that end, Jim has opened the bar.'

She made a grand gesture, a sort of visual 'ta-da!' Jim, his face fixed in a determined smile, stood in front of a grand array of bottles, including a couple of rare and expensive small-batch bourbons that I had never before seen in England. I gave Alan a startled glance. He smiled and went to get some for both of us.

My mother had a philosophy that guided her through many a rough time. 'Only worry when you can do something about it – whatever it is. Then it's not worry, it's thinking things through, trying to decide what's best. When there's nothing you can do, it's just plain worry, and it's pointless and self-destructive.'

There was certainly nothing I could do about our present predicament, and I've always enjoyed bourbon. Alan learned to like it years before I met him, when he was on an assignment in Washington, DC. It's still a fairly unusual taste in England, where scotch (called just whisky, with no *e*) or gin is the preferred spiritous liquor. I like them all, but when I need a stiffener, bourbon is my choice.

And so we sat and drank and talked. In the interests of acting 'civilized', we avoided all talk of corpses, skeletons, mummies and assorted horrors. We felt free to talk of storms; surely the weather was a staple of drawing-room conversation. The English talked about the 1987 hurricane, a storm of epic proportions that paled, however, by comparison with the one we had just suffered. The Americans chimed in with 'can-you-top-this' stories, a competition I felt I won with the famous Blizzard of '78 that buried parts of Indiana with over three feet of snow in a single night – though some of the tornado tales came close.

I fear we all drank a bit more than we should. Perhaps it was inevitable, given the strain we'd been living under. It wasn't gone, either. We had chosen to ignore our problems for a little while, but they'd be back in the morning, in full force. So it wasn't surprising that we grew a little too loud, a little frenzied, a little too like Blitz parties or dancing on the deck of the *Titanic*. Ed started coming up with more and more outrageous puns, with Pat topping them. I found myself laughing so hard at one of Ed's groaners that I realized it was well past the time I should have switched to soda water.

I don't remember who first noticed that the rain had stopped, or who broached the idea that we should build a bonfire and burn the guy, but once suggested, the scheme caught hold and spread, if the simile can be forgiven, like wildfire. If we had all been entirely sober, cooler heads might have pointed out that our supply of dry wood was limited, and it might be better to save it to keep us warm until power was restored.

Or then again, they might not. We had been making do, camping out (if in luxurious surroundings) for what seemed like months. We were all in a mood to cut loose, and what better excuse than Guy Fawkes Night?

So the men broke into agitated discussion of the best site for the fire, and exactly how to build it, and whether to use any of the newly-fallen wood ('...but some of it was dead anyway – that'll be dry enough to burn...'). They finally decided on a hilltop overlooking the river, on the far west side of the property, and trooped to the outbuildings to find wood.

The women, meanwhile, flocked like homing pigeons to the kitchen to make piles of sandwiches with whatever we could find. The Aga was nearly cold, so there was no hope of cooking anything, but there was plenty of cheese and ham and cold roast beef, and if bread was in short supply, crackers (in the American sense) and biscuits (in the English sense) would do. I managed to find some popcorn tucked away in a pantry and popped it, sort of, over the dying kitchen fire as my contribution to the decidedly unconventional supper. Some of it burned and quite a lot didn't pop – I'd never have succeeded as a pioneer woman – but with lots of butter melted over the top it smelled great and would taste OK.

Joyce asked Pat to 'help her find' the guy. 'My dear woman, if you've forgotten where you put it, how can I help?'

'Well, I think I know where it is, but...'

Pat uttered something between a laugh and a snort. 'Ah. I see. Yes, I'll come and help keep the vampires at bay.'

Well, I would have been afraid myself to tramp through that dark house alone.

As we packed up everything to take out to the bonfire, I ate a few crackers, on the principle that starch soaks up alcohol. I don't know if the theory worked, since the stuff was obviously in my blood stream already, but my head did feel a little clearer as Lynn and I tramped up the hill together, baskets in hand.

'If anyplace is dry enough for a fire, that hilltop should be,' I commented, somewhat breathlessly. The hill was steep.

'Mmm. Did anyone tell the rest where we were going? The vicar, and the Bateses?'

'I heard Jim say he was going to. I wish the vicar had been able to come. I think he might be rather fun in other circumstances. But obviously he couldn't leave Laurence for so long.'

Lynn, who was leading the way with a lantern, stopped so suddenly that I stepped on her heel.

I stopped too, perforce, and put down my heavy basket. 'Sorry! What's the matter?'

'Nothing. I mean, *everything*, but nothing new. Dorothy, what's going *on* here? Why are all these awful things *happening*? I tried to cooperate with Joyce, poor thing, and pretend this was still a party, but you mentioned Laurence and it all came crashing back down on us. I don't understand anything about it, but I thought *you* would have figured it out by now.'

'Hey, have a heart! I've been here … what, three days?'

'Or a century.'

'I know, but things just keep on happening, like … like that popcorn. I barely thought I had a handle on the skeleton – so to speak – when up popped more awfulness. Dave Harrison died, and Julie hid in that shack … and Mike … and Laurence – poor man, I hope he'll make it.'

'He'd stand a lot better chance if he could get some medical care.'

'He's at the heart of this, Lynn. That's the only thing I'm sure of. He and the house are the centre of the whole mess.'

'How do you work that out?'

I thought about that. 'I'm not sure, actually. I hadn't stopped to follow my train of thought. You know how your mind jumps around, relating things that don't seem to have anything to do with each other?'

'I know *your* mind does.'

'That,' I said with dignity, 'was uncalled for.'

Lynn giggled.

'Anyway, I haven't thought it all out, but I know – I feel in my bones, Lynn – that this house is at root of everything.'

'You,' said Lynn, picking up her basket and continuing up the hill, 'are getting as bad as Ed. Bones and roots, indeed.'

That didn't deserve a reply. Lynn was back to pretending it was a party. I saved my breath for the climb.

NINETEEN

The men were just lighting the bonfire when we got to the top of the hill. They had somehow contrived a huge pile of wood, and they must have doused it with kerosene, because when they tossed in a couple of matches, the flames leapt up immediately.

It was beautiful, and warm – hot, in fact. I hadn't been truly warm for days, but after a few moments I had to move away from the fire. It was also more than a little frightening. The ancients thought of fire as one of the four elements, and there was certainly something elemental about this fire, something alive and menacing, as it devoured its fodder, roaring, crackling, almost smacking its lips. Tongues of fire, the Bible called them, and certainly one thought of tongues as the fire licked out to find something new to consume.

'A good fire,' said Alan, by my side.

'Yes,' I said a little doubtfully. 'But is it a good idea?'

He looked at me enquiringly.

'I mean – it's Guy Fawkes. Bonfire Night. If anyone sees this, will it make them think everything is normal over here? Just the folks at the big house having a good time?'

'Might do. On the other hand, bonfires aren't as common as they used to be. And they were once signals, you know.'

'I do know. But they could stand for either good or ill, if I remember. Come, all is well, or stay away – danger.'

'Remember your mother, love. We can't do anything about the way the message is taken, so enjoy the fire. I believe Lynn brought some marshmallows to toast. You Americans do eat the oddest things.'

So we had our picnic and ate our marsh-mallows (at least the Americans did), and tried not to think about bodies piling up back at the house, about our continued isolation, about Mike and his grand, doomed gesture.

We tried not to think about those things. I, for one, wasn't successful.

Neither was Alan. For when we had eaten what we wanted of the not very wonderful food, and the guy had been dutifully admired (it was an effigy of a former, not very popular prime minister) and burned, and the bonfire was beginning to die down, Alan went quietly to Jim's side and spoke briefly to him. Jim looked slightly startled, then nodded and took off down the hill, almost at a run, Alan right behind him.

Lynn, who was sitting on the ground close to the fire, got up with one of the lithe, grace-ful movements I envied, and came over to me. 'What are they up to?' she asked bluntly.

'I don't know for sure, but ... well, Alan had an idea this afternoon. I'm not going to tell you about it, in case it doesn't come off. If it does, you won't need to ask.'

And that was all I would say.

In a few minutes Jim and Alan trudged back up the hill, carrying between them a large box, which they carried near the fire and set down.

Jim then climbed up on top of the box and said, 'Ladies and gentlemen!' in a voice I'd never heard before from him, a voice that reminded me he was a highly paid, valued executive of something-or-other.

'Ladies and gentlemen,' he repeated, a little more quietly now that he had everyone's attention. 'We were to have had a fireworks display tonight. Unfortunately, those plans were cancelled by the storm and ... other events. However, Alan has reminded me that fireworks and flares are essentially the same – pyrotechnics, both, one simply more spectacular than the other.

'We need, pretty badly, some communication with the outside world, and there seems to be only one way to, possibly, attract the attention of someone in Branston Village. Alan and I propose to set off some rockets, the least flamboyant of my collection, in an SOS pattern. If someone sees and understands, our isolation may be nearly at an end.'

'If,' said Pat with unusual sombreness.

'Yes, if. We can but try. So I'll ask you all, please, to step back at least thirty feet. That's ten metres to you politically correct Brits,' he added with a ghost of a grin. 'Neither of us is an expert at this, and we don't want to set anybody on fire or put any eyes out.'

So we moved back obediently, the six of us. Pat and Ed stood together, while Tom and Lynn and I kept Joyce company. Six of us. There should have been a crowd there, the other five of our house party, and the Bateses, and however many came from the village. And the display should have been beautiful, fabulous, not a few puny rockets for a puny few people.

We watched in silence as Jim picked out nine smallish rockets and lined them up in groups of three. Then Alan, using a long match, touched flame to the fuses of the first three, allowing a second or two between.

Ffft. Ffft. Ffft. The first three went off in rapid succession and exploded, with loud reports, in showers of red sparks.

The next three, lit at longer intervals. Ffft. Silence. Ffft. Silence. Ffft. Explosions. Sparks.

Then the final volley.

'We'll do another set,' said Jim. 'Stay where you are until we're done.'

After all the sparks had died away and the smell of gunpowder had dissipated, we waited on the hill. Waited for what? I wasn't sure. For some response, I suppose, some sign that our message had been seen and understood.

There was nothing. No answering flare, no gunshots, no – what – smoke signals?

After a while we drifted back to the house and went to bed.

'He's awake!'

'Mmm.' I turned over and pulled a pillow over my head to shut out the unbearable light. Alan pulled it off.

'He's awake, love.'

'I'm not,' I mumbled. 'And I have a head-ache.'

'Then have some coffee and a painkiller. I'm going to talk to Laurence.'

He didn't slam the door. Alan doesn't slam doors. But he closed it with a definitive click that penetrated my consciousness. I sat up, squinting against the light, hands to my throbbing temples. Ooooh! How much had I had to drink last night, anyway?

Then, finally, his words reached my brain. Laurence. He was going to talk to Laurence. It was Laurence who was awake!

I fell back on to the pillows. I was in no shape to cope with the implications.

Furthermore, I didn't have to. I was supposed to be having a nice holiday. Let somebody else deal with Laurence, somebody who didn't have a hangover. And what an undignified condition for a respectable woman my age! It had been years since I'd got myself in this state. I certainly knew better, but ... well, put it down to stress. In any case, I needed coffee. I needed ibuprofen. Then I was going back to bed to nurse my aching head. I groped for my bathrobe and made my cautious way down to the kitchen.

No one was there, thank heaven. I didn't want to talk. I wasn't sure I could. There was, however, a large Thermos on the table. As I hoped, it contained good strong coffee.

After three ibuprofen and two cups of coffee, I acknowledged the fact that I could not just go back to bed. I was not only, I hoped, a respectable woman but a responsible one, and hangover or not, I had obligations. Several people were depending, at least in part, on me to help ferret out the truth.

Ferrets were rat-catchers. Well, there was at least one rat i' this particular arras, and he needed to be caught.

What, I wondered with gross irrelevance, was an arras?

I hoped not a hidden room. I did not intend to think about hidden rooms.

Enough! I told my wandering mind. Get dressed, madam, and then be up and doing, with a heart for any fate.

Eventually, and most unwillingly, I took myself to Laurence's room, where I found almost the entire household gathered to hear what the poor man had to say. Only Julie was absent. She was probably still huddled in her room, stuck fast in whatever terror, or just confusion, held her there.

Someone had made Laurence a pot of tea, and Joyce was making sure he drank it. It was doubtless loaded with enough sugar to loosen every tooth in his head, but he needed sustenance, after nearly three days without eating.

'So, go on,' said Alan. 'You talked to the vicar and then went for a walk.'

'Yes. I needed to think. I ... well, there was a decision I needed to make, whether—'

'Yes,' Alan interrupted. 'I know about that. Then what happened?'

'I don't remember very well. I think I walked toward the river ... the river to the south, I mean. The water meadows. It was ... the destruction was ... may I have a little more tea, please?'

'I'll make fresh,' said Joyce, putting her hand to the pot's cheek. 'This is cold.' Rose Bates moved to take it from her, but Laurence shook his head.

'That'll do just as well. My mouth is a bit dry. Cold is fine.'

I gave Alan a worried look. He shook his head, ever so slightly. 'You must be hungry, as well,' he said gently. 'Shall I have Mrs Bates boil an egg or two for you?'

'I'm not very hungry. My head aches a bit.'

'Well, she'll boil the eggs, and if you don't want them, I'm sure someone else will. Now, sir, can you tell me anything at all that happened as you walked toward the river?'

He shook his head, winced, and closed his eyes. 'I remember seeing the ruined gardens, and Mr Bates getting fresh wood for the fires. And there's something ... I heard something ... but I can't remember.'

'Alan, don't you think—' I said at the same time that the vicar said, 'Really, Mr Nesbitt—'

We cancelled each other out, but Alan nodded. 'Yes. It's time he rested. Mr Upshawe, we're all very glad you're feeling better. Now ... oh, yes, here are some ibuprofen tablets to wash down with some of that cold tea. We'll talk again after you've had a nice sleep.'

He shooed us all out, all but the vicar. I saw the two of them hold a brief conversation, but I couldn't hear what they said. Then Alan closed the door – and to my astonishment, locked it behind him.

'The vicar has the other key,' he said. 'He can get out if he needs to, but I've told him to stay until he's relieved. By me. And to wedge the door and respond only to a coded knock.'

And then I saw, and smacked my forehead, and immediately regretted it. 'What he heard,' I said, when the waves of pain receded. 'You don't want anyone to get to him before he's had a chance to finish about what he heard.'

'Yes. And anything else he might have seen. Anything, in short, that he hasn't yet told us.'

'So that's why you had everyone else in the room. And I noticed you didn't let him talk about his conversation with the vicar.'

'He did try, before you came in, but the vicar and I managed between us to suggest that the conversation dealt with private spiritual matters.'

'Which, in a way, it did.'

'Yes, but I didn't want the details revealed at this point. I did want to make the point, very publicly, that he had told us all he knew.

Unfortunately, it didn't work out quite that way. So until he can talk to us again, I want him guarded. I wish I had several stout constables to take the duty, instead of one elderly vicar and one elderly retiree, but I must make do as best I can.'

I sighed. 'No reply from the mainland, then?'

He snorted. 'You're in your Agatha Christie mode again, aren't you? No, they've all been told to ignore any signals from— what was the name of the island?'

'Indian Island. *Ten Little Indians*, remember – the other title.'

'Yes. Well, to answer your question properly, no, we've heard nothing. Though how could we hear anything? The village is too far away for a loud-hailer, even if they possess such a thing. No phone, no email—' He held up his hands in frustration. '*If* anyone saw, *if* anyone understood, we'll know only when they come to us, and that can't be until the roads are clear. Hence the melodramatics with locked doors and so on. And Dorothy –' he turned a very serious look on me – 'I want you to be very, very careful. Don't go anywhere alone. Everyone knows you're trying to puzzle this thing out. You're in danger, my girl, or you could be.'

'That's the trouble!' I said fiercely. 'Everything is ... is misty, amorphous. I could be in danger. Or maybe not. Maybe Dave Harrison was murdered. Or maybe not. And if he was, maybe it was Laurence who did it. Or maybe the other way around. And there's the skeleton and the mummy and Mike – and Julie – and I did want to see the fireworks!'

And I burst into tears.

Alan gathered me into his warm, safe arms and let me cry. When I had reached the stage of hiccuping little sobs, he pulled out his handkerchief, mopped my face, and said 'Blow.'

'That was really a big help, wasn't it?' I said mournfully. 'All you need on your plate right now is a weepy woman.'

'All I ever need is this particular woman,' he said, which nearly sent me over the edge again. 'You're still feeling a bit fragile, I suspect.' He pronounced the last syllable to rhyme with mile, and it summed up exactly how I felt. 'Suppose you go back to that bed I dragged you out of, and sleep it off. Don't forget to lock the door, though. I'll knock like this.' He tapped a pattern on my sleeve. 'And, Dorothy, if you feel afraid or worried about anything – no matter if you think it's foolish – scream like the devil's after you, and I'll be there. Promise?'

I nodded, feeling foolish already, and trudged back to our room.

TWENTY

I woke from one of those dreams, the complicated kind that go on and on and plunge one deeper and deeper into the labyrinth. I was just about to find the way out, nearly there, but someone kept hitting croquet balls into my path. Tock. Tock. Tock-tock. I wished whoever it was would stop, but they kept coming. Tock. Tock. Tock-tock.

'Dorothy. Dorothy, are you awake?'

'I am now,' I said, and got up to let Alan in. 'I thought you were playing croquet. But I was just about to figure it all out.'

He grinned. 'Have a nice nap?'

'I feel better, anyway. Alan, if I'm ever tempted to drink that much again, stop me. I had dreams ... well, nightmares, really.'

'Where did the croquet come in?'

I yawned. 'I can't remember anymore. But it was all very vivid at the time. And speaking of remembering...'

Alan shook his head. 'Nothing very useful. He thought he heard something – perhaps a footstep – behind him as he walked down to the river. But it was still windy, as you recall, not a gale but a steady wind, and between the whistle of the wind itself and the sound of debris being blown about, he can't be sure what he heard. And of the scene at the river he remembers nothing.'

I gave a great sigh. 'Is he telling the truth?'

'I think so, and I've had some opportunity of judging. You know a head injury often wipes out the memory of preceding events.'

'Sometimes the memories come back.'

'But not always, by any means.'

'Have you told him Harrison is dead?'

'No,' said Alan, 'and I've told the vicar not to say anything. At this point that's my one hope of triggering his memory. If I tell him the right way, it might be enough of a shock to bring back ... whatever happened.'

I began to pace. 'Another maybe. Another misty thing. Alan, I think I'm going to go talk to Julie again.'

'Not alone.'

'No. Anyway, I don't think I'd get anything out of her by myself. And she's afraid of you, for some reason. Oh!'

'Yes, I thought about that myself, but I never pursued it. Why is she afraid of me? I've never harmed the woman; I scarcely know her.'

'She's afraid,' I said slowly, 'because you're a policeman.'

'I was a policeman.'

'Yes, but she may not know the difference. I hate to say it of Joyce's sister, but Julie's none too bright. Probably comes of living with Dave all those years. And I'm sure she's heard stories about the omniscience of the English police.'

'All true,' said Alan smugly.

'Right. But if she believes that you know everything, and she's afraid of you, that means she has something to hide.'

Alan gave me that grave look again. 'I'm not sure I want you to talk to her.'

For once I didn't give him a flippant answer. 'I know. And I agree, in principle. If Julie Harrison has done something criminal, I want nothing to do with her, to be honest. But if she *has*, somebody has to talk to her. Somebody has to worm it out of her. We've agreed you can't be the one. Who else, besides me and Pat?'

'She talked before to the vicar.'

'She was in a state of hypothermia and exhaustion. Now she's fine, except she's terrified of something – or someone. It isn't just you, but she hasn't given me the slightest clue about who or what it might be. No, it's probably not the vicar, but would he know the right questions to ask? And would he pass along the answers? You know that tender conscience of his. And you have to remember, too, that she talked pretty freely to Pat. Which seems to exonerate Pat of ... whatever it is that worries Julie so.'

'I'm not sure your logic holds up there. I wish I could do it myself.'

'So do I. But you can't. So it has to be Pat and me.'

'All right, I suppose. But I intend to be right outside the door. And it can wait until after

189

lunch. I assume you can eat something now?'

'So long as it doesn't have much taste, or any smell at all.'

I stayed out of the kitchen. Alan brought me some very mild cheese and rather tasteless crackers, and had thoughtfully made a glass of iced tea for my strange American tastes (apparently the freezer was still cold), and reported as I nibbled that the Bateses were back at work and apparently feeling quite normal, except that Mr Bates wasn't quite as urbanely courteous as usual, and his wife was rather quiet.

'Embarrassed, I suspect,' he concluded. 'A big man like that doesn't care to remember that he fainted at the sight of ... that he fainted, and in front of a lot of people.'

'I would have, too, only I couldn't see very clearly. He was right in front of that ... thing.' I shuddered and put down my glass. 'I really think that's all I can manage for now. And if I don't go talk to Julie soon, I'll lose my nerve. I don't think I can face kitchen smells, though. Could you find Pat for me and ask if she's willing to act as prosecuting attorney again?'

'Counsel for the Crown,' he murmured, and left the room.

Pat was more than willing. She was, in fact, hovering in that uncertain state between boredom and nervous excitement that makes it impossible to settle to anything. 'I feel like Kipling's rhinoceros,' she said as she walked in the door, giving an impatient wriggle of

190

that magnificent body.

'Cake crumbs under your skin?'

'Exactly. I want something to happen, but I'm afraid of what it might be. I understand you want me to tackle Jovial Julie again.'

'I'm hoping that she may be chafing enough under her self-imposed restraints to open up a little more. Especially if you provide some further ... um ... lubrication.'

Pat held up the bottle she had thoughtfully brought along, an unopened litre of a premium bourbon. 'Will this do the trick, do you suppose?'

'Yipes! That's way too good for the purpose. I do hate to see that stuff poured down an unappreciative gullet.'

'Perhaps you'd like a taste first?' asked Pat with a wicked smile.

'Ouch! No, I won't have a hair of the dog, thank you very much. If somebody's going to get a splitting head from that stuff, better her than me. Excelsior.'

We headed down to the far end of the wing, Alan right behind us. He had obtained the key from Rose, assuming that Julie was still barricading herself. I couldn't say I blamed her. If I hadn't had Alan to sustain me, I would have locked myself up, too.

'Dorothy, look.' Pat pointed with the bottle.

Near the end of the long corridor, a lighter area showed, as if a door was open, letting in, not direct sunlight, since that side of the house faced north, but the glow of reflected light.

191

Julie's door was open, and a glance told us she wasn't in the room.

'Bathroom, probably,' said Pat.

'There's an en suite bath for every bed-room, remember? Every one that's in regular use, anyway.'

'Then she's gone in search of something to eat.'

'I'm sure Mrs Bates brings her food. Something to drink, more likely,' I said, by way of calling the kettle black.

'She'll be back soon, anyway. Should we close the door so she won't know she has a reception committee?'

'Not when she left it open,' Alan put in sensibly. 'Leave everything as it was, but stay out of sight of the doorway.'

Feeling as if I'd walked into an Inspector Clouseau movie, I took a position against the wall beside the hinge side of the door (hoping Julie wouldn't bang it into my nose when she returned). Pat stepped into a corner, easily visible but not until one was in the room. And Alan, who was there simply as guard dog, stepped into the unoccupied room across the hall.

We waited, scarcely daring to breath. The hall was carpeted with heavy Oriental runners and the floors, though very old, were very solid. Julie's footfalls wouldn't make much noise, and we didn't want to be caught off guard.

I began to get a cramp in the calf of my left leg. I tried to wiggle it out, but it only got worse. In agony, I had to walk it out. 'Cramp,' I mouthed, pointing to my leg, when Pat glared at me. I walked as quietly as I could and returned to my post as soon as the cramp eased itself.

Pat's nose began to twitch. At first I thought she smelled something peculiar, so I sniffed myself, but could detect nothing but the slightly stale aroma of a room that had been shut up for too long with someone who hadn't bathed for a while. Then Pat sneezed, a sneeze that was all the more explosive for being suppressed.

We both waited anxiously for the sound of footsteps running the other way. Nothing.

I sighed, inaudibly I hoped, and settled down in silence again, changing feet now and then to avoid cramp.

I don't know how long we stood there before it dawned on us that Julie had gone farther afield than the kitchen or the library liquor cabinet. At any rate, I was the first to give it up.

'This is pure farce,' I said aloud, slumping away from my rigid pose beside the wall. 'Julie's up to something, and I think we'd do better trying to find her and figure out what it is.'

Pat agreed. 'My skin was beginning to crawl in earnest. I don't think of myself as a fidget, but when one can't move, one instantly wants to.'

'Well, let's get Alan and decide what to do.' Alan, hearing us talking, left his lair and joined us. 'The bird has flown?'

'Hopped away, more likely,' I replied. 'I doubt she's gone far, but we'd better find her.'

'Yes. Why don't I take up my surveillance from across the way again, and you two check the rest of the bedrooms. And bathrooms. Because on past form...'

He didn't need to finish the thought. If Julie had managed to get hold of another bottle, she might well have found another comfortable bathtub.

It would be tedious to detail our search. It was slow and thorough. We looked in every bedroom, occupied or not (in a couple of cases waking nappers), and their adjacent bathrooms and sitting rooms. We checked two linen closets and found nothing but sheets and towels. We even peered down the shaft of the dumbwaiter.

No Julie.

'She could be keeping one step ahead of us, you know,' said Pat as we sank down on the canopy bed in the last vacant bedroom. 'One could play that game forever in a house this size.'

'Yes, but why? I can't think why she'd want to hide, not from us. In fact, I can't think why she'd leave her bedroom at all, not for any length of time. She only had to ring for anything she wanted, and she's been so scared of whatever-it-is.'

'Cabin fever. She got fed up with being by herself.'

'Maybe,' I said dubiously. 'Or else...'

Pat sighed. 'Yes. I was hoping we could avoid that speculation. Or else, you're thinking, she didn't leave her room willingly.'

'I think Alan's had that idea for some time.'

So we trooped back to where Alan was keeping his futile watch. 'No luck?' he asked. But he knew the answer.

'What now, boss?' That was Pat. I was rapidly becoming too worried to be cheeky.

'Where have you looked?'

We told him. Pat summarized, 'She isn't anywhere on this floor. We've exhausted all the possibilities. And ourselves,' she added.

'Did you study her room at all?'

I took that question to myself. 'No. I thought you'd rather do that. At a quick glance, I didn't see anything to show whether she left of her own accord or ... not. But you'll know better than I what to look for.'

'First,' said Alan, 'we need to determine that she is not still somewhere in the house.'

'Yes, we'll—'

I never got to finish the sentence. 'I hope that you, my dear, will have nothing to do with this search. You've done your part. Please, I want you to go to our room, lock yourself in and stay there. Do I need to spell out why?'

No, he didn't. Nor was I, for once, disposed to argue. With Julie's disappearance the nightmare had overshadowed us completely. There was no more question of pushing it out of our minds, pretending that all the horrors were in and of the past.

We were now living in fear, genuine, un-adulterated fear.

'Alan ... you won't do anything silly?'

'By which I assume you mean heroics. No, love, I won't. I'll be with other people – more than one other person – the whole time. Now Pat and I will see you back to the room. I don't like the idea of her being alone, either. Then she and I will go downstairs, tell the others, and organize search teams.'

I didn't learn until later that Alan had excluded the Bateses from the search, even though their knowledge of the house probably surpassed anyone else's. His stated reason was that someone needed to be available in case, by a miracle, some outside help arrived. His real reason, I knew, was that they were not entirely above suspicion. Neither were Jim and Joyce, but Alan had to have someone who knew the house reasonably well. So Jim had gone with Allen, along with Lynn, and Joyce led Mike, Pat and Tom.

Neither of the Moynihans knew as much about the hidden parts of the house as John Bates, but they knew what one might term the surface very well. Both groups searched the same areas at different times, in case someone spotted a trace – a tissue, a bit of cigarette ash, a thread – that the others had missed. They searched all the living areas, the cellars, the outbuildings. They ranged over the devastated gardens, peering under promising bushes and into the pits left by upturned shrubs and trees. They looked in and under everyone's cars, including the trunks/boots and under the hoods/bonnets, and made sure that all the cars were where they should be.

They found neither Julie nor any trace of her.

TWENTY-ONE

Alan knocked on the door. This time I was wide awake and recognized his code. I knew as soon as I saw his face that the news was not good.

'You didn't find her.'

'No, but that's not the worst of it.' And he related to me the scene when the searchers returned and told Rose Bates that Julie had now to be counted as missing. 'It seems Rose has been busy conducting a search of her own. She said that food was missing from the kitchen – portable food, cheese and biscuits and apples, that sort of thing – and that Mr Bates had reported that two bottles of whisky were gone. Well, Pat confessed that she had taken one of them, and put it back on the kitchen table. But Rose said bourbon wasn't whisky, so there were still two bottles un-accounted for.' Alan heaved a sigh. 'Which would have been the end of it, except then Pat commented that it was apparent Julie was gone, and the only question remaining was whether she had gone of her own free will or been spirited away. And at that Rose flew into a kind of hysterics. Jim and Joyce are still trying to calm her down, so far as I know.'

'But why should that have touched her off? It's no more than we've all been thinking ever since we found her room empty.'

'"Spirited",' said Alan with another sigh. 'Pat meant nothing in particular by the word, but it seems there's a streak of good old country superstition in the competent and efficient Mrs Bates. All the unfortunate things that have happened in recent days have worked on her fears, and the mention – as she thought – of spirits was the crowning touch. She has decided, from what little sense I could make of her ravings, that the house is cursed, or possessed, or something of the kind. God only knows what's going to happen without her in the kitchen. She has been the glue that kept the household together, and now...' He raised his hands in a helpless gesture and sat down heavily on the bed.

'There's no chance she'll come to her senses?'

'Oh, eventually, I suppose. I wish we could give her a sedative. When she does come out of it, she could be in a bad way. I'm no doctor, but I've seen full-blown hysteria before, and it's not easy on anybody.'

'Poor Joyce.' I sat down beside him.

'Why Joyce, more than any of the rest of us?'

'Because she's the hostess. She'll feel it her job to try to keep things going, and it's hopeless. I wish—'

'No.' Alan said it with a finality that cut me off in mid-sentence. 'You will not attempt to cook for this crowd. You will not organize a rota for the household chores. You will stay in this room until help arrives.'

'Her master's voice,' I said with a lightness I did not feel. His face didn't change. I studied it for a moment and said, 'You're really worried, aren't you?'

He sighed. 'I am. I didn't mean to shout at you, Dorothy. But I have *no* idea what's going on here, and until I do, I'm genuinely frightened. For everyone, not just you. Until someone responds to our calls for help...'

'That could be a long time,' I said meekly. 'What are we going to do about food?'

'I'm going back down in a moment. Tom and I will pack boxes of non-perishables for everyone. Fortunately there's plenty of food, though the variety may leave something to be desired. We will distribute them to everyone, and then my recommendation is that everyone keep to his or her or their own room – with the door locked. I do not intend this to turn into that novel you keep citing, with all of us being picked off one by one.'

'Your recommendation.'

'Well, love, I can't give orders to any of these people, much as I'd like to.'

Only to me, I thought but didn't say.

'I can only advise them, strongly, that there

is someone very dangerous among us, and we need to take sensible steps for self-protection.'

Thus began our siege. I wondered what the single people in our party would do, and then decided not to wonder. Laurence Upshawe was still under the care – or guardianship – of the vicar, Paul Leatherbury. Jim and Joyce had each other, Tom and Lynn, the Bateses. And if Pat Heseltine and Ed Walinski decided that sharing a room was less lonely and frightening, good luck to them. I certainly didn't intend to poke my nose into their activities. I had Alan, after all.

Or I would have, when he returned from his commissary duties. I wished, the minute he had left, that I had remembered to ask him for some books. I can endure almost any period of enforced inactivity if I have enough to read. There were books in the room. Joyce was too good a hostess not to see to that. But the ones I hadn't already read didn't interest me. I thought about taking a nap, but I was too tense to sleep. I wanted to *do* something, find some way out of this nightmare.

I started counting casualties. Two recent deaths, three if Julie had met the fate we all suspected. Two much older deaths, the skeleton and the mummy. (I shuddered at the thought of her and forced my mind to move on quickly.) Laurence injured. Mr Bates shocked into a faint.

Seven. Seven human beings killed or injured in this house. *By* this house?

No. That was too fanciful, too much like Rose Bates's terrors. This wasn't Hill House, with its evil, ghostly inhabitants. But there seemed to be an evil, malevolent presence here, all the same. Only it was human.

Which one? Which of the inhabitants of this house had killed, and killed again, and again?

I went to the lovely little writing desk in the corner and opened the top drawer. Sure enough, there was a small cache of stationery, paper, envelopes, even stamps. The paper was thick and lovely, meant for invitations, thank-yous, gracious correspondence. I had nothing else to use for a list. I pulled out several sheets and the pen, also thoughtfully provided, and headed the top one 'Events'.

The first listing there was obviously the skeleton. I was about to write it in when I had another thought. Really the first odd thing to happen was Dave Harrison's conversation with Julie, that first night, and then his drunken outburst just before dinner.

Julie had shut him up on that occasion. Why? What had he said, exactly, that she wanted to cut off?

I headed a second sheet 'Queries' and wrote that one in, and then went back to the skeleton.

There were plenty of questions about him. It seemed likely that the first question, his identity, had been answered. But assuming he was Harry Upshawe, who killed him? Why? When? And another one that just occurred to me: why had the pilot of that aircraft not tried to contact Harry when he didn't show up for the planned trip?

Maybe someone had called the pilot, someone pretending to be Harry, saying he could not make it after all. That could be important, a lead...

And then I realized it was only another dead end. We couldn't question the pilot; he had gone down somewhere near São Miguel.

Nevertheless, I wrote the question down. There might be some way to check fifty-year-old flight plans. I doubted it, but Alan might know.

Lots of questions. No answers. I went back to my Events page.

The next things, in the order they had happened, not when I learned about them, were the complicated series of events involving Laurence, the vicar and the Harrisons. I began to note them down with some care.

The first was Laurence's conversation with the vicar. I wrote down the gist of it, as best I remembered. Alan, who had a policeman's memory for detail, could correct me. Then Laurence had started on his walk.

Meanwhile, Dave and Julie, in their irrational state, had decided to try to get away. They heard Laurence's – confession was too strong a word – his narrative. Julie, somewhat surprisingly, was bright enough to realize the implications and warn Dave – who then went off after Laurence.

And then what? Julie could have told us. Julie had disappeared. Laurence could have told us. Laurence had received a blow to the head that wiped out his memory.

At this stage of my unproductive exercise, Alan rapped on the door, and I let him in. He carried not only a large crate of food, but – bless him – a canvas bag full of books.

'Sorry I was so long, love. Tom and I delivered everyone else's first.'

'How are they all holding up?'

'As one might expect. The Bateses are inclined to be a bit resentful; I am abrogating their responsibilities, after all. Mr Bates is testy; his wife is defensive but more inclined to cooperate.' He took a box of cereal out of his crate, and a couple of cans of peaches.

'I suspect Mr Bates is still feeling a bit poorly, after that faint. It was only yesterday, wasn't it? Time is behaving very oddly.'

'It does. Yes, it was yesterday, and Mr Bates is obviously feeling "poorly", as you put it. The rest are bearing up, though Jim and Joyce are desperately worried, and feeling guilty.'

'That's ridiculous. Nothing they did caused any of the awfulness.'

'They assembled the house party. And of course we're just assuming that—'

'Alan!'

'I like them, too, but I think like a policeman, love. I can't help it. Where were Jim and Joyce when Harrison met his death?'

I tried to think back through the eternity that had passed since last Friday. 'Napping! A bunch of people did that afternoon, remember? None of us had had much sleep.'

'Exactly. And presumably they'll vouch for each other. As evidence, it's useless.'

'Well, but what about...' I paused to think about the other victims. Laurence's story was allied with Dave's. Julie had run off to hide, the first time and possibly this time, too. Mike, poor idiot, had gone his own ill-advised way. But...

'The skeleton! And the mummy! Jim and Joyce couldn't have had anything to do with them.'

'Probably not. But we're assuming that both old deaths took place longer than two years ago. Until we get a forensics expert in here, that's not a proven fact.'

'Harry Upshawe died fifty years ago!'

'Probably, but we have not yet proven – *prove*n, I said – that the skeleton belonged to Harry, nor indeed that Harry is dead, rather than living in happy senility in America somewhere. I have to put Jim and Joyce in the category of suspects. Unlikely, I agree, but not impossible.'

'We've eaten their salt!' I was beginning to be very angry indeed at my husband's stubbornness.

'Nevertheless.'

Ever since I was a child, I've wept when I was furious. I hated it then; I appeared to be full of misery when I was in fact full of rage. And I hated it now. I felt the tears start and turned my head so Alan wouldn't see. We almost never quarrelled, and maybe there was some misery involved with my tears, after all. I fumbled blindly for a book and took it to the farthest corner of the room.

He knows me rather well. He said nothing, but continued unpacking the groceries and stowing them away as best he could.

'Sandwich?' he offered when he had put all the food away.

'Thank you, no.' I was starving, but unwilling to let go of my anger. I turned another page I hadn't read. In sudden dismay, I glanced at the book to make sure I wasn't holding it upside down. It was right side up, but it was a book of Victorian sermons. Probably Alan had brought it so we could laugh over it together.

Another tear squeezed out and rolled down my cheek.

It was Alan who patched it up. He must have heard my stomach growl; I was really very hungry. He came over to me, gently took my book away, and said, 'I imagine your head and stomach would be happier with tea than a glass of wine, my dear. Darjeeling, perhaps? And a chocolate biscuit or two?'

My stomach spoke again. I swallowed. 'Yes, please.' There were still tears in my voice.

Alan sat down next to me. 'Dorothy. I'm exceedingly sorry. You married a stubborn man, my dear.'

'And you a stubborn woman.'

'And we're both still convinced we're right, but we can't ... Dorothy, I never want anything that trivial to come between us again.'

'Trivial? A question of murder?'

'A difference of opinion. I fully concede that I've been wrong before, particularly when it came to my opinion about a suspect versus yours, and I may be wrong this time. Now, may I make you some tea?'

I took his hand. 'And several sandwiches. I was ready to eat those sermons.'

TWENTY-TWO

It had grown dark by the time we finished our tea/supper. Alan lit the lantern and a soft glow permeated the room. If I sat close to the light, I thought I might be able to read, for a while, at least.

'I'll trade you the sermons for something a little more frivolous,' I said.

'Agatha Christie?'

I shuddered. 'No. Too topical. There would not be any P.G. Wodehouse?'

He rooted in the box and handed me a large volume of Jeeves stories.

'Perfect. I can't read more than one or two at a sitting – it's like consuming too many desserts – but one will certainly lighten the gloom. Where are you going?'

For Alan had put on his coat and hat.

'To fetch some wood, for a start. The fire's nearly dead, and it's getting distinctly chilly now that the sun's gone down. We'll need more tea presently, and I don't think I could boil water over those embers. Then I thought I'd get Jim to help, and try again.'

'Flares?'

He nodded. 'Maybe three volleys, if the supply will hold up. Most of Jim's stash is more spectacular stuff, not terribly suitable for the purpose, but we'll try.'

I could have made a remark about collaborating with a murder suspect. I didn't. The sore spot was still tender. Leave it alone. I contented myself with a caution. 'Be careful with those things. I'd simply hate to have you blinded, or worse. And come back soon, love. It's ... creepy in here without you.'

And cold. When I had locked the door behind him, I put on my coat and hat, moved the lantern to a table near the dying fire, and settled back close to both, trying to pretend I was warm.

I found I couldn't concentrate on 'Jeeves Takes Charge' with much more success than I'd had with the Reverend Entwhistle's sermons. I knew the Wodehouse text almost by heart; perhaps that had something to do with it. I did wish Alan would come back with the wood. Arthritic hands never turn pages easily. Cold arthritic hands have a really hard time. I dropped the book twice, the second time on my foot. Thirty-four stories in one book pack a punch. I gave it up, carried the lantern over to the bedside table, and climbed in, clothes and all, bringing my earlier lists with me.

Studying them by the soft lantern-light, I saw that they weren't very useful. The questions had no answers, or none that I could find. The events made no sense, individually or collectively. I picked up a third sheet of expensive stationery and headed it 'People'.

Begin with Jim and Joyce. What did I know about them? *Know* – not surmise.

I thought about ruling some columns and decided the paper wasn't big enough for that, and anyway, my mind doesn't work that neatly. I think in narrative.

So I wrote down their ages: fifty or so, both of them, at a guess. Americans. Lived at Branston Abbey for about two-and-a-half years. Extremely wealthy. Jim was retired – no, I was assuming that, I didn't know for sure. Tom and Lynn would know. They would also know where he had worked, or was still working, and where they had lived before coming here. Not in America for quite a while, I was guessing. Or ... wait. Had Tom or Lynn said something about the Moynihans moving here to get away from the Harrisons? I couldn't remember for sure.

I needed to talk to them. Surely Alan would rule *them* out as suspects? Well, whether he did or not, I was going to invite them to come share our food and our fire, and pick their brains.

What else did I know about Jim and Joyce? They loved England. They loved trees and beautiful gardens and old houses. They had excellent taste in furniture and food, and enjoyed tradition – witness the planned Guy Fawkes celebration. They were cordial and thoughtful hosts, trying to make the best of a well-nigh unbearable situation.

They were childless. Did I know that, for sure? I wracked my brains, but couldn't remember being told that. Maybe I only surmised it; I had seen no family photos. I added another query to the list I needed to ask Tom and Lynn and lay back, dissatisfied.

So far there wasn't a thing known about the Moynihans that could clearly exonerate them from any except the oldest deaths, and those did not, necessarily, have anything to do with the modern ones.

'Bosh!' I said out loud. My instincts were usually reliable about this sort of thing. The house and its troubled history was at the root of the whole conundrum. I was as sure of that as … well, I was sure.

Tom and Lynn, Alan and I. Well, I knew I hadn't murdered anybody, and I would go to my death swearing Alan hadn't. And Tom and Lynn didn't know the Moynihans well, or the house at all. They were in their early sixties, and hadn't moved to England until about thirty years ago. So even if they'd had motive, which was a ludicrous idea, they couldn't have disposed of the skeleton. For I was utterly convinced that the skeleton was Harry Upshawe's, and that meant it had been under that oak tree for fifty years.

Scratch Tom and Lynn. Not that I'd ever had the slightest notion they'd done any of these things, but I was trying to adopt Alan's skepticism. Without a great deal of success, I realized. My partiality was not to be squelched.

All right. Let's list the rest, just for something to do. Mike Leonard, alias Michael Leonev. Dancer extraordinaire. Gay or giving an excellent impersonation. Funny, quirky. Had reason to be angry with Julie, and maybe with Dave by extension. Older than he tried to appear – nearing forty, at a guess – but still far too young to have been responsible for the skeleton. No known motive for attacking Laurence, with whom, indeed, he was reported to have been flirting. But – any possible suspicion attaching to him (and there wasn't much, in my opinion) was destroyed by his own actions. He had given his life in an effort to bring us help.

Or ... oh, for heaven's sake! Had he committed suicide because he had killed Harrison?

I had to admit that if Mike had planned suicide, he would have wanted to do it in some highly spectacular fashion. It could be. It just could be. He could have killed Harrison. He was strong and fit, and Dave had been flabby and, moreover, probably drunk at the time.

A variation: he killed Harrison and was trying to escape, but drowned in the attempt.

But for what possible reason? Julie had grossly affronted him, and he would have had every right to be angry. But angry enough to kill? That seemed out of character. I thought Mike might have been capable of deep feeling. If he had fallen in love, he would have fallen hard, and he might have done almost anything to protect someone he loved. If he had loved Laurence, he might have been incensed enough to attack Laurence's attacker – if that was the way the riverbank scene had played out. But I didn't think, from his actions in the very few hours I had known him, that he had been in love with Laurence. That left pique with Julie as a motive, and it just wasn't enough.

People have been known to kill for what seem to reasonable people to be woefully inadequate motives, said Alan's voice in my head.

Still – it was possible. Not probable, but possible. I left Mike's name on the list, reluctantly, and somewhat pointlessly. There is little satisfaction in discovering that a recently dead man is a murderer. Except that it exonerates others. With a sigh, I pressed on.

Ed Walinski. I knew almost nothing about him, really, except that he was a great artist, a hard worker – I'd watched him working with the others at repairs to the house and grounds – and an inveterate punster. Oh, and he had punched Dave Harrison in the nose. That, I suspect, simply proved that he was a sensible human being. If I'd been of an age and physique to do any punching, I might well have done the same thing. Really, John Donne to the contrary notwithstanding, Harrison's death seemed to be a blessing to mankind.

Except for the destruction that followed in its wake, I reminded myself.

Anyway, I'd not known Ed to lose his temper on any other occasion. And was he a sly enough character to shove Dave in the river and then spend the rest of the weekend cheerfully turning his hand to whatever might help?

Boom! Boom! Boom! The reports startled me considerably. I had forgotten about the flares. And hadn't Alan planned to bring firewood in first? I looked out the window in time to see the second volley, spaced a few seconds apart, and then the third one in rapid fire. They let about a minute elapse, and then did it again. And yet again.

The booms died away, and though I opened the window and strained my ears, I could hear no answering thunder.

I closed the window with cold, stiff fingers, and hurried back into bed. I wouldn't do any more with my lists until Alan brought the firewood. I was too cold, and I wasn't getting anywhere anyway.

It was only a few minutes before Alan's knock came at the door. I opened it wide, and he came in – empty-handed.

'Jim is bringing the wood?' I said, shivering and hurrying back under the covers.

'There is no more dry wood.' Alan divested himself of his outer clothing and his shoes. 'It's all been burnt. Tomorrow when it's light

Jim's going to investigate the attics and see if there's any valueless old furniture up there that can be cut up and burned. Meanwhile, bed is going to be the only warm place.' He turned the lantern down until the flame wavered and died. 'Move over, love.'

TWENTY-THREE

We found an agreeable way to keep warm and at the same time patch up the last shreds of our quarrel. I fell asleep in his arms.

We had gone to bed very early, so I woke long before the chill November dawn. My arm had fallen asleep; I pulled it out from under Alan to shake it into feeling again, and then got up to go to the bathroom.

Something about the house was odd. I couldn't put my finger on it until my stocking-clad feet hit the bathroom tiles.

I wasn't cold.

I used the toilet and then turned on the hot water tap. It wasn't too long before the stream became warm, and then hot.

I hightailed it back into the bedroom. 'Alan! Someone's found a way to get the Aga going, and I think even the furnace! There's hot water, and the house is warm!'

Alan wakes all of a piece, the result, I suppose, of years of irregular hours as a policeman. He threw back the covers and raised his head, rather like a cat sniffing the air before venturing forth. He cocked his head to one side. 'The central heating is certainly on. I wonder...' He put out a hand to the bedside lamp and turned the switch.

'Light!' I'm not sure God on that first day found the light any more wonderful than I did at that moment. 'Alan, that means we have power again! And oh, dear heaven, you don't suppose – a telephone?'

I picked up the one on the bedside table while Alan found his mobile.

'Nothing here,' I said. 'Yours?'

He shook his head and began pulling off the remainder of the clothes we'd worn to bed. 'I,' he said, 'am going to take a bath.'

I let him go first, and then I basked in a hot tub. What bliss to be clean and warm again! One doesn't fully appreciate the benefits of civilization until they're missing for a while.

We had to put on clothes that were considerably less than fresh, but we could soon wash everything. Calloo, callay – electricity!

We forgot that we were supposed to be isolating ourselves. We forgot, for a little while, that there was a murderer among us. I collected all our dirty clothes except for the ones we had on and headed downstairs, recklessly turning on lights as I went, in search of Joyce's washing machine. Alan was right behind me, singing a little tune in which the word 'coffee' featured largely.

The kitchen was brightly lit when we got

there, and savory smells filled the air. I didn't know what Rose Bates was preparing for breakfast, but my mouth watered. She beamed at us. 'Isn't it wonderful? You're the first ones down, but I know all the rest will be here soon. Breakfast is nearly ready. I'll serve it up in a minute – in the dining room – but first, shall I take those things to the laundry for you, Mrs Martin?'

'Just point me in the right direction. I'd hate to take you away from whatever concoctions you have brewing.'

'Through that door. I washed towels the minute I got up, so the machine is ready for you. I knew all the guests would be dying to use it.' Then she heard what she'd said, and her smile wavered a little.

I hurried to the laundry and tried to ignore the thoughts she'd conjured up.

We did full justice to that wonderful breakfast. Rose had created a sort of breakfast pudding, an airy combination of eggs and ground ham and I don't know what else that tasted like food for angels. There were sausages, not the bland, cereal-filled ones that desecrate so many English breakfast tables, but real bangers, browned to a turn and bursting merrily when pierced by a fork. There was bacon, both the English and the American variety, perfectly cooked. There were grilled mushrooms, and some sort of fish soufflé, and baked apples with cream, and toast and marmalade and coffee and tea and orange juice. I ate as much as I could hold and wished I could eat more.

A bright blue sky contributed to the holiday mood. There was literally not a cloud in sight, and though the air was cold, it was still. Our dark and stormy weather appeared to be at an end.

It was Alan who, regretfully, reminded us that the situational climate was not so serene. When we had all eaten our fill, and Rose had come in to clear, he stood and tapped in his coffee cup.

'That was a magnificent meal, Mrs Bates, and we all owe you our most hearty thanks.' There were cries of 'Hear, hear!' and a little round of applause. 'I'm all the more sorry, then, to introduce a discordant note, but I must remind you that the restoration of electricity, though welcome, hasn't materially changed our circumstances. A number of serious incidents remain unexplained, and until we can sort them out, I must urge you, once more, to be on your guard. We hope that help may arrive soon, but there's no guarantee of when that might happen.'

'You're not going to confine us to quarters again, are you, darling?'

That was Pat, naturally. I was growing used to her style and tried to take the 'darling' in my stride.

'I have no authority to do that, and I doubt you'd pay attention to me even if I tried to "confine" you. I will ask – I will plead – that none of you go wandering off by yourself. I've no desire at all to cope with yet another disappearance, or worse.'

That sobered even Pat. 'Well, Ed,' she said with a grimace, 'do you want to read in the library, or shall I follow you about as you take some pictures? It's a fine day, at last.'

I didn't wait to see which alternative they chose. The sparkle had gone out of the day. Rather drearily, I followed Alan to the lovely little panelled den where the Moynihans had installed an anachronistic television set. 'Will anything be on the air?' I asked, without much hope.

'We can but try. I should think it's quite possible. Auntie is quite a power in the land, you know.'

'Auntie' being a quasi-affectionate term for the BBC, I had to agree.

Alan unearthed the remote, turned on the set, and found the news – '...power restored to much of the south-east this morning. Work continues on the mobile transmission masts and it is expected that most, if not all, will be back on service by this afternoon. Fixed lines will create more difficulties, since it takes time to determine the exact location of down-ed wires.

'In other news, looting in outlying areas of London has been largely contained, as the restoration of electricity has reinforced police efforts. The Metropolitan Police say that there are still some isolated problems in parts of Brixton and Lambeth, but police response has been restrained and little violence has en-sued.'

The announcer went on talking, but I had stopped paying attention. 'Phones, Alan! Communication!'

'And not a moment too soon,' he said heavily. He turned off the TV and stared into space.

'Dorothy,' he said at last, 'when the police do get here, I'm going to feel like the world's prize ass. Bodies to the left of me, bodies to the right of me, and I haven't a clue who's responsible for any of them. Not to mention two persons missing, presumed dead. If I hadn't already retired, I'd probably be sacked.'

'Well, you're not alone,' I retorted. 'I have not figured anything out, either. I've been making lists, but...' I raised my eyes to the ceiling.

Unexpectedly, Alan laughed. 'Lists, eh? Then I know you're functioning normally. I'd like to take a look at those lists of yours, but first, how would you like to go for a walk? Knees up to a longish stroll around the grounds?'

'Pining for the exercise,' I said gratefully. 'And if I get tired I can always turn back.'

'Not without an escort, my girl. Don't forget—'

'Yes, I know. There's a murderer walking around loose somewhere. Do you have any idea how tired I am of remembering that?'

'No more than I am of saying it.'

'I suppose that's why we're going for our nice little stroll. To try to find Julie, right?'

'I didn't marry a dunce, did I? But keep quiet about it when anyone else is around, just in case.'

'Aye, aye, sir. Fire when ready, Gridley.'

It was actually a beautiful day, the first we'd had in a long, long time. The air was very mild for early November, the sky that shade of pale aquamarine that I associate with Paris, almost never seen in America and seldom in England. When it's punctuated with a few fluffy clouds Alan and I call it a 'French Impressionist' sky – life imitating art again. There was no wind at all.

We did not, however, have a pleasant walk. I had to lean on my cane and on Alan's arm much more heavily than I would have liked, because the ground was still spongy from more than a month of solid rain. It was also littered with obstacles. Leaves and twigs, larger branches, bushes torn out by their roots covered what had once been the beautifully smooth lawn. Near the house there were slates, broken glass, unidentifiable bits of masonry. I soldiered on, unwilling to let my slight disability force Alan to turn back.

'Where are we going?' I asked. For we were not wandering aimlessly; Alan, though moving slowly in consideration of my knees, was clearly making for some destination. 'Where do you think she might be?'

'She *might* be anywhere, dead or alive. I've given some thought to the question however, and my idea is that she's alive and hiding.'

'That was exactly my conclusion!' I said

triumphantly.

'I would be interested to hear your reasoning.'

'That door was locked, always. She was scared to death of someone. She wouldn't have just taken a fancy to leave her room, not when she could ring for anything she needed and be sure who was at the door before she opened it.

'Now. There is another key to her room, the one kept in the kitchen for the Bateses to use. Suppose she realized that anyone could take that key and get into her room. She's not a terribly intelligent woman, but she has a certain amount of cunning, and even if she's been drinking, she could have worked that one out.'

'That could be what happened. Someone took the key and dragged her away.'

'It could. But I can't see it. For one thing, she would have screamed the house down.'

'Not if she was drugged,' Alan pointed out. 'Someone could have slipped something into her glass.'

'But then they would have had to drag her, literally, and as you're in a good position to know, she's not a light weight. No, if I were someone who had wanted to get Julie out of her room, to ... to kill her, or do her harm, I would have tried to entice her out. But she wouldn't have enticed all that easily – or at all, if the person she was afraid of were trying it. I think she decided in that muddled mind of hers that she was more vulnerable in the house than out of it, and left for another hiding place. But where that place might be, I have no idea at all.'

'I agree with your reasoning. That's the way I worked it out, too, except I do have a little idea about her hiding place.' He tapped his temple.

'Little grey cells functioning, are they? OK, tell me.'

'I have an unfair advantage, you see. I've covered more of the estate than you, most of it searching for someone. I seem, indeed to have spent most of the weekend searching for someone!'

'You poor dear. And this was supposed to be fun.'

'Yes, well. I began to ponder the Harrisons' idea of tunnels.'

'But Alan, we're much too far from the sea for smuggling to have been practical.'

'That isn't the only use to which tunnels were put, you know. Think about it, Dorothy. The house is, according to Jim and Mr Bates, riddled with secret rooms and so on...' He paused suggestively.

'Priest's holes – oh, how utterly stupid of me! Escape tunnels!'

'Or passageways to a church. Remember Mr Leatherbury commented about the High Church tendencies of the Upshawes? I asked him, while you were off somewhere the other day, whether there was a good deal of Anglo-Catholic sentiment in the parish. He said it had died out a bit now, but that according to parish records most of the communicants were, in the seventeenth and eighteenth centuries, very Catholic-minded. And that implies to me—'

'That they were actually Roman Catholic!'

'Or had been at one time. They – the brave souls who professed that faith – would have had to hide it, naturally. Hence the priest's holes. Now, often a Catholic household would have, somewhere in the house, a chapel, or at least a place where Mass could be said. But the vicar said he had never heard of a chapel here at the Abbey.'

I giggled. 'A secular bunch of monks, they must have been.'

'Now, now. Obviously there was a church here when the Abbey was functioning as such. But it was apparently destroyed when Henry shut the place down, leaving only the cloisters of the old religious establishment.'

'And the papists, later on, wouldn't have dared use any place that was so obvious for their clandestine Masses.'

'Naturally not. So the vicar's best guess is that they used the parish church itself, but approached secretly by dark of night. Hence a tunnel.'

TWENTY-FOUR

'Oof.' I tripped over a root and grabbed Alan's arm. 'Could we slow down a little? I'm fine, really, but I wouldn't mind sitting for a bit. If there's any place to sit.'

'Sorry, love. You should have said something.'

'I was perfectly all right until that last root. It reached up and grabbed my ankle. Reminded me of those trees in *The Wizard of Oz*. Remember? They struck out at Dorothy and Toto.'

'Downright malevolent, some trees are.'

We sat on a felled trunk while I caught my breath. 'So where do you think this tunnel is?'

'Well, it would have come out in the parish church, which is just across the river. The vicar says that end has apparently been blocked up; at least he's never been able to find it. And the entry, in the house, has kept its secret all these years, according to both the vicar and Jim. *But.*' He tented his hands and went into his lecturing mode. 'A long tunnel like that would have had air vents built in, and very likely an escape hatch.'

'Sure! Rather like an animal's burrow. Various ways in and out so that, if an enemy was at one hole, the badger or whatever could get out the other.'

'Exactly. And on one recent foray I found what looked very much like one of those emergency exits. It's not much farther now; do you think you can make it?'

'I told you I'm fine. But Alan – you're not going to make me go into a tunnel, or a cave, or anything like that?'

'Would I do that to you? No, I just thought I'd rather have you along. I hated the idea of leaving you back at the house all by yourself.'

He sounded apologetic. We've worked hard to keep a decent balance between his desire to protect me and my need for independence. Every now and then I get testy about his hovering, but on the whole I find it rather endearing – when not carried to extremes. I patted his arm and we continued amicably.

We were nearing the river now. I could hear the rush of water and smell the freshness. 'It sounds not quite so … fierce, I guess is the word.'

'It's gone down a bit,' Alan agreed. 'Now watch your step here.' He guided me around a fallen tree, to the edge of what seemed to be a grassy cliff, if there is such a thing.

'Erosion of some kind?' I asked, dubious.

'I don't think so. I think it's a kind of ha-ha.'

A ha-ha, as I learned on a trip to Bath some years ago, is a landscaping device serving the purpose of a fence without creating a barrier to the view. Imagine a lawn sloping away from the manor house towards a meadow where sheep or cows are grazing. It's a lovely, pastoral scene, but plainly you don't want the animals coming up and eating all your flowers and shrubs. Nor do you want to see an ugly affair of posts and rails in the middle distance. So you have your army of gardeners (we're in the eighteenth century at this point, and you're rich as Croesus) – you have your gardeners terrace the slope so that rather than a smooth incline, the lawn levels off for a few yards and then drops off suddenly, forming something very like a cliff perhaps six feet high. The vertical wall is reinforced with brick or stone, and there you have it. From the house the difference in level is invisible, but the beasts on the other side can't get to your garden. Somewhere you build a flight of steps so people can get down, if they want to.

'This is the wrong sort of place for a ha-ha,' I objected. 'No lawn, no vista, no livestock.'

'That's why I think it's what we're looking for. I think they – whoever "they" were, back during the Civil War perhaps – they built this to make possible a concealed door into the tunnel. Or rather out of the tunnel; it would have been used as an exit rather than an entrance.'

'And you've found the door?' This was getting exciting.

'I think so. There aren't any steps left, if there ever were any. I'll have to lift you down.'

'Don't be silly. Help me sit.'

Sitting on the ground isn't easy when you

have titanium knees. They don't flex as readily as your original equipment. And getting up is even worse. You have to kneel, and that can be very painful. However, I wasn't going to give in. With Alan's help I sat, awkwardly, on the muddy, leafy ground and scooted to the edge. Then, using my cane as a prop, I slid down on my bottom.

My slacks would never be the same again, but I made it.

I insisted on getting up without Alan's help. That required a good deal of manoeuvring, grunting, and at least one yelp, but I was at last standing upright. 'OK,' I said, still panting. 'Show me.' I brushed some leaves off various bits of clothing.

'You see that bit of stone? It looked odd to me when I first saw it. Not a match to the rest of the rock nearby.'

I moved closer and scrutinized it. 'Well – maybe not exactly the same colour. But different rocks are different colours. Aren't there different sorts of rocks, most places? I never studied geology.'

Alan grinned. 'It is refreshing, if I may say so, my dear, to discover something you don't know. In many parts of the country you get a mix of sedimentary and igneous rocks. Those are—'

'I know what they are. I'm not quite a dunce. Rocks compressed from silt, and rocks created by fire.'

'Roughly, yes. Well, the fact is, here it's all sandstone. But this is a piece of much harder stone, and it looks as if it was once part of a building. It doesn't belong here. So when I discovered it, I tried to work out what it was doing here, and when I came up with the idea of a door, I came back to try to find some way to shift it. I couldn't, but if I'm right about this, Julie may well have wedged it somehow to elude pursuit. So a spot of force seemed indicated.' He pulled out of an inner jacket pocket a small but efficient-looking crowbar, and from another pocket a piece of what looked like old lead pipe, and flourished them. 'Now, if you will hold the pipe a moment while I position the lever ... good. And I wedge the pipe over the end, thus—'

'Yes, to extend the crowbar and give yourself more leverage. That much science I know.'

'Keep your hair on, woman – I wasn't showing off my male superiority. At least I don't think I was. You'd best stand back a bit; if Julie mucked about with the hinge points, I may well pull some of the bank down on us.'

He braced himself as well as he could in the mud, took hold of the pipe with both hands, and pushed hard toward the wall to force the business end of the lever outwards.

It was as well I obeyed his injunction to step back. He did bring down part of the bank, but that wasn't the real surprise. It was the torrent of water that gushed out, shoving the heavy piece of granite aside like a falling domino, and knocking Alan off his feet.

He wasn't hurt. That was the first thing I

checked, the only thing I cared about. Sopping wet, muddy, and smelling like a swamp – an *old* swamp – he got to his feet with difficulty only because the footing was so slippery.

When I was sure he was intact, I studied him as he looked at me. We both burst into somewhat hysterical laughter. 'You look like the Tar-Baby,' I said when I could speak.

'And you like a most disreputable bag lady. We shall have to creep into the house by a back way.'

'What I'd like to do is get to the laundry room, strip, and wash all our clothes on the spot. But getting up to our room—'

'—stark naked, through several acres of stately home—'

That set us off again, but we sobered as we clambered up the bank and squelched off toward the house.

'You were wrong,' I said to Alan.

'I was,' he admitted.

'It was a great idea, though.'

'It never occurred to me that the tunnel would have flooded, though I should have thought of it, given the rains we've had.'

'And the tunnel runs under the river, and might have developed a leak or two in the past several hundred years.'

'Yes. In any case, Julie could certainly not have hidden in there. I was wrong.'

'Or,' I said grimly, 'if she did, and the flood came later...' I didn't need to finish the thought. I went on, hurriedly. 'But assuming she *is* alive and hiding – or being hidden – somewhere, the question is, where?'

And to that question, neither of us could come up with an answer.

When we got back to the house, we managed to sneak up to our bedroom without seeing anyone. I was tired, and nearly as wet and dirty as Alan, but when I had shed my impossible clothes and cleaned up a bit, I wanted some tea.

'Alan,' I called into the bathroom, where he was relishing a hot bath – his second, the first having removed only the top layer of grime. 'Alan, we're out of tea. Will you disown me if I go down to the kitchen?'

'You could ring.'

'I'm not very good at that, and besides, I want to talk to Rose. She seemed, this morning, thoroughly recovered from whatever fit of superstition assailed her last night, but I'd like to make sure she's OK. I promise I won't let anyone lure me into a closet, and if I'm not back soon, you can come looking for me.'

'And don't think I won't!' he growled.

I headed for the kitchen.

'Mrs Martin, what can I do for you?' Rose Bates was once again her cool, efficient self, disposed to resent my presence in her kitchen.

'I'm pining for some tea, and I'm sorry, Rose, but I'm just not used to asking someone else to do what I can perfectly well do for myself. It seems really rude to ring a bell and summon you to my side when you're busy doing something else. Is the kettle hot?'

She pursed her lips. 'It will be in a moment. I'll get a tray.'

I had thought we had established friendly relations, and wondered why she was now snubbing me. Maybe now that she had her electricity back and could cook properly, she didn't want help or companionship. In any case, I'd been put firmly in my place. I sat on a kitchen chair, feeling foolish, while she prepared a tray: cloth, cups and saucers, spoons, sugar, lemon and a plate of biscuits. I didn't dare protest that after that breakfast I wouldn't need food for a week. Nor did I comment on the lemon, assuming that the milk was used up, or sour. Electricity or not, it would be some little time before the household routine was back to normal.

When Rose had poured the boiling water and put the pot on the tray, I murmured my thanks and escaped to our bedroom, where Alan was pacing, in his dressing gown.

'Safely returned from my dangerous mission,' I said, and put the tray down. 'My love, I really am sorry to worry you, but you know me.'

'For my sins,' he said, but with a smile. 'You can't have had much of a talk with Mrs Bates. I've only just got out of the tub.'

'She wouldn't talk at all – back on her high horse. I don't think I'll ever be an Englishwoman, Alan. I just can't get the hang of "dealing with the servants".'

'Good job we don't have any, then. I gather

she was so annoyed with you she forgot the milk?'

'I didn't dare ask, but I imagine we've run out, or else it's turned. And I didn't really want the biscuits, but I didn't want to offend her. I'm sure they're homemade, and they look delicious.'

'They are,' said Alan, popping a second one into his mouth. 'Go ahead. You walked off your breakfast.'

'I'd have to walk home and back to walk off *that* breakfast,' I retorted, taking a biscuit. 'And speaking of home...'

'Yes. I tried once while you were downstairs. No signal. But I'll try again.' He found the cell phone, pushed the button for Jane Langland's number, listened, and shook his head. 'A signal, but full of noise,' he said, closing the phone. 'It's progress of a sort. Now, are you ready for a nap, or do you want to do some more exploring with me?'

'Not outside! I just got clean. I have to start our clothes washing, but after that – what did you have in mind?'

He leered at me and twirled an imaginary moustache. 'What I often have in mind – but later, m'dear, later. For now, how about the case of the hidden mummy?'

TWENTY-FIVE

'It's not so bad with lots of light,' I said in some surprise. We were in the bedroom with the hidden room, and Alan had opened the concealed door – carefully, so the grisly contents wouldn't fall out again. Alan had invited Tom and Lynn along, so he would have some help moving the mummy, and Ed, to take pictures of all the stages, and of course Pat came along with Ed. Jim and Joyce were there, too – it was, after all, their house, and their mummy, so to speak. So we were quite a little party, missing out only Laurence, who was still keeping to his bed, and the vicar, keeping watch over him.

The room was very cold. Either the central heating hadn't yet extended to this room, or it hadn't been turned on here. I shivered, not only from the cold.

Lynn wasn't terribly thrilled about seeing the horrid thing again, but neither Alan nor Tom would allow her to stay alone in her room, so she and I stayed in a corner of the room, looking the other way, while the men very carefully moved the body out of its prison and placed it on a writing table, Ed documenting every step of the way. Jim and

Joyce watched with, I thought, great distaste, while Pat was frankly enjoying the proceedings.

'I don't *quite* understand about the preservation of the body,' said Lynn. 'I thought mummification was a complicated process, embalming and wrapping and all sorts of gruesome proceedings.'

'I don't know a lot about it either, but I'm sure I read in some book or other that natural mummification can take place when the conditions are right. It would be very dry in there, next to the fireplace, and surely hot when there were fires. The dryness would help, but I would have thought the heat would cause decay, rather than preservation.'

'But there would have been very little heat, actually,' said Joyce, who had drifted over to join us. 'This was one of the rooms that was apparently never used, or not for the past many years, anyway. No one ever told us why not. I suppose I thought it was simply a matter of too many rooms to look after, and never having enough guests to need the space. I know when we first looked at the house, this room and several of the others in this wing looked like Miss Havisham's parlour, right down to the spider webs. Ugh!' She shuddered. 'It almost put me off the place for good.'

'It's a pity,' said Lynn. 'It's a lovely room, and once you get the grounds cleaned up, the view will be spectacular.'

'Yes, but don't you see?' I was getting excited. 'There might have been a very good reason why this room, and the adjacent ones, were shut up and never used. If someone in the family knew—'

There was a subdued commotion in the other corner of the room. 'Eureka!' said Pat softly, and Ed chimed in 'Gloriosky!'

We looked over to see Alan looking gratified. He held in his hands a small dark object, while from his fingers dangled a black chain.

'We've covered her face, ladies, so you can come and see without becoming unduly distressed.' Alan talks that way when he's reverted to policeman mode. We moved nearer. I sniffed cautiously, not sure how much of this my stomach could take, but to my surprise the only smell was a faint mustiness, so I got close enough to see properly.

'This,' said Alan, holding up the chain, 'has been blackened by soot, but it will clean up nicely, I think, as I believe it's gold. I don't know if you can tell, in its piteous state, but it seems to be a locket. If there are pictures inside, and if they are well-preserved, it may be of great help in identifying our young lady here. However, we may not need it for purposes of identification.'

With the air of a conjuror producing the rabbit, he held out Exhibit B. 'We found this wallet in her pocket. It contains money, in the old currency. We haven't counted it, but I saw a pound note and a half-crown. Those haven't been around for a while, which will help us date the corpse. Most important, however, is this.' He showed us, in a cracked vinyl window pocket, what was unmistakably a driving licence. 'Issued in 1958 to one Annie Watkins, born 1940, address Branston Abbey, Branston, Kent.'

There was a quick intake of breath from someone in the room. I couldn't tell who, and neither, from the look on his face, could Alan. In that moment he might have been a hound who had caught a faint whiff of fox. His head came up and I could almost see his nose twitch. 'Did that ring a bell with someone?' he asked, calmly enough.

Pat. It had to be Pat. She was the only one whose history in the village went back far enough. She would hardly have been born in 1958, I thought, but she might have heard something, might know the family name. She said nothing, however, and her face was utterly bland – which in itself was enough to tell me she was hiding something.

'Very well. If you think of something, any of you, come and tell me at once, please. I ask this for your own protection. Knowledge of a crime—' He was interrupted by a loud noise out on the lawn, loud and getting louder. 'Is that what I hope it is?' he asked, and strode to the window.

Just settling on the lawn, with that gentle lightness that always seems so inappropriate for something its size, was a small blue-and-white helicopter marked POLICE.

Alan sprang into instant action. 'Tom, I'll ask you and Jim to stay here with our poor Annie. Dorothy, I'd like you with me, if you will.'

Leaving the rest to do as they liked, which was to trail after us, Alan sprinted out of the room at a much faster pace than I could manage. 'I'll catch up,' I called to him. He said something and disappeared around a corner. It was left to Joyce to guide us through the maze of corridors and staircases and out the terrace doors.

Alan was shaking hands with the two people who had climbed out of the helicopter. The rotors had, mercifully, been turned off and were slowing to a stop. I panted up to Alan, and he turned to me. 'Dorothy, these are Detective Constables Price—' he nodded to the attractive woman – 'and Norris. My wife, Dorothy Martin.' We shook hands all round, and Alan went on. 'The constable in Branston saw our signals and sent for help, and this is the handsome response.'

'I can't possibly tell you how glad we are to see you,' I said, nearly in tears from the relief. 'I don't know what Alan has told you, but we've been having a pretty bad time here.'

'I've not said anything beyond that. Miss Price, Mr Norris, if you will come into the house – oh, this is our hostess, Mrs Moynihan – perhaps we can take a few minutes to put you in the picture.'

The detectives followed us back to the house, and I heard Mr Norris say, 'Retired CC – watch your step.' I think Alan heard, too, but he made no sign.

Once we were settled in the drawing room,

Alan kept his attitude of command. He had no intention, I knew, of stepping on the Kent Constabulary toes. On the other hand, he wasn't going to cede entire control of the case to a couple of young constables who knew nothing of the nightmare we'd been through.

'With your permission, officers, I think it might be wise to assemble the entire house-hold to hear the story. I may forget something, and it will give you the opportunity to decide what's best to be done. Agreed?'

DC Norris was inclined to resent being told what to do. 'With respect, sir, we have no idea why we've been called here, or what your wife means by "a bad time". As I'm sure you must know, there are more emergencies out there than we can cope with, and we're all very tired. We're merely responding to an SOS.'

'I do appreciate that, Mr Norris, and I sympathize. That's why I want to save as much of your time as possible.'

Norris gave a brief nod, and Alan touched the bell. We sat in uncomfortable silence until Mrs Bates appeared. Alan explained the situation to her and said, 'If you will, I'd like you to bring everyone else in the house in here, including you and Mr Bates.'

'Mr Upshawe, sir? And the vicar?' She sounded disapproving.

'If Mr Upshawe is well enough, yes. This shouldn't be too taxing for him, I hope. And please take DC Price, here, to the ... I don't know what it's called, the bedroom where we found the mummified body—'

There was a stifled exclamation from both the constables.

'—and tell Mr Moynihan and Mr Anderson to come down, too. Miss Price, here's the key to that room; you'd best lock it behind you.'

I was hard put not to giggle. The release from the strain of the past several days was part of my light-headedness, but I was getting a real kick out of watching Alan bossing around two police officers over whom he had no authority whatever. 'I'll bet you were a holy terror to your own troops,' I whispered to him. He merely lifted an eyebrow.

It took a little time, but we were finally assembled, all of us. All of us who were still among the living and could be found, that is. That was the first point Alan addressed.

'Now, I'm sure you'll want to begin this interview in your own way, Mr Norris, but you should know that three of our original party are not here. One is dead and two are missing, one at least of those presumed dead.'

DC Norris seemed about to strangle. 'Mr Nesbitt! There is a body upstairs, apparently long dead. Now you're telling me there's another body around here somewhere, and two more possible deaths? What the bl— what on earth has been going on here?'

'Oh, and there's the skeleton under the tree,' Alan went on, blandly, 'but we'll come to that in due course. As to what's been going on, that's what I hope you can help us determine.'

Slowly and carefully, with some occasional

prompting from one or another of the assembly, Alan detailed all that he knew about the eventful weekend. He kept strictly to what was known, leaving out any speculation. Beginning with the storm and the discovery of the skeleton, he led the rapt constable through the death of Harrison and the injury to Upshawe, the disappearance and re-appearance of Julie, Mike's presumed drowning, Julie's second disappearance, and the discovery of the mummy.

'So you see,' he said finally, 'why we were rather desperate to get help. I do apologize for usurping your job, but I thought it would be easiest to explain the complicated business all of a piece, as it were. Now I'm sure you have questions for all of us.'

There was a strained silence. Finally DC Norris cleared his throat.

'As I'm sure you'll know, sir, we were detailed to respond to a distress call, not to investigate a multiple homicide. If that's what this can be called.' He sounded uncertain about the number of actual homicides involved. As well he might.

'We need to check in with our commander for orders. If the mobiles are working, we can call. Otherwise, I'm afraid one of us, at least, will have to return to Shepherdsford. We're going to need the full SOCO team, and with everything else that's going on...' He shrugged helplessly.

'Yes, I understand. There couldn't be a worse time for you to find this mess in your laps, could there? Your commander would be—'

'Superintendent Westley, sir.'

'Ah, yes. And your CC is Sir Robert Bunyard, if I remember correctly.'

'Yes, sir.' He swallowed and tried to turn it into a cough.

'Well, you might just tell one or the other of them that I'd be most grateful for any help they can supply. We're not in danger of life or limb here – at least I don't think so – but we *are* badly in need of technical expertise. I've done what I could, but with no forensics team – and no authority – I haven't accomplished a great deal.'

For the first time since the police had arrived he sounded tired, and worried. He ran his hand down the back of his neck in a familiar gesture and then smiled at me in reassurance. I was not greatly reassured.

TWENTY-SIX

Mobile service still being unavailable, DC Norris decided to stay with us while DC Price returned with the helicopter to get more help. Norris had, then, a nice decision to make. Should he stay with one of the bodies (recent, mummified, or skeletal), guard the living victim/suspect (Laurence

Upshawe), or keep an eye on all the rest of us (potential victims/suspects)?

In the end he opted to guard Dave's body, I suppose on the principle that a recent murder, even if not proven, was of more interest than two very old ones, even though they were almost certainly the results of foul play. What forensic evidence there was should be protected. Besides that, Laurence was already being guarded, and there were far too many of the rest of us for one man to make any difference.

I suspected, too, that the poor constable had decided we were all a pack of lunatics, and the corpse in the garage was more congenial company.

So the pack of lunatics dispersed, each of us left to our own devices. Rose Bates returned to her kitchen, undoubtedly offended by the disturbance to her routine. Her husband went about whatever mysterious tasks he chose to undertake. Pat wandered off toward the library and Ed, camera in hand, to find some good shots while the sun still shone. Laurence went straight back to bed, this time with Jim to keep him company, while Mr Leatherbury took a well-deserved nap and Joyce tried hard to think of some way to keep her imprisoned guests amused and happy. Tom and Lynn went for a walk.

In short, we were back to where we were, almost, except that the presence of one young constable had, perhaps irrationally, eased our fears and our cabin fever. Soon, now, we were going to know what had happened. Soon we would be able to go home. Soon our lives would be back to normal.

Except for Dave Harrison's. And Julie's. And Mike's.

With a heartfelt, Scarlett-like vow not to think about them, I proposed to Alan that we revisit the mummy.

'I thought you found her pretty grim, darling.'

'I do. But I have a theory about her, and I'd like to know if there's anything to be seen that justifies my idea.'

Alan shook his head. 'Unsound practice. You don't formulate a theory and then look for facts to justify it; you collect facts and then—'

I made a rude noise. 'Don't be stuffy. You know perfectly well every policeman in the world forms theories ahead of the facts. You'd never get anywhere with tough cases if you didn't. Anyway, you're going to do the looking, not me. Nothing in the world would get me to look at that grinning skull again.'

John Bates was in the hall outside the drawing room door, hammer raised, preparing to board up one of the broken windows. 'Oh, J— Mr Bates,' I said. 'Is Mrs Bates feeling well? I thought she seemed a bit ... distressed, earlier.' *Testy* was what I really meant, but it didn't seem politic to say so.

'She is quite well, thank you, madam, but a bit upset, owing to her work having got so far behind.'

'Well, you tell her for me that we all certainly understand, and she's not to worry.'

He gave a little bow. 'Thank you, madam. I will give her your good wishes.'

'He is so exactly like Jeeves, I sometimes thinks it's Wodehouse I've walked into, rather than Christie. I didn't think they came like that anymore.'

'A *rara avis*, certainly,' Alan agreed.

We took the lift to the third floor. That fruitless little expedition this morning had been harder on my knees than I cared to admit; Alan could tell, though. He unlocked the door to the forsaken bedroom – I had begun thinking of it in those terms – and turned on the lights.

I avoided looking at the table where the mummy lay. 'Alan, I was serious when I said I didn't want to look at her unless I absolutely have to. But you're trained to observe. I want you to describe for me, in detail, exactly what her hair looks like, and what she's wearing.'

'She's rather nicely dressed, or would be if her clothes weren't covered in dust. Everything is black. Her jumper – sorry, sweater to you – is knit in some very fine-gauge yarn, not wool but a synthetic, I think. No moth holes, at any rate. It fits well and has a little lacy-looking collar, removable. It has yellowed over the years, though, and cracked a bit. Starched, I suppose.'

I cheered inwardly, but made no comment.

'You understand I'm describing the way I imagine her clothes would have looked when she was put in here. Her body has shrunk, so the fit isn't good now – but I think it was. Her skirt is of a different fabric, rather thin, and is – I don't know the word – it flares out from the waist.'

I risked a look. 'Unpressed pleats,' I said. 'Quite full, and hemmed just about at the knee. They don't make clothes like that any-more. And black stockings. Alan, I can't make myself touch her. Could you check to see if they're pantyhose – tights?'

I couldn't watch, either. It seemed like such a violation, an invasion of her privacy. Which was foolish. She was dead, had been dead for a long time. Still – she'd taken the trouble to dress nicely. She wouldn't have wanted some strange man pulling up her skirt.

'Tights,' Alan reported. 'Black, fairly coarse – dancers' tights, I'd say, not regular street wear.'

'Yes,' I said absently to myself. 'That would fit. I wore those about then, I remember.' Aloud, I asked one more thing.

'And her hair, Alan?'

'It's gone brittle over the years, and lost its colour. Some of it has probably broken off – the forensics team will be able to tell us more. But it was long, and she wore it pulled back, with a black ribbon, Alice-style. If I had to guess, I'd say she was a blond. All that black would be attractive on a blond. Oh, and she's wearing earrings, small gold hoops – at least I think they're gold.'

'Pierced ears?'

'No. Clip-ons.'

I hated to ask the last question, but I thought I knew the answer, anyway. 'Wedding ring?'

'No. No rings at all. Her fingers are shrivelled, though. It's possible any rings might have fallen off. I'll check.'

He had brought a powerful flashlight. He shone it around every crevice of the poor girl's tomb.

'I don't see anything, and I can't grub around in there without incurring the ire of the SOCOs. I shouldn't have removed her, by rights, but I had no way of knowing the cavalry was on its way, and I didn't like the idea of leaving her to the mercy of anyone who might think it a good idea to do a little cover-up. Now, what does all that tell you, my dear Miss Marple?'

'It tells me when she died, and tends to confirm my theory about why.'

'Ah.' Alan looked at me with that mixture of admiration and indulgence he uses when I'm being sleuthly. 'And are you going to share your insights with a poor dogsbody of an ageing detective?'

'Yes, let's – Alan, do cover her up. It's obscene, somehow, sitting here talking about her in front of her.'

To his credit, Alan did not smile, simply unfolded the sheet he'd used to cover her face and laid it gently over her. We went to a settee that gave off clouds of dust when we sat on it, and I explained my conclusions.

'We know the mummy – Annie, poor girl – we know she was still alive in 1958, because her driver's licence was issued then. Now. The other death, the skeleton – Harry – almost certainly took place in 1960. I thought it would be really strange if they were not somehow connected, so I thought about how to tell when she died.'

'The clothes,' said Alan, enlightened.

'The clothes. They are the fashions of the late fifties into about 1961. After that Mary Quant reigned supreme among the young Englishwoman who cared at all about clothes, so Annie here would have been wearing a miniskirt.'

'How do you know all this? I never thought of you as a fashionista.'

'I'm not now, but I was young then, just a little younger than Annie, if I'm right. We were a bit behind England in catching up with Carnaby Street, but I read the magazines and wished those styles would come to southern Indiana. Anyway, this girl was plainly young, nineteen or twenty, I'd guess.'

'Clothes again?'

'Partly, but mostly her hair. No one wore an Alice band much after twenty, even in Indiana. I never did, in fact. My hair was always thick and wavy, and not even ironing it could give it that lovely straight, shiny fall. I remember – but that's beside the point, which is that Annie was young, and tried to look her best, even though she didn't have much money.'

Alan was stymied by that one.

'The collar, Alan. That detachable collar. I'm betting it's plastic, yes?'

'*Plastic?*' He went back to Annie, turned back the sheet, and gingerly touched the collar. 'Well, I suppose it's possible.'

'Aha! I do know more than you about some things, even English things. When Mary Quant was first starting out, she opened a little shop in London, and one of her special things was little white plastic collars. You could take a plain black sweater and turn it into something chic, just by fastening on the collar. Easy and cheap.'

'And she started selling them – when?'

'The mid-fifties, I think, but they died out around 1960 or '61, when the mini was about to become all the rage. You'll note that Annie's skirt is much shorter than the calf-length that prevailed during the fifties, but not yet above the knee. Also, she wore dancer's tights, because she wanted black, and what we Americans call pantyhose – street tights – didn't come into use until miniskirts made them a necessity. *Et voilà!* She was twenty or so and dressed conservatively, but definitely fashionably, on a tiny income. The sweater, by the way, is probably Dacron. It was really popular for a while, knitted up very fine-grained, and was very inexpensive.'

'So she died at about the same time as Harry. Is that what you're saying?'

I had been a trifle elated by my discoveries, but I came back to earth with a thump. 'Yes, poor thing.'

'And – the wedding ring? Or the lack there-of?'

'This is the hard part, Alan. She doesn't show any obvious injuries, does she? I mean, she wasn't shot, or hit over the head, or what-ever?'

He already knew where I was going. 'There are lots of ways to kill a person and leave few traces. Poison, for one.'

'Yes, I know. And the forensics people will have to take everything into account. But I'm betting, Alan – I'm betting she was one of Harry's victims. I'm betting she either killed herself, or died in childbirth. Harry's child.'

TWENTY-SEVEN

'It's the wildest speculation,' said Alan after a long silence.

'But based on a good many facts. Her age. I know that from the way she's dressed and the way she did her hair. Or, OK, Mr Police-man, I surmise that. One is allowed reason-able deductions from the evidence.'

Alan made one of those see-saw, yes-no-maybe gestures.

'And given her age, we know when she died. And it was about the same time that Harry died. Isn't it really hard to believe that the two events were simply coincidental?'

'It's a house of cards – but you know that. Go on building it.'

'I think I'm done,' I said, deflated now. 'But it isn't quite a house of cards. Is it?'

He was quiet for a long time, making little puffing motions with his mouth, as if he still had his pipe. Finally he said, 'You're suggesting that Harry seduced this girl, she bore his child and died in her travail, or killed herself for shame, and Harry decided to flee the country – but someone killed him before he could get away.'

'More or less, yes. I know it's awfully thin, but—'

'Thin! It's tissue paper! We don't know for sure that the skeleton is Harry's. We know nothing about this girl but her name. We don't even know how she met her death. We can't—'

'Alan.' I put out my hand. 'Stop thinking like a policeman for a minute. What if my hypothesis – OK, my wild guess – is true? What if Harry did make this girl pregnant? And just suppose, just for one moment, that she had been your daughter. What if he'd done that to Elizabeth? And she'd died of it. What would you have done?'

Another silence. Then Alan said, softly, 'I'd have beaten him within an inch of his life.'

I held up my hands in the universal 'There you have it' gesture.

'All right,' he conceded. 'It's still thin as skim milk, but I'm beginning to believe it might be possible. We'll have to get—'

249

'—the forensic evidence. I know. If Annie, here, turns out to be *virgo intacta*, we drop the theory. But she won't. Poor Annie. No baby, no lover, no life left.'

But there, as it happened, I was wildly, seriously, wrong.

It was nearly lunchtime. I didn't know if Rose was up to cooking us anything, but she produced a masterpiece of a meal, as usual. I couldn't imagine how she kept on feeding us with no fresh groceries, but she managed to come up with a salad of canned and frozen vegetables, a pasta dish fit for the gods, and a chocolate mousse that I would have sworn had a dozen eggs in it. I raised my eyebrows at Joyce, who simply shrugged in helpless wonder.

'I don't know how she does it,' she said, shaking her head. 'Like Peter Wimsey with respect to Bunter's coffee, I don't want to know. If it's witchcraft, I'd rather remain ignorant.'

'If it's witchcraft, she's a white witch,' I replied. 'And in any case, a treasure.'

'And Mr Bates – he's just as wonderful. There is nothing he won't turn his hand to, and do it well. He doesn't even need to be told; he just sees what needs doing and does it. Jim and I couldn't possibly keep this place going without him.'

After lunch what I wanted more than anything else was a nap, but I resisted and went to the library to hunt down Pat. For once she wasn't there. A volume of Thackeray lay bookmarked on a table, which, given her taste in literature, told me she had probably been there, but she had fled. I noted with approval that she didn't leave books face down, and went to hunt for her.

It took me a while, and the siren song of that nap was sounding ever more clear and appealing, when I finally tracked her down, of all places, in Laurence's room.

Ed had taken Jim's place, and for a moment I wondered if I was interrupting something. Pat and Ed were definitely hitting it off well together; perhaps they had found a cozy place to ... but Laurence was up, sitting in a chair and wide awake, and Ed was on the other side of the room. Pat sat by Laurence's chair with a small notebook in her hand.

'I'm sorry, all,' I said, hesitating at the doorway. 'I was actually looking for you, Pat, but you're obviously busy.'

'Yes, but come in, Dorothy. I have a feeling you'll want to hear this. Laurence's memory's come back.'

She was right. I did definitely want to hear, and I thought Alan should, too. For once I remembered that there were servants in the house, and rang for Mrs Bates. John answered, though, and fetched Alan with his usual efficiency.

'Now, then, ducks, where were we?' said Pat.

Laurence smiled a little. He was plainly still in pain, and still in need of the long-delayed medical attention – good grief, we should have sent him back with the helicopter! – but he was ready and eager to talk.

'I've told you the first part of it,' he said. 'I talked to Mr Leatherbury, and was still very perturbed in my mind as to what I should do. You know about that part, sir,' he said to Alan, 'and Miss Heseltine has suggested that perhaps I shouldn't talk about it freely.'

'Quite right,' said Alan, nodding approvingly at Pat. 'Go on, please.'

'I told you, I think, that I walked toward the river, to the south, and was appalled at the destruction everywhere. I was never very fond of this house, but the gardens and meadows were lovely, lovely. They will never be the same.' His voice broke, and I was glad neither Jim nor Joyce was there.

'Well. The next part is very clear in my mind now, very. I became aware, gradually, that someone was walking behind me. I don't think I consciously thought "following" me, simply that someone was walking the same way I was. I turned around, and to my surprise it was Mr Harrison. I had not put him down as a nature lover, and I wondered what he was up to.'

He cleared his throat. 'I don't know why that attitude occurred to me – that he was "up to" something, except that he was walking in what I could only think was a furtive manner. I had turned around rather suddenly, I suppose, and he darted behind a tree, only just too late. He saw that I had seen him, or he must have done, because he came out and walked toward me, quite fast. His gait was unsteady, and I thought he had been drinking.'

'He usually was,' Pat put in, *sotto voce*.

'He came up to me and – really, accosted is the only word. He took hold of the front of my jacket and nearly spat in my face. He reeked of whisky. He was so drunk, and speaking so fast, that I could barely understand him, but he seemed to be threatening me. "You'd better not," he said, again and again, but I couldn't make out what it was that he didn't want me to do. All this time – well, I suppose it was only a minute or two, but it seemed a long time – he was holding me close to him and breathing whisky fumes into my face.

'I had finally had enough. I was not in a happy frame of mind to begin with, and it was just all a bit too much. I pushed him away, or tried to, but he had a strong grip, and though he stumbled – we both did, I think – he didn't loose his hold. And if he was angry before, now he was in a fury. He unleashed a stream of profanity and struck me, hard, on the jaw.' Laurence put a hand up to explore the bruise, now brilliantly coloured and swollen. 'Not broken, luckily, but it was a narrow escape. I saw the blow coming, but couldn't twist free to avoid it. And that's the last I remember until I woke here, in this room.'

'And where were you when this confrontation took place?' Alan asked.

'Fairly near the river, we must have been, because I remember seeing that the water meadows were flooded, and the water was running fast.'

'Were you able to strike back, at all, or defend yourself?'

'I made a pretty poor show, didn't I? Tussling with a drunken man, and laid out with one fist, like a baby in her cradle. No, I wasn't prepared for what he did, and after that one blow – well, as I say, I remember nothing more. I believe the Americans have an expression about a glass jaw?' He looked at me with the ghost of a grin.

'So, Laurence.' Pat leaned forward, her chin on her knuckles, her eyes intent. 'This is really important. Did you get any hint – noise, movement, anything – that anyone else was present at the time Harrison confronted you?'

He thought hard. 'It's possible, I suppose. There was a lot of noise from the wind in the trees. There were sounds, but I was a trifle too preoccupied to analyse them.'

'The wind in the trees?' asked Pat.

'Well – the rustle of leaves and so on.'

I looked at Alan. Pat looked at both of us and then back at Laurence. 'I believe,' she said gently, 'that the wind had died down that afternoon. You went out after tea, right?'

'Yes, I— by Jove, I think you're right! I do remember thinking that the floods would recede when they were no longer driven by the wind. So the rustle I heard...'

'Could have been an animal, a twig falling, almost anything,' said Alan. 'But it could also have been a third person.'

'Who didn't come to Laurence's rescue,' I pointed out.

'Well,' said Laurence, 'but there's no need to rely on my memory. If Harrison wasn't too drunk to remember anything, you can ask him.'

Oh. Oh, dear. Nobody'd told him.

Alan took a deep breath. 'I'm so sorry. There hasn't seemed to be a good time to tell you. Harrison is dead. He drowned that afternoon, near where you ... were.'

I knew he'd started to say 'fought'. But fought wasn't exactly the word, when the fight had consisted of one blow from one of the men.

If Laurence was telling the truth. But I thought he was.

He frowned. 'He fell in the river? He could have lost his footing, I suppose, but we weren't very near the edge. Unless perhaps the bank gave way – waterlogged – the water was running fast—'

'We don't know exactly how he died,' said Alan, 'only that he was found in the river. We won't even know for certain that he drowned, actually, until the medical examiner can have a look at him.'

'You don't know how he died,' Laurence repeated in a flat voice. 'And I've just told you that he struck me. I claim to remember nothing after that, but...' He looked hard at Alan.

'You have had someone in this room with me ever since I woke up. And before that?'

'You were never alone, from the time we found you and brought you in. The vicar kept watch most of the time, but he's taking a break, poor fellow.' He returned Laurence's gaze. 'And yes, your companion was there as much for our sakes as for yours. You were very badly hurt. We weren't sure, at first, that you would live. Your skull wasn't fractured, so far as I could tell, but there could have been a subdural haemorrhage. I wanted you watched very closely for any change.'

'But you also thought I might be involved in Harrison's death.' Still those flat tones. 'But— just a moment!' He sounded suddenly livelier. 'A fractured skull? Subdural bleeding? Harrison struck me on the jaw, not the head, and as flabby as he is – was – surely a blow from a fist couldn't cause any serious skull injury.'

'You were found, you see, very nearly at the edge of the swollen river, with your head on a large rock. Which was quite sufficient to cause serious head injuries.' Alan sat back to watch his reaction to that.

'Good Lord! No wonder I've been having God-awful headaches. Concussion, almost certainly, and you're very lucky I didn't have that bleeding, or you'd have yourself another dead villain.'

TWENTY-EIGHT

'But I don't think he did anything,' I said to Alan as we went back downstairs – using the elevator; my knees were getting very tired of all those stairs.

'Except, of course, to lie to us all about recognizing the skeleton.'

'Well – yes. There is that. But I can see why he did that. He knew that Harry had left the country in 1960. Had died in a plane crash. He'd known those things all his life. To be confronted, suddenly, with evidence to the contrary – it was too much to assimilate all at once. He told you, told us all, the story he'd been told as a boy.'

'Dorothy, that's what I'd like to think, too.' He ran his hand down the back of his neck. 'Damn it, I like the man as much as you do. But he could also have been telling the story because he'd already worked out the implications and didn't want anyone to know.'

'In that case – thank you, that elevator door is hard to manage – in that case, why did he go tell the vicar the whole thing later? No, I'm sorry, Alan. Laurence lied to us, yes, but I find it absolutely impossible that he had any reason to kill Dave Harrison. I believe he

257

tried to push Dave off because he was getting impossibly belligerent, and got himself pasted, but I don't think he ever struck Dave again. I think all that with Dave going into the river, and the rock, and so on, happened later, after Laurence was knocked out, and I think it was that other person who did it.'

'The rustle that might have been a squirrel? House of cards again, Dorothy?'

I stuck my tongue out at him, and would have said more, but we had reached the drawing room, and Mr Bates materialized at our side in his disconcertingly silent way. 'The authorities have arrived, sir, madam. They await you in the library.'

'They want facts, don't forget, Dorothy,' said my loving husband in an undertone as we went through to the library. 'No castles in the air.'

'But where else is one to build card houses?' I whispered.

The police had sent a large detail, in two large helicopters. Evidently the 'old pal of the CC' routine had accomplished exactly what Alan had intended, and got us the cream of the crop. I forget who all showed up, but beside the forensics people (complaining about working away from their lovely labs, but getting right down to it, anyway), there were at least two Detective Inspectors, several Detective Constables, and other lesser lights: sufficient force, one would have thought, to patrol the City of London after a terrorist threat. They were sufficient, at least, to make me feel more secure than I had since the moment I found the skeleton.

It would be tedious to relate the questioning and cross-questioning that went on for the next few hours. Everyone was interviewed separately, one at a time, while constables kept an eye on the rest of the group to make sure nothing of any consequence was discussed. We went into our activities, and our reports of everyone else's activities, for the past five days. Much of it seemed, to me at least, to have happened in another life. I'm sure I contradicted myself over and over; my memory was never terrific, and it hasn't become any sharper with advancing years. And how, for heaven's sake, was one supposed to remember, or even know, what had gone on in a rambling old house with probably thirty bedrooms and innumerable nooks and crannies? The entire cast of an axe-murder film could have been hiding in Branston Abbey going about their ghoulish work all weekend, and no one would have known. 'We wouldn't even have heard the screams,' I said to myself, and didn't realize I'd spoken aloud until the rather bored detective who was questioning me jumped to the alert, and I had to explain I was just wool-gathering. I'm not altogether sure he believed me. He looked very relieved when he sent me back with the rest.

'Headache, darling?' Alan asked me presently. We had been talking about Shaw's *Pygmalion* versus *My Fair Lady*, Pat joining in

with spirited opinions, and I was a little startled, but Alan's pressure on my hand warned
me.

'Oh, love, I didn't want to bother you, but
yes, it's been getting worse and worse.' I put
a histrionic hand to my temple and hoped
that was what he wanted. He sighed, stood
up, and went to speak in a low murmur to the
PC in the corner.

If he'd been anyone other than a distinguished retired chief constable, I doubt
he'd have got by with it, but the constable,
a young woman who looked to be barely
out of training, was awed by the whole situation – multiple deaths in a listed building, an
epic storm, and then an eminent policeman
among the personnel. She licked her lips and
looked around for someone to ask, but all her
bosses were in other rooms.

'You're quite welcome to come along,' Alan
said a little louder, 'if you feel it's necessary,
but I really do need to get her to bed. She's
apt to experience some nausea with these
wretched things, you see, and no one would
want...' He artistically left the sentence un-
finished, and the constable gave in.

'I mustn't leave here, sir,' she said nervous-
ly, 'but I'll ask DI Collins to send someone. I
hope she feels better soon, sir.'

'We both do, Constable. Thank you for
being so kind.'

That almost ruined it. The PC looked as if
'kind' wasn't in her job description, and she
wasn't sure she'd made the right decision.

But by that time Alan had solicitously helped me out of my chair and I'd assumed, I hope, the suffering-but-brave-about-it expression of someone with an almost unbearable migraine.

We kept it up all the way to our room. One never knew when someone was watching, or listening. Once inside, Alan gestured me to the bed, wrung a washcloth out in cold water, and handed it to me. 'In case someone comes,' he said in that low tone that is so much less carrying than a whisper.

I lay down, cloth at the ready, and said, 'All right, what's this little charade all about?'

'Mostly, I wanted to get out of there. It's the first time I've ever been on the receiving end of a group interrogation, and I had no idea how wearing it is on the nerves.'

'Most unfair of you to pull rank that way. Unfair to the others, I mean.'

'Indeed. But the other thing was, I wanted you to know that they're taking Laurence away—'

'Alan!'

'Keep your voice down! You're ill, remember? Not to arrest him. I knew you'd think that, and I wanted you to know before you learned it from someone else. The police doctor is worried about that head injury and wants him in hospital, at least until they're sure there are no permanent brain injuries. He'll have a constable with him, if only because he might possibly remember something else.'

I wanted to ask if Laurence was still under any suspicion, but there was no point. We would just repeat everything we'd said before. So I just smiled and said, 'That's good. I've been worried all along about the poor man going without medical attention.'

Alan patted my hand. 'And the other news is, Dave Harrison died of drowning – there's water in his lungs – and was almost certainly pushed into the river, probably with a tree branch or something of the sort. There's a small but nasty bruise in the middle of his back, slightly abraded.'

'So that settles that, at least. He was murdered.'

'That seems to be the inescapable conclusion.'

'But what a clever way to do it! His murderer never got close enough to leave fibres or let Dave scratch him – no DNA to match up.'

'And every single one of us was manhandling tree branches that day, so evidence of bark or wood fibres on the hands is worth sweet Fanny Adams. As for the weapon, it's probably part of a fine dam somewhere downstream by now. Yes, it looks like the perfect crime. And that, my dear, is why I wish I could get you away from here. We know for certain, now, that there's a murderer on the loose in this house, and you could so easily annoy him into ... something unpleasant.'

'Or her,' I said in an odd bit of feminism. Insist that the murderer could just as well be a woman? Maybe not quite in the spirit of the thing. And besides – 'So you find me annoying, do you?'

'Terribly.' He moved over to nuzzle my ear. 'And extremely distracting. It's a pity—'

The knock on the door sounded peremptory. We sprang apart as guiltily as if we were a couple of teenagers caught necking on the front porch. 'Come in,' he said, reaching for a tie to straighten – except he was wearing a turtleneck and sweater.

'PC Bryan, sir, just checking on Mrs Nesbitt.'

'Mrs Martin, Constable,' said Alan with a straight face.

'Oh, yes, sir?' The young woman's face reddened slightly as she looked around the room so obviously occupied by two.

I was pleased to see that the young could still blush, but it was a shame to tease her. 'I kept my own name when we married, Constable. It confuses many people.'

'Yes, ma'am. I hope you're feeling better, Mrs Martin.'

Now it was my turn to be embarrassed. I had completely forgotten our little ruse. I picked up the cloth, which had left a wet spot on the bedspread, and dabbed at my temples with it. 'Thank you. My medication is usually quite effective, if we catch the headache in time.' Which was the absolute truth.

'Um ... good. I came to tell you, Mr Nesbitt, that we've had a call from Superintendent Westley.'

'Oh, the mobiles are back in service now?'

'Yes, sir. We told him that Mrs N— Mrs Martin is ill, and he said you may both leave if you wish. I'm afraid it won't be possible to drive out for some time, but the rail service from Shepherdsford has been restored, and there's a direct line to Sherebury.'

There was our dream come true, just like that. Home. Away from this dreadful funhouse with its skeletons and mummies that popped out on every occasion, with its murderer happy in the knowledge of having committed the perfect crime.

This house with its unhappy host and hostess, facing years, probably, of repairs and rebuilding that would never erase the memories of this weekend. This house with its complement of other guests, all of whom wanted to get home every bit as badly as we did.

Alan and I have been married only a few years, a second marriage for both of us, but we have achieved in that short time a certain level of wordless communication. I looked at him and he at me, and I made my decision. 'Please tell the Superintendent that it's very good of him, and we're grateful, but I really am feeling much better, and we would just as soon stay until ... that is, until the drive and the roads are open.'

Alan squeezed my hand.

'I expect we'll be back downstairs shortly.' I smiled at the constable, and she smiled back and left to pass the word.

'I couldn't, Alan. Not when I'm really fine.

264

It wouldn't be fair to the others. And besides—'

'And besides, you want to unravel the rest of this tangled web.'

'Do you mind too much?'

'I'd rather have you safe. I'd always rather have you safe, but I can't cage you up.'

'Anyway, love, with all the police in the house, I feel as safe as the Queen. No one but a fool would try anything with all those minions of the law around.'

'As an American police officer I once knew was fond of saying, however, "most criminals are not rocket scientists".'

'You're saying he – she – the murderer might try to strike again, even with all the cops around.'

'You have to consider his – for convenience' sake, let's stick to a single gender – his state of mind. If he doesn't know for certain that we now know Harrison was murdered, he must realize we soon will. He thinks he's committed the perfect crime, but doubts and fears will keep nagging at him. What if he left something at the riverbank, something incriminating? What if someone saw him? Worst of all, he knows *why* he committed the crime – and *he doesn't know if we've figured it out.*'

'We haven't. Or at least I haven't, and I've been thinking of nothing else all the time we've been here.'

'But he doesn't know that. He may think we're about to close in. Whoever he is, he's in a state of extreme nervous tension, the worse since he must conceal it. He's like one of those rockets we didn't get to set off Sunday night – just ready to explode. That's what I meant, Dorothy, when I said you might annoy him. You ask questions, you know. Lots of questions. You might just ask them of the wrong person, and set fire to that fuse, and then...'

'Maybe I'd better let you ask the questions.'

'That would certainly be more sensible, but I have no confidence at all that you'll remain meekly one step behind me. You have too much in common with the cats, and with the Elephant's Child. Just be very, very careful.

'And now I think your headache must be just about gone, so let's rejoin the rest, shall we?'

TWENTY-NINE

It all looked so peaceful when we got back to the library, so normal. Pat sat reading one of the classics, Ed an art book. Mr Leatherbury, looking rested, had found that book of sermons I had brought back downstairs and was reading it with every appearance of enjoyment. To each his own.

Tom and Jim sat at a chess game, playing at that glacial speed that characterizes real experts. They were, now that I came to think of it, both extremely successful businessmen, which I suppose requires something of the chess-player's mind. Joyce and Lynn, in front of the fire, were studying an old piece of needlepoint, apparently with an eye to repairing the frayed bits.

Just a normal group of people, intelligent, well-to-do, with nice manners and varied interests.

And one of them – one of us – was a murderer.

Who, who? Well, it wasn't Alan, and it wasn't I. And Tom and Lynn are some of my oldest friends. Scratch them.

That left our host and hostess, the Bateses, Ed, Pat and the vicar.

Take the easiest one first. I suppose the saintly old vicar was the least likely suspect, so there ought to be a reason why he was the villain of the piece. But for the life of me I couldn't find one. He really was the vicar, known to Pat and the Moynihans, and had held the living for years.

Suppose, though ... I glanced at Alan, deep in last week's *Times*. I wished I could have this conversation with him, instead of just with myself, but the presence of the policeman in the corner of the room, unobtrusive though he was, effectively stopped any open speculation about the crimes.

Suppose, then, that Mr Leatherbury had known all along about the skeleton – that his predecessor had told him about it. Never mind, for now, how the previous vicar had found out. Suppose the present vicar had known all about it, including who put it there.

But, the more logical part of my brain insisted, one or the other of them would have gone to the police with the knowledge.

But maybe not, if ... if the murderer – the original murderer – had something to do with the church. A curate? A chorister? The churchwarden? A major benefactor?

That last was the most likely. Let's see. Mr Upshawe – Laurence's father – kills his nephew so that he will inherit Branston Abbey one day. The vicar finds out. Mr Upshawe tells him that it was more-or-less an accident, really, and he – Upshawe – will leave the parish a large sum of money to replace the church roof if the vicar tells no one.

Oh, good grief. That one was as full of holes as the roof of the cloisters. For one thing, that particular Upshawe had little money. Sure, he was going to inherit the Abbey, and the estate, but it would probably take every cent he could put together just to keep the Abbey's fabric in good repair, never mind the parish church. And he didn't leave anything much in the way of money to his son, remember. Laurence had to pension off the servants because he couldn't afford to keep them on.

If Laurence was telling the truth. Always if Laurence was telling the truth. And Laurence had displayed an ability to lie.

Well, but there could have been little money

left because Laurence père gave a lot of it to the church. And that was easy enough to check. Find out if the church, fifty years or so ago, had a new roof put on – or any other major repairs, I reminded myself; the roof was a figment of my imagination.

As was the whole of this scenario. Not only that, but even supposing the idea had some basis in fact, why would that give Mr Leatherbury a reason to kill Dave Harrison? I sighed and started off on another tack. Pat Heseltine.

Pat really was, on the face of it, a possible candidate for the role of Second Murderer. (I had to concede that she was too young to have done in the skeleton and/or the mummy, unless everyone was wrong about when those two unfortunates met their demise.) Pat was intelligent. She was an attorney, with the means and, I thought, the will to find out everything about everybody in Branston. Such people are dangerous, even when they don't have a face and body Helen of Troy might have envied.

She could have known about the skeleton. In fact, with the exception of Laurence, she was by far the most likely person to have known about the skeleton. The only thing was, suppose she did. Suppose she knew when and how and at whose hand the owner of the skeleton had perished. Why then would she need to kill Dave?

As for Ed Walinski – I looked at him and shook my head. Ed was a foreigner who had probably never heard of Branston Abbey until he met Jim and Joyce. How had they met, by the way? I'd never asked, but it was irrelevant. Ed was a photographer, devoted to his art. I could, just, imagine him taking pictures of the scene by the river as it played out, but I couldn't imagine him taking part. No, I should have made him the least likely suspect. Even my devious mind could not come up with a reason for Ed to kill Dave Harrison.

The trouble was, why would anybody kill Dave Harrison, except on the grounds that he was insufferable?

Well, now, there was actually an idea. I nudged Alan, who gave a start and opened his eyes.

'Aha! I thought you were much too interested in week-old news.'

He yawned. 'It's a fair cop. What's on your mind, love?' He gestured with his eyebrows in the direction of the constable.

I nodded to show I understood his warning. 'It's just that I was thinking about Julie. Are any of these stalwarts out looking for her?'

'I should think so. You remember that I have no role in this investigation.'

And it's killing you, I thought but didn't say. I contented myself with a sympathetic smile. 'But you told them she was missing, right?'

'Yes, dear,' he said, in the tone husbands have been using since Eve first asked Adam a silly question.

I kept my voice very low. 'It's just that I wondered – I mean, a spouse is usually—'

The warning look was more pronounced. 'I'm sure the detectives are taking all possibilities into account,' he said rather more loudly than necessary. 'And isn't it just about time for tea?'

It was well past teatime, actually, the police activities having disrupted our normal schedule, and I was hungry, but I couldn't get Julie out of my mind. It was terribly frustrating not to be able to talk about her to Alan, or anybody else, for that matter. But nobody could stop me thinking about her.

Where could she be – if she was still alive? Alan's idea about the tunnel was a good one, but it hadn't worked out. All the outbuildings had been checked, including the shed where she had hidden the first time. The house had been searched.

The house. This great, rambling house with thirty or so bedrooms, closets, attics – how thoroughly had they searched? And wasn't it possible, as Pat had suggested, that Julie could have been playing with us, going from one room to the next to stay hidden? I had pooh-poohed the idea at the time, but I was beginning to like it.

How could I suggest to the police that they look for her in the house? Request a word with one of them in private? I didn't want to do that without consulting Alan. Well, why not? If we were free to leave, surely we were free to have a confidential conversation. Except that it would look odd to the others if we just walked out.

I was glad the police were there, I reminded myself. Very glad indeed. But they were cramping my style something fierce.

And now more of them were arriving! I heard the whap-whap of helicopter blades drawing near, nearer, deafeningly just outside.

'What the—' Alan exclaimed, and went to the window along with the rest of us.

'Oh, no!' said Joyce, and Jim swore.

'It was inevitable,' said Tom. 'Are we allowed to talk to them?' he asked the constable who was minding us at the moment.

For the media, in force, had arrived. This was pure jam for them. The most exciting seams of the storm story had been mined and played out. They needed something to keep the readers and the viewers titillated and buying their advertisers' products, and here was a beauty of a new story. It had everything except sex and royalty, and I had no doubt the more creative members of the Fourth Estate would find a way to bring them in somehow.

The knock sounded at the door.

'I'll go,' said Joyce to the constable. 'This is still my house, regardless of what has happened here. I'll ask them to wait in the library, shall I, until your ... er ... your superior can decide what to do with them.'

There ensued a lovely hullabaloo. DI Bradley, the chief of the officers who had descended upon us, herded the media crowd into the library and began issuing stern instructions about all the places that were off limits to them. The men and women of the press were, by turns, intrusive, rude, noisy and insensitive, but they certainly supplied a grand distraction just when I most welcomed it.

'Alan,' I said in his ear, 'I think I know where Julie is.'

He looked at me sharply.

'I think she's in the house somewhere, probably on the third floor. I think she's been there all the time, just skipping from one room to another while we were looking for her.'

'It's possible, I suppose,' he agreed. 'But, as I recall you saying when she went missing, why would she do such a thing?'

'She's not particularly logical, you know. She's frightened of someone or something, and her idea may be to keep everyone guessing so whatever, or whoever, she's afraid of can't catch up with her.'

'Childish,' said Alan.

'Yes, but she is childish in many ways. Oh! That reminds me. Joyce said something, a while back, about her relationship with Julie. The two never got along, and something happened to annoy Julie even more – only Joyce never said what it was. Do you think the Bill would let you ask her what it was?'

'You, my dear, are beginning to display an alarming gift for English slang. Yes, given my position as a retired officer, I imagine Her Majesty's Constabulary would allow me to interview one of the suspects.'

I was about to object to the word when I saw the twinkle in his eye. 'And can I be there?' I asked, pushing my luck.

He sighed. 'I suppose, since you are now free to do as you please and go where you please, you could sit in a corner. I don't see what Joyce and Julie's childhood have to do with anything, though.'

'I don't know that it does,' I admitted. 'It's just a loose end, and I don't like loose ends.'

So, when Joyce had freed herself temporarily from the minions of Fleet Street and the Beeb, Alan diverted her to the dining room, and I followed. He closed the door, and we all sat around the table.

'Joyce, I feel a trifle awkward, since I'm here as your guest,' Alan began, 'but my wife thinks there may be some use in asking you to finish an anecdote you began earlier.' He sketched out what I had repeated to him, and then asked, 'Would you tell us what it was that further estranged your sister?'

'Oh. I can't imagine that it's useful in any way, but I'll tell you. It's just a little embarrassing, that's all.' She took a deep breath. 'I told you,' she said, looking at me, 'that the two of us never got along. Julie was always jealous of me, of the attention I got from our parents, of my appearance – I was always prettier, though what it matters now, at our ages – well. The worst thing happened when I was nineteen. There was a great-aunt, my mother's aunt, who had quite a lot of money. She never married, and I was her first niece –

274

named after her, as a matter of fact. She was fond of me, and I of her. We did things together, went places. I think I was almost a daughter to her, and when she died, I was really ... well, it hit me hard. And then I found out she had left me all her money.'

She fidgeted. 'Julie was just sixteen then, a bad age for that kind of thing. She'd always felt left out, because Aunt Joyce never paid much attention to her, and she thought it was grossly unfair that I should inherit a fortune and she got nothing.'

'Oh, dear,' I said from my corner.

'Yes,' said Joyce, sighing. 'She got really mad, and even ran away from home for a little while. I didn't know what to do. I didn't really think it was unfair. I had loved Aunt Joyce, and she me, and my mother – her only other relative – didn't need or want the money. Julie had never paid Aunt Joyce the slightest attention except to whine when an expedition was planned and Julie wanted to go.'

'That might have been somewhat unfair,' I ventured.

'You'd think so, but it wasn't, really. Julie had a knack for spoiling things. If we went to the county fair, Julie would eat far too much, cotton candy and corn dogs and funnel cakes and all, and get sick and have to go home. Or we'd go to an art gallery and Julie would whine about not having fun and her feet hurt and she was sleepy and ... well, you get the idea. She didn't really want to *do* any of the things Aunt Joyce and I did, she just wanted to tag along. So it wasn't long before Aunt Joyce and I decided it was easier for everyone to go by ourselves.'

'Yes, I see. A difficult child. But you were saying, about your inheritance...'

'In the end I talked to my mother about it, and made arrangements to give part of the money to Julie. You might have thought that would make her happy, but no – she wanted half. And you can call me selfish if you want to,' she added with some defiance, 'but I wasn't prepared to give in to her.'

'I don't see any reason why you should have,' I said warmly. 'You'd already done far more than you had to, legally.'

'Julie never cared a whole lot about what was legal,' said Joyce, and then covered her face with her hands. 'And how can I sit here talking about her this way, when she may be lying dead out there somewhere this very minute!'

'That's another thing—' I began, when Alan interrupted.

'I think we've taken up enough of Joyce's time,' he said. 'The media are probably slavering to talk to her again. Thank you, Joyce, for your candour. It can't have been easy for you.'

She simply shook her head, and we left her to whatever trial came next.

'And did that little exercise do any good?'

'I don't know. It cast more light on Joyce's character, anyway. But bells keep ringing at the back of my mind, begging to be answered,

276

and when I try, they go away. Pat says those kinds of stray thoughts are like cats, who need to be ignored to appear again.'

'And how right she is. Look, love, we never had any tea, and I for one am pining away. Shall we?'

THIRTY

But we were destined that day to have a somewhat longer wait before the tea we both craved. When we entered the drawing room, we were met by DI Bradley. 'A word, sir?' He said it politely enough, but his look plainly excluded me from the conversation.

'I'll just excuse myself, then,' I said, glancing in the direction of the downstairs powder room.

I really did need to use the facilities, and when I came back into the hall, I was very glad I had, or the sight that met me might have led to a regrettable accident.

For assembled there was the whole boiling of us – guests, hosts, staff, police and the media. And in the centre of the buzzing swarm was none other than Julie Harrison.

In handcuffs.

The moment I appeared, the ladies and gentlemen of the press swarmed my way.

Here was a new quarry/fount of information/ victim – as you choose.

'What is your relationship to the accused?'

'Are the murders here the work of a serial killer?'

'Are you a guest here, or a resident?'

'How do you feel about ghosts?'

The last came from a young man who had, I think, detected an American accent in my brief 'No comment' replies to all queries.

For I smilingly refused to answer anything. This was a new experience for me, and not very pleasant. I knew, too, that anything I said might be twisted to suit the purposes of the reporters.

America has its own gutter press, the sort of publications you see in checkout lanes, with headlines about aliens impregnating movie stars (or political figures, depending on who's the hot news at the moment) and the latest sex scandals in Hollywood, and sometimes even rumours-reported-as-fact about British royalty. But the slimiest American 'news' papers pale by comparison with the English. Certainly there are a good many well-respected papers, *The Times*, the *Telegraph*, the *Guardian* among them. But the worst of the rags in my adopted country print not only the salacious stories you can find in America, but pictures, as well, that would be treated as pornography in many places.

Well, all of us had our clothes on, and no one, so far as I could see, had an arm around anyone inappropriate, but I still wasn't going to say anything at all. Silence can be mis-construed, but not as badly as an inadvertent remark.

I finally managed to reach Alan, who was surrounded by his own phalanx of tormen-tors, and was also keeping a prudent silence. I couldn't ask him what was going on, with all those eager ears listening, so I simply clung to his arm, letting them take what picture they would – who had a better right to cling, after all? – and waited.

It was only a moment until DI Bradley cleared his throat and spoke in a voice that rivalled my best quiet-the-sixth-grade efforts in my schoolteacher days long ago. 'Ladies and gentlemen! Your attention for a moment, if I may.'

His voice had a nice tone of command. He was, I thought, going to rise even further in his career. The crowd quieted and he smiled kindly.

'Now I do realize that you all want to know what has happened. Well, there's quite a story here, and it will take some time to tell. Nor have I the eloquence to do it justice. And speaking of justice, you all know that there are laws about what can and cannot be pub-lished under certain conditions.'

Murmurs ensued, and they were not happy murmurs. He couldn't be talking about the *sub judice* law, could he? Because that pro-vision barred publication of details about a case once it had gone to trial, but we were a long way from that, surely. I looked questioningly at Alan, but he simply patted my hand.

'So, given the fact that we are dealing here with a citizen of the United States, who is under the protection of her embassy, I can say little except that we will be taking Mrs David Harrison with us to help us with our enquiries. Thank you.'

'What about Michael Leonev?' One reporter's voice rose above the others. 'I understand he's disappeared, possibly drowned.'

'Yes, that's our understanding. We will, of course, be on the lookout for him. But if he has indeed drowned, it may be some time before his body can be found. Next question?'

'They're arresting Julie?' I asked Alan, under cover of the volley of questions.

'That isn't quite what he said,' Alan answered, infuriatingly. And when I looked daggers at him, he went on, 'Let's get out of here. They're not paying attention to us at the moment; I think we can escape.'

We edged our way to the library, went in, and closed the door, and I exploded. 'Alan, what is going on? Where did they find Julie? What did he mean, help us with our enquiries?'

'Slow down, love. One thing at a time. They didn't find Julie, she found them. She simply walked down the stairs, went up to the nearest uniform, and confessed to the murder of her husband.'

I sat down.

'Alan,' I said when my head stopped whirling, 'I really, really need that cup of tea.'

'There's nothing whatever to prevent us going upstairs to make some. That would certainly be easier than getting the attention of either of the Bateses at this point, don't you agree? Let's go through the garden.'

The library was at the end of the south wing, the Palladian section of the house, and had a terrace outside the doors. I'd never used that way out, but once outside I turned to look at the amazing architecture, completely unlike the front of the house. White pillars, a small dome over the second story (this part of the house had only the two), restrained Greek-influenced decoration everywhere – 'It looks like a miniature version of the Capitol!' I said in awe, and Alan nodded agreement.

We moved down a couple of terraces, the better not to be seen from the house, rounded the west end, and entered by way of the servants hall where we had come in when we first arrived a hundred years or so ago. The elevator took us quietly to the second floor and we got to our room unobserved.

'Now tell me everything,' I demanded, and Alan did his best to comply, meanwhile turning on the kettle and setting out the teapot and appurtenances and the large box of biscuits he had raided from the kitchen – was it only last night?

'There isn't a lot more to tell, unfortunately. Almost as soon as Julie appeared and made her amazing statement, the vultures were on her, and nobody else could get a word in edgeways. The moment he could, Bradley exercised his authority, spoke a word or two in her ear, handcuffed her – and then you came on the scene and know as much as I do.'

That was profoundly unsatisfactory. 'Well, but ... where had she been hiding all that time?'

'No idea.' He put two of those big, squishy tea bags in the pot and poured in the boiling water.

'Did she say how or why she had killed Dave?'

'Not a word.' He picked up the pot and swirled the water around.

'I admit I thought she might have done it. I tried to tell you—'

'I understood, but I had to stop you because we weren't supposed to talk about the deaths with anyone else around.'

'Well, but ... oh, hand me a biscuit, will you? Maybe it's sugar my brain cells need. They don't seem to be functioning at all.'

Alan finished making tea in silence, poured it out, and handed me a cup prepared almost to my satisfaction, save for the unavailable milk. I drank it eagerly, drained the cup, poured myself another, and said irrelevantly, 'We should have asked them to bring us some groceries.'

'Which "them"? The police or the press?'

'Either. Both. I don't suppose they run errands for people, though.'

'Probably not. I wouldn't be surprised if Bates finds someone to send a message to some good friend in the village. If one of those mosquitoes downstairs belongs to a local rag, he'll want to keep in with the gentry, even if they are Americans. You may have your milk sooner than you think, my dear.'

'How long do you think it might be before the roads are clear and we can all leave?'

'Another day or two, I should imagine. The police can't use those helicopters forever; there are never enough to go 'round. They'll want the drive cleared and some sort of bridge rigged, and Bradley will get what he wants, sooner rather than later. He's a mover, that lad.' I nodded, and Alan finished his last cup of tea. 'I sincerely hope that by the time the road is clear, our problems will be, as well, and we can all go home.'

'But,' I said, my head swimming again, 'but I thought they *were* cleared. Julie has confessed—'

'My dear woman!' Alan turned on me a look of sheer astonishment. 'You don't mean to say you believe her?'

I opened my mouth, closed it, and glanced at the little clock on the mantel. An anachronism in the room, being of French and almost certainly eighteenth-century provenance, it was nevertheless beautiful. It showed the time to be five thirty, or nearly. 'Alan,' I said calmly, 'I think I am in need of something a little more sustaining than tea. Did you happen to bring any bourbon up with you last night?'

I sipped at it, slowly. I had no intention of repeating my folly of Sunday night. I'd barely recovered, nearly two days later. But I was feeling as though I'd been spun around rapidly, then blanket-tossed and walked through a darkened maze and left abandoned there. 'A riddle wrapped in a mystery inside an enigma,' I remarked. 'Didn't somebody say that about something?'

'Winston Churchill, referring, I believe, to Russia. Come now, Dorothy! This isn't that bad.'

'All right, tell me again, slowly. Julie Harrison has confessed to the murder of her husband. The police have taken her off, in handcuffs. But you – and presumably they – don't believe her. Explain, please.'

'I don't speak for the official police, my love, but I would be very surprised if DI Bradley believes a word of what she said. There are no flies at all on that young man.'

'I had that impression, too. He'll go far. But if he doesn't believe her, why did he arrest her?'

'Oh, you should be able to work that out, at least until you've had another few wee drams of that stuff. Think I'll have some myself.'

'Well, let's see.' I scrounged around and found some nuts to go with my bourbon. Maybe hunger was part of what was wrong with me. 'Julie hides all night, the night after Dave is killed. You find her and bring her back to the house, where she's scared to death of everybody except Mr Leatherbury. Eventually she opens up some to Pat and me. Then when we go to ask her more, she has disappeared. We look everywhere, can't find her. Then lo and behold, she comes prancing right out from wherever she's been and turns herself into the police.'

'You're doing fine so far,' said my maddening husband. 'Go on.'

'She turns herself in,' I said more slowly, 'and the police take her away ... oh!'

'Exactly. They take her away.'

'Away from whatever has scared her so. Away from ... from the person who really killed Dave?'

'I think the conclusion is warranted, don't you? And that's why DI Bradley let her, apparently, pull the wool over his eyes. She confesses, he takes her away, she's safe, the murderer thinks he's safe. Very neat.'

'I wouldn't have thought she was that smart,' I reflected.

'She may not be well-educated, but I think where self-preservation is concerned, our Julie is very smart indeed.'

'Except when it came to choosing a spouse. Her instincts let her down badly there,' I argued. 'And that's why I think she may be pulling a double bluff. She could have decided that Dave was such a bad bargain, she'd be better off without him. And then when his death wasn't accepted as accident, she hid out until she could work out what to do. Alan, that could explain why she was so scared of

285

you, in particular. You represented the Law!'

'Yes, we talked about that once before, as I recall. It doesn't explain why she would be so eager to walk into the arms of the real authorities the minute they arrived on the scene.'

'Well ... she'd had time to work out what to do. She might know that, as an American, she stood very little chance of getting into real trouble. I'll bet she's on the phone to the Embassy right this minute, especially after that very clear directive the good inspector was so careful to give her.'

'It could be you're right. It's all speculation at this point, in any case. It's been a trying day, love, and it's not over yet. What would you say to a nap till we can decently go down for dinner?'

THIRTY-ONE

As it worked out, Alan was in a moustache-twirling mood and we slept only a little, but were greatly refreshed, and much more cheerful, when we went down to dinner. Alan had told me what to expect, but it was still pleasant to find that our police presence had disappeared. 'There'll still be some officers in the house, Dorothy, but they don't intend to make themselves conspicuous. The idea is to let the real murderer think he's got away with

286

it. He may get careless.'

The media had also departed, thanks be to God. I knew we would find ourselves all over the evening news, if we turned on a television. No one did.

Dinner was therefore an enjoyable meal, even though we still had no fresh food. I hoped, for Rose's sake, that supplies would be forthcoming soon. An artist grows despondent when deprived of her best colours. Mr Bates was at any rate in good spirits again, serving with his usual deftness and style. Everyone was full of excited talk about going home, speculation about how soon that might be, plans for when they arrived.

Even knowing what I knew, my thoughts also turned to Sherebury. Alan had been trying at intervals to get through to our neighbour and cat-sitter, and finally achieved a static-filled connection. He handed me the phone.

'Jane? I can barely hear you. This is Dorothy. What? How are the cats?'

'Cats are fine. House is ... but they think ... sounds like ... disaster...'

And silence. 'Hello? Hello? Are you still there?' Nothing.

'Well,' I said, handing the phone back to Alan, 'that was some use, I guess, but not much. The cats are OK, but I got the impression something disastrous had happened to the house. I wish we could get back.'

'Jane will cope,' said Alan calmly.

'She will,' I agreed. 'Jane's specialty is

287

coping. I still want to see the worst and figure out what we're going to do.'

'Meanwhile, you can exercise your talent for – I won't say snooping—'

'You'd better not!' And I went off to snoop.

Pat was back in the library, back to Dorothy Sayers. 'I abandoned crime while we were immersed in it,' she said. 'Too topical. Now that we've light and heat and the other essentials of civilization, I can enjoy murder and mayhem again.'

'There's no murder in *Gaudy Night*,' I pointed out.

'Oh, don't you think so?' She smiled enigmatically.

'Anyway, I came to ask you something, but I'm interrupting your reading.'

'Never mind. I know the book by heart. What can I tell you?'

'Well.' I settled down in a squashy leather chair. I'd need help getting free of its embraces later, but meanwhile it was supremely comfortable. 'It's about the house – the estate, I suppose I mean. Someone, I think it was the vicar, said Laurence went to New Zealand in 1982. The Moynihans didn't buy the place until a couple of years ago. What was happening to Branston Abbey in the meantime? Surely it wasn't just sitting empty? And if Laurence was paying wages and taxes and maintenance all that time...'

'I wondered,' said Pat, 'when that was going to occur to you.'

I refrained from throwing a cushion at her,

though I thought about it.

'My firm, in fact, handled the sale of the estate. Both times.'

'Both?' I tried to lean forward, but the chair defeated me. 'The house was sold twice?'

Pat touched the bell push. 'This story is going to require some lubrication. Yes, the house – the estate – was sold twice. Laurence never did care much for living here. Oh, thank you, Mr Bates, I'd like some brandy, please. Dorothy?'

I shook my head. I'd learned my lesson the other night. 'Just some orange juice, please. Go on, Pat.'

'Laurence,' she continued, 'had qualified as a doctor by that time, but the practice here was occupied by the same man who'd delivered most of the babies for miles around. He didn't need an assistant. Laurence was champing at the bit. As there were no opportunities for him around here, he began to look around for other practices, and someone told him they were in great need of doctors in the Antipodes. So he went out there to see for himself, and never came back. He found a city, Christchurch, that suited him beautifully, with a good hospital – he's a surgeon, you know – and took up his new life then and there.'

'He never married, then?'

'No. There was a girl here he would have quite liked to marry, while he was still in medical school, but she was a flighty little thing then, not willing to wait for years until

289

he started earning decent money, not willing to leave Branston, sure she'd have plenty of better chances. She turned him down.'

Pat sipped thoughtfully at her brandy, and I started putting two and two together. Pat was about ten years younger than Laurence, and very beautiful, still, in middle age. When she was young ... ah, well, she didn't seem inclined to tell me any more, and it was none of my business.

'When Laurence was settled in Christchurch he wrote to my firm, asking us to sell the estate as soon as possible. I hadn't passed the Bar yet, so I wasn't formally associated with the firm, but I knew what was happening. Laurence wanted to sell. He was less concerned with the money than with ridding himself of the responsibility. Almost all the servants had been pensioned off by then, or found better jobs, and there were no tenants on the farms or in the cottages any more, so there were few complications.

'But.' She took another sip. 'There were also few buyers for a large estate with a very old house that would require thousands of pounds spent, regularly, for maintenance. The months went by, the years. The only people living on the estate then were John Bates's father, who was the caretaker, and John. He was a small boy then, but he helped his father as much as he could. We hired cleaners and gardeners and so on, to keep the place from deteriorating, but it was all extremely frustrating.'

'So John has actually lived here all his life?'

Pat nodded.

'But aside from his family, the house was essentially empty until the Moynihans ... but no, you said the house was sold twice.'

'Yes. A few years after Laurence left, we were beginning to consider the National Trust. They don't pay much, but they do assure that the property will remain intact and well-preserved, and the Home Secretary's office was getting a bit impatient. You know they oversee the preservation of listed buildings?'

'I do know, as it happens. My house is listed, and I had a go-round with them some years ago when it needed a new roof.'

'Then you'll understand why they were rather breathing down our necks. At that point, however, a holding company stepped up with an offer. Not a fantastic offer, but a way of getting it off our hands, and enough money to pay for some needed repairs and leave a bit for poor Laurence, who by that time had, I think, despaired of ever realizing anything from it.'

'A holding company? What did they plan to do with it?'

'They had in mind an institution of some kind, a school or retirement home or something. But apparently the plans fell through, because nothing was ever done.

'A few years later – around 2000, that would have been – the elder Mr Bates died and John took over as caretaker. He and Rose had just married, poor things, and the full responsibility of looking after the estate fell upon their shoulders.'

I shuddered. 'Not a burden I'd care to have thrust upon me.'

'Nor I. But they have done a yeoman job, prevailed where many another couple would have foundered. I doubt that even these past few days have offered the greatest challenges those two have had to face. Only a genuine love of the house could have kept them here. Now, where was I? Oh, yes, in due time the holding company decided to sell. The matter came into our hands again, and this time the Moynihans bought it.'

'I imagine everyone concerned was glad to get an offer this time.'

'Yes.'

Pat was looking at me with a rather peculiar expression. I had the feeling she was waiting for something from me.

'I suppose theirs was the only offer?'

She relaxed. Apparently that was the right question. 'No, in fact it wasn't. There was one other, but it was far below the asking price, and Jim and Joyce offered full price, with no haggling, so there was no contest, really. A pity, in a way. Most of the old estates have already passed out of the hands of the original owners, which couldn't be helped when the families died out, but I do hate to see them go to foreigners. Not that Jim and Joyce aren't perfectly nice people, but...' She shrugged.

'That's more the kind of sentiment I'd expect from the vicar, enamoured as he is of old houses.'

'You don't think I'm a sentimentalist? Well, perhaps the role does fit me rather oddly. Are you sure you won't have a little brandy?'

It was a clear dismissal. I said something about bed and left Pat to her Dorothy Sayers, but I wasn't sleepy.

The conversation had been interesting chiefly for what Pat hadn't said. Was she, in fact, the 'flighty young thing' who refused Laurence Upshawe's hand all those years ago? I could always ask the vicar, but he was a good friend of Pat's and might not tell me, even if he knew – the thing had happened before he came to the parish.

And even more interesting, who had underbid the Moynihans for Branston Abbey? It was easy to deduce from what Pat had said that he, she, or they were English. Could it possibly have been the vicar? Or Pat?

Hardly the vicar. The clergy in the Church of England don't usually have much more money than clergy anywhere else. There are exceptions, but very, very few could come up with the kind of money this pile must have cost – not to mention what it would continue to cost in upkeep.

Pat, then? Pat, who appeared to be cool and professional and yet hated to see the old estates fall into the hands of foreigners. Lawyers made good money, some of them, but a village solicitor? And what on earth would a single woman do with a place this size, anyway? True, Jim and Joyce were only two people, but it was likely they planned to use the house to entertain largely, in the interests of Jim's business, whatever that was – I kept forgetting to ask Tom.

And if either Pat or Paul Leatherbury had tried and failed to buy the house, in what possible way could that fact connect with the death of Dave Harrison, let alone with a skeleton and a mummy?

I gave it up, found Alan, and had that brandy after all.

THIRTY-TWO

I must have dreamed that night, though I have no memory of what my subconscious cooked up. I only know that in the morning I knew the answer. All the answers. Who killed Dave and why, who buried the skeleton, who hid the mummy away and why – and a lot more. It remained only to prove all of it, and that might well be a big problem.

I tackled Alan over our morning tea. 'How old would you say John Bates was?' I asked, without preamble.

'Early thirties, at a guess. Why?'

'And Rose is maybe a little younger?'

'I suppose so. What does it matter?'

'Just confirming my own ideas, that's all.

294

Are you about ready for breakfast?'

It was a beautiful day, and we had a beautiful breakfast. Alan had been a true prophet. Somehow or other John Bates had obtained fresh supplies. A bowl of fruit adorned the breakfast table, oranges and bananas and kiwis and even a couple of pineapples, quartered and then sectioned. There were fresh eggs, plainly new-laid, the yolks mounding handsomely above the whites in Rose's perfect fry-up. Milk for my tea and for the vicar's cereal.

'How is this possible?' I asked Rose in awe.

She smiled. 'John has friends. He sent a message back with the *West Kent Chronicle*, and a man brought a boat around to the water meadows this morning. I told him I'd cook him a very special lunch by way of thanks. The river's gone down a lot in the past day or two. By tomorrow that part of the meadow will be all mud, and by the next, anyone who wants could walk out.'

I smiled and shook my head in silent admiration, but I felt a little panicky. I didn't have a lot of time. And I had to be very, very careful.

As soon as breakfast was over, I sought out the vicar. I found him, as I thought I might, sitting on the bench in the ruins of the garden, reading the morning office.

'Please don't let me interrupt you, Mr Leatherbury,' I said. 'In fact, may I join you? I know some of the responses, at least.'

He beamed, and patted the bench beside

him. 'We can share the book. I should be delighted.'

So we read the Psalms together, and the canticles, and prayed for peace, and grace, and I felt quite a lot better when we had finished.

'You are an Anglican, my dear.' It was not a question.

'By adoption, as it were. I was an Episcopalian back in the States, but we're all in the Anglican Communion. At home I attend Sherebury Cathedral; it's right in my backyard.'

So we had a pleasant little chat about the Cathedral, and its Dean, whom Mr Leatherbury knew, and various church practices. Then he gave me a clear-eyed look. 'But you did not come out here for the office. Are you cold? Shall we go inside for our talk?'

'You're right. I came to talk to you. And unless you're cold, I'd rather talk here, where it's private.'

He inclined his head courteously and waited for me to continue.

For a moment I found that hard to do. I began tentatively. 'I hope you'll believe that I don't ask these questions out of curiosity. I am ... I think I am on the verge of knowing what has happened here, not just these past few days but over the past many years, but I need confirmation.'

Again he nodded.

'Very well, then. Pat told me about a woman Laurence wanted to marry, years ago. She turned him down. Was it Pat, herself?'

Somewhere a bird sang a wintry little snatch of song. Another answered. I waited.

'Yes, it was,' said the vicar with some reluctance. 'It all happened before I came to St Michael's, but Pat told me about it a long time ago. We're good friends.'

I tucked away that bit of information. 'Yes, I had realized that. She is a remarkable woman, I think. I won't tell anyone, I promise.'

'Thank you.'

'Pat also told me that the Moynihans were not the only ones interested in buying the house at the time they did buy it. She did not tell me who the other party was, but I think I know.'

Now his face was shut.

'I thought for a bit it might have been you, with your love of old houses, but I didn't think – forgive me – I didn't think you could afford it.'

'Nor would I have bought it if I had been able to raise the money. I am a priest of the church. I dearly love beautiful old houses, but it would be most unseemly for me to live in one. Remember what Christ told the rich young ruler.'

I nodded assent. 'Then I thought of Pat, but I doubted even she, who must have a good income, had that kind of money. And a single woman – what would she do with a house this size?'

Now his eyes were wary.

'I went to bed thinking about it, and this

morning I knew. Or at least I think so. It was John Bates, wasn't it?'

He said, heavily, 'I am not privy to the confidential dealings of Pat's law firm.'

'No. But you know, all the same, don't you?'

He sighed and nodded. 'It was very difficult for Pat. She knew and respected John and Rose, and knew how much love and labour they had put into this estate. She felt they, of all people, deserved to live here as owners, not mere servants. But they simply hadn't the money, nothing like enough. I believe John had been saving every penny he could, ever since he was a boy, actually, in the hope that one day it could be his. But alas, one must be a millionaire many times over to own an estate like this and keep it in proper repair. It was always a pipe dream.'

I could not speak for a while. Finally, I said, 'I hope you will pray for all of us, sir. We need it.'

'I do, and I shall.'

I had expected to feel some satisfaction. I now had all the pieces I needed to complete one part of the puzzle, but all I could feel was sadness. And as for the other part – I went to find Alan.

He was in the library, surrounded by a nest of newsprint. 'Look, love! Mr Bates managed to get some papers in this morning, along with the groceries. He is truly a man of parts.'

'Yes. Alan, what did you do with that locket? The one you found on the mummy? Annie's locket?'

If he was surprised by my lack of enthusiasm about the newspapers, he didn't remark on it. 'I gave it to the police. To DC Price, since she was the one who had to sit with the poor thing. Their experts need to take a look at it, see what they can learn from it.'

'Is she still here? DC Price, I mean?'

'No, I believe she went back with the helicopter late last night. Why?'

'Would she still have the locket, or would she have handed it over to one of her superiors, do you think?'

Alan put down his paper and gave me his full attention. 'Dorothy, what is this all about?'

'I want to know more about Annie, and that locket might tell me.' I hated being devious with Alan, but I wanted to do this my own way, and if I told him everything I knew – all right, everything I suspected – he would certainly interfere.

'Are you plotting something?'

'I suppose you could say that,' I answered reluctantly. 'Is it all right with you if I ask DI What's-his-name about the locket?'

'You're not going to get into some kind of trouble, are you?'

'What kind of trouble could I get into with police swarming all over the place?'

It wasn't an answer, and Alan knew it. He also knew that I needed my independence and that I had, so far, managed to wiggle out of whatever trouble I got myself into. I waited.

'You'll find DI Bradley in one of the third-floor bedrooms. I don't know which one. And Dorothy.'

'Yes, love?'

'Don't go and do anything stupid.'

I was sure he would consider what I was planning to be stupid, but I didn't.

Well – not very stupid, anyway.

I took the lift to the third floor. My knees were beginning to shake a little, and I didn't want them to give out on me.

There were twelve bedrooms on this floor. Heavens, I thought, what must it have been like, back in the days when all of them might be occupied at once! And no running water in those days. Hip baths, with the water having to be heated on the stove and brought up the stairs – no lift – by hapless chambermaids. And then there were the chamber pots to be emptied every morning—

I refused to follow that train of thought any further.

Which room would I choose, if I were a policeman in hiding? Not the mummy room, because that was the obvious one. I'd choose the room next door, or the one across the hall. Close, in case someone wanted to pull something funny.

The mummy room overlooked the back of the house. That's where the helicopter would land when it came back. That's where he would be, next door, with almost the same view. And he would have stationed one of his minions across the hall, to keep an eye on the front of the house and any comings and goings there.

There would undoubtedly be someone at the ends of each wing, as well. It wasn't going to be at all easy to do what I meant to do.

If I was right.

I found DI Bradley where I expected to. He was not, at first, best pleased to see me. 'I hope, Mrs Martin, that you haven't told anyone else that I am still here. Our presence is meant to be inconspicuous.'

'And it is,' I assured him. 'Alan did tell me you hadn't left, but I simply worked out where I would be if I were you, and there you were.'

'Ah. On the principle of the missing horse.'

'Exactly.'

'Will I seem rude if I ask you, now that you have found me, to go away again? If our voices are heard—'

'Certainly.' I lowered mine another notch. 'I came for a purpose, though. There was a locket – Alan found it on the mummy's body and gave it to DC Price. Did she turn it over to you?'

'She did.'

'If you still have it, Mr Bradley, I'd very much like to see it.'

I held my breath. There was no reason in the world why he should show it to me.

The thing hung in the balance for a long moment. Then he reached into his pocket and pulled out a small plastic bag. 'The chief asked me to give every consideration to Mr

Nesbitt – and to you. He apparently has a good deal of respect for your abilities, and your discretion.' He sounded extremely dubious, but handed me the bag. 'You may not take it out, you understand.'

'May I open it? Still in the bag?'

'If you can.' He sounded even more dubious. 'It's very dirty; the catch may be corroded.'

With very great care, I manipulated the locket, through the thin plastic of its container. Getting a fingernail in the crack between the two halves, I pressed the catch.

It opened, showing itself quite clean on the inside. The tiny gold ovals on either side framed two pictures. One showed a young girl with flowing blond hair pulled back with a blue ribbon. She was beautiful, with a classic profile, lovely bones, a gracefully shaped head held high, proudly. She wore small gold hoop earrings and a locket around her neck. The other was of a man a good deal older than she, handsome in a weather-beaten sort of way. He had a stern, unsmiling face.

'Thank you,' I said, and handed the bag back. I didn't close the locket. Let that be remembered in my favour when St Peter reckons up the score.

THIRTY-THREE

Now I knew what I had to do. I didn't like it at all, and I had no idea how to go about it, except that I must do it alone.

I would have liked a little quiet time in the cloister, but the men were out there working. I peeked out from Julie's old room that had such a splendid view. I could hear the braying of saws, could see, through the holes in the roof, Ed and Mr Bates man-handling a branch of oak here, Jim hauling away a pile of debris there, Tom and Alan setting up a sawhorse, even Laurence and the vicar gathering up broken glass with gloved hands.

No possibilities there.

I went to my room, put my coat on, and went outside by the kitchen hallway. Savoury smells were coming from the kitchen, and I heard Rose humming as she worked. I felt slightly sick.

The sun was bright, but not warm. Winter was coming. The grass, even after all the rain, was becoming dry and brittle. Leaves on the few trees still standing were fading from their autumn grandeur to winter brown or gray, or falling from their living branches to lie in melancholy silence on the dying earth.

I walked south to the water meadows. Here the mud lay thick, a fetid brown slime covering all the vegetation. A dead fish, stranded by the receding waters, stared at me with its dull eye. A boat was pulled far up on the shore, its sides mud-splattered, heavy footprints all around testifying to the unloading of provisions.

Walking was treacherous. I had foolishly not worn wellies, nor had I brought my cane. I turned back. There was no respite here, either.

My head was throbbing. The pain hadn't yet begun, but the pounding was growing stronger.

So unfocused was my mind that the helicopter was in sight before I recognized the sound for what it was, and then it was too late to hide. Whether the arrivals were more police, or the media again, I didn't want to talk to them. I didn't want to talk to anybody except Alan. Alan the forbidden confidant, Alan the one person I must not even be near lest I say too much.

But the person who stepped out of the helicopter, who was helped out of the helicopter by a man with a microphone, hobbling on crutches and smiling broadly, was Michael Leonev, aka Mike Leonard.

I rubbed my eyes and looked again. It was still Mike.

He struck a pose, using one crutch like a royal staff. 'Hail the conquering hero comes!' he shouted. 'Or rather, not so terribly heroic, and not the conqueror of anything in particular – but definitely, my dear, I have arrived!'

He snapped me out of my daze. I knew everyone in the house would be out here in seconds. I ran to him, faster than I knew I could move, and pulled his head down so I could make myself heard over the rotors and the clamour of the reporters.

'Mike, listen! I'm terribly glad to see you, but all that has to wait. Can you keep everyone occupied for fifteen minutes, at least? Longer if possible, but fifteen minimum? And *in the house!* As far away from the kitchen, and from the back windows, as you can manage.'

'Dear lady! Mine not to question why, mine but to ... yes, my dears! This thy son was dead and is alive! Kill the fatted calf! But do let's save felicitations until we're inside and I can sit down, or better yet lie down. I confess to a trifling fatigue.'

The women, being nearest, had arrived first and clustered around Mike, chattering and laughing and questioning – and being questioned by the eager media. I slipped away unnoticed and lay in wait for my quarry.

As I had half-expected, he was the last out of the cloister, walking slowly, as if reluctant to leave the work even to welcome back one we had believed dead. I cut him off from the rest.

'Mr Bates, there's something urgent in the kitchen. Can you spare a moment?'

He smiled at me, that movie-star smile, that

heartbreaking smile so like the smile in the locket, and gestured for me to precede him.

When we were safely inside, I saw the last of the house party vanish up the stairs in Mike's wake. Two of the men were carrying him, to the accompaniment of great hilarity. Only then did I began to speak, very quietly, in case any policemen were within earshot.

'John, I know all about it. I know the whole story, what you did and why, but I'm not going to tell anyone just yet. You must leave, you and Rose, you must leave *now*! Take your friend's boat and go.'

'Madam, what are you talking about?' He clung to the Jeeves persona. I admired his nerve, but I could have shaken him.

'Don't waste time!' I hissed. 'There are still police in the house. They'll figure it out soon, and then it will be too late for you. You have two options: stay and be arrested for the murder of Dave Harrison, or leave this place and save yourselves.'

He had a third option, but I hoped he wouldn't think of it. We were alone in that part of the house, and he still carried the hammer he had been using in the cloister. If he kept his nerve—

But he didn't. He saw the certainty in my face and broke.

'I— it wasn't murder! I swear it. I never meant— Rose, tell her!'

We had arrived in the kitchen, where Rose was stirring a heavenly-smelling pot. She looked from one of us to the other, turned pale, and dropped the spoon. It clattered to the floor.

She started to speak, but I held up a hand. 'Rose, listen. I know everything. John's family story, his love for this house, everything. And because I have a good deal of sympathy for both of you, I'm giving you this chance to get away. If you don't take it, it means a long prison term for John, and maybe for you, too, if you're convicted as an accessory. *Please* listen!' I was near tears of desperation. 'You only have a few minutes before everyone will come back downstairs, and they may come to the kitchen. You don't have time to decide, or explain, or pack up. Just *go*!'

John put his arm around Rose. She leaned close to him as he cleared his throat. 'It's very good of you, madam, but life away from this house would have little meaning for me. I will not leave.' Jeeves was back in perfect command of himself. 'But I cannot allow you to believe that I am a murderer. I must explain what happened. There is no great hurry. If you would come with me?'

I followed him to the part of the kitchen wing I had never seen, the Bateses' private quarters. The cozy sitting room had no fire in the fireplace – no dry wood, I remembered – but it was beautifully warm. On the mantel above the cold hearth were pictures, among them a large copy of the tiny photo I had seen in the locket.

'She was my grandmother,' said John, following my gaze. 'You probably knew that. But do please sit down, Mrs Martin.'

'I thought she must be. Did she die in childbirth?'

'She died,' said John with precision, '*of* childbirth, but not in the process. She killed herself when she realized the father of the child was not going to marry her, as he had promised.'

'The father being Harry Upshawe.'

John nodded.

'But John, who raised the child, then? The child who became your mother?'

'The child was a boy, who became my father. He was raised by the man who gave him his name, the man who should have been my grandfather, Samuel Bates.'

And the last little piece clicked neatly into place. 'They were engaged, then?'

'They were before that devil from hell came along. Annie Watkins was parlourmaid here then. There was still lots of money, and they had a large staff. Not what it had been before the wars, but big enough. It provided a lot of employment hereabouts, did Branston Abbey. Annie lived here, and that was the death of her. She fell in love with "the young master".'

His tone of voice splashed the phrase with vitriol.

'She was sure he would marry her. He was full of charm, so they say, and full of promises. But he wanted to make sure, he said, that the baby was a boy. He wanted an heir, and though the village was littered with his bastards, they all happened to be girls.

'So Annie turned down Samuel Bates and waited for Prince Charming to walk her down the aisle.'

'And instead he told her he was going to America,' I said sadly.

'He didn't even have the courtesy to tell her. She found out from one of the other servants. And then, as my grandfather – as Samuel Bates told the story, she dressed herself in her best black, kissed her baby, and took a bottle of sleeping pills.'

'And Samuel Bates went to have it out with Harry Upshawe. Samuel worked on the estate, too, I presume?'

'Head gardener. He meant to beat Harry within an inch of his life, but...'

'But he went that extra inch too far, and so Harry had to be buried under the oak tree. It would be easy for a gardener to disguise the digging. And your grandmother, a suicide, couldn't be buried in consecrated ground, so Samuel walled her up in that bedroom – for spite, I suppose. But wasn't there talk, in the village and on the estate? Questions about what had become of her body?'

'There was. Samuel was a large, powerful man, and he had a temper when he'd taken a pint too much. Nobody much crossed him. And Samuel never told anyone what he had done, not even my father or me. He simply said he'd taken good care of Annie, and he hoped she'd haunt the Upshawes to the end of their days. That was why—'

I heard voices and laughter. The hungry crowds were assembling for lunch. We had very little time.

'And ... Dave Harrison?'

'Mr Harrison,' said John, again in that cold, precise tone, 'was an arrogant fool. He thought he could push ahead his scheme about some sort of holiday camp. It would never have happened – this is a Grade One listed building – but he was about to kill Laurence Upshawe to keep him from talking about Harry. I have no great love for Upshawe, but he was of the estate. My claim as heir is better than his. I am the son of Harry Upshawe's only son. But the present Mr Upshawe did inherit, according to the law. I stopped Mr Upshawe being killed, but Harrison had already struck him with that stone. We struggled. Harrison slipped and fell in the river. He couldn't swim. I reached out a branch to him, but it was too short.'

'And you led the searchers to Laurence, so he could be found and cared for.'

'I should have taken them there sooner, but I was afraid everyone would think what you did think. I bear the guilt for that, if Mr Upshawe suffers any permanent damage. But Rose bears no blame. She knew nothing about it until yesterday. I thought it as well to tell her, with police in the house. She will carry on here until I can return.' He kissed her, then straightened his back. 'May I ask you to excuse me, madam? I must go to find a police officer.'

THIRTY-FOUR

'There was talk in the village, of course, even years later when I was old enough to understand.' Pat held the floor as we sat in the drawing room over postprandial drinks. It was our last such gathering. With a mummy, a skeleton, a recent body, and a limping dancer to transport, not to mention various pieces of evidence and, of lesser importance, a good many house guests, the police had commandeered workers from every available source to clear the drive and put a temporary bridge in place. Tomorrow we could all go home.

The media had come again, and gone again. The police had gone, taking John Bates with them. They promised to release Julie in the morning and bring her back here. I didn't envy Jim and Joyce having to deal with her.

'No one knew for certain what had become of Annie Watkins,' Pat went on. 'Some said old Samuel had disposed of her body in the convenient river. Some doubted she was dead at all, said she'd fled to cousins in Canada.'

'Not to her parents?' asked Lynn.

'She was an orphan. That's one reason she lived at the Abbey.'

'And Samuel never told anyone?' Alan asked.

'Old Samuel could be an offensive fellow in his cups. John Bates holds him in high esteem, as well he might, but the villagers didn't like him much. There were even those who said he'd walled Annie up in the Abbey alive.'

'Not so very far from the truth,' I said with a shudder.

Pat nodded. 'At any rate, I gather there began to be an odd feeling about the Abbey in the sixties, talk of ghosts and so on.'

'Was that why it was so hard to sell? I'm a bit surprised Laurence stuck it out as long as he did.'

'Perhaps there were other attractions in the neighbourhood,' I said, for her ears only.

She took a long pull at her drink and said nothing.

'What I don't see, Dorothy, is how you figured it all out.' That was Lynn again.

'It was the mummy, really, the mummy and Mr Bates's reaction to it. He's not a fainting man. Annie wasn't a pleasant sight, but neither was the skeleton, and Mr Bates dealt with it with his usual aplomb. So when he fainted at the sight of Annie, I thought it must be because he knew who she was, and had some association with her. He was far too young to have put her there, and anyway he would scarcely have showed her to us if he knew she was there. So I went about working out what the relationship might be, and ... Bob's

312

your uncle.'

'What will happen to him, Alan?' asked Joyce.

'It depends on whether the jury believes his story. The injury to Dave's back doesn't jibe with what Bates told Dorothy, but that could have been caused accidentally. It's a pity there were no witnesses to the thing. If I were guessing, I'd say there will be a conviction for manslaughter, voluntary or involuntary, depending on the jury's reaction. If he gets a lenient judge, he may be let off with a relatively short sentence.'

'I sure hope so!' Jim set down his glass with a thump. 'Just thinking about running this place without him gives me a backache.'

'I hope ... that is, are you going to have unpleasant associations with the house, now?' I couldn't help feeling that if I'd left well enough alone, some of that unpleasantness might never have come to light.

'I thought about trying to sell,' Jim said frankly, 'but Joyce talked me out of it.'

'It was Rose, really,' said Joyce. 'She came to me in tears, begging us to stay on. She plans to organize a team of John's friends to do his work while he is ... away ... and said we would be put to no trouble.'

'She could get a far better job elsewhere,' said Tom. 'Even tonight, upset as she was, she prepared food fit for the angels.'

'I told her that,' said Joyce, fighting tears, 'and she said, "John would die in prison if he didn't know he had this house to come back to."'"

It was time to change the subject. I looked across the room at our dancer, who was sitting in a chair by the fire, his foot propped up on a cushion. 'Mike, we managed to spoil your homecoming, didn't we? Or rather I did. The others have heard your story, I suppose, but I haven't.'

'Oh, I don't mind telling it again. The stripped-down story, this time. I did *rather* embroider it earlier, I'm afraid.'

'All right, you don't need to spare my feelings. I did ask you to spin it out as long as possible, and you performed nobly. It's not your fault if it did turn out not to be necessary. Go ahead and give us the penny-plain version.'

'Well, I jumped across the river, as you knew I was going to. And all would have been well if the opposite bank hadn't been so littered with leaves. I slipped on landing, and near as nothing ended up in the river. However, I managed to hang on to various bits of vegetation – what sort, I have *no* idea, not being a countryman. When I got to my feet I realized I'd damaged myself, twisted an ankle or something of the sort.'

'Mike! Were you badly hurt? Will you be able to dance again?'

'All in good time, dear lady. I was in some pain, but a dancer learns to work through that, so I started walking. I had no choice, really. I could sit there on the ground and howl till the cows came home, and no one would come to pick baby up and carry him home to mummy. Oops, sorry, poor choice of words.'

Someone snickered.

'Fortunately the road was more-or-less clear of traffic. Because I had just reached it when I stepped on something that gave way under me, and that's all I remember until I woke up in hospital in – is it Shepherdsford? That just-bigger-than-a-village place not far from here?'

The vicar nodded. He looked very tired, I thought.

'And there was a *beautiful* doctor's face looking into mine. Unfortunately he was only checking my eyes for the proper response, to make sure I wasn't dead or something. I'd been unconscious for quite some time, I gathered. Some kind person had found me by the side of the road and brought me in, and I gather all the doctors were horrified, I do mean *horrified*, my dears, when I told them how far I'd walked on what turned out to be a broken ankle.'

'Mike, enough,' I said, interrupting. 'Tell me this minute, will you dance again?'

'They say there's no reason why not, if I'm a good little boy and do as I'm told. It seems a good clean break heals much better than torn muscle tissue. In fact that ankle may end up being stronger than the other.'

He had dropped his affectations for a moment. This was a serious matter. 'I'm delighted to hear it,' I said in great relief. 'I'm waiting to see you dance Siegfried. But go on.'

'Well, that was Saturday. I was more or less *non compos mentis* for a day or so, raving like a loony, they told me, and then they eased off those *lovely* pain meds, and I remembered why I came, but there was no way they could notify anyone here, because the phones were still out. I wanted them to go and rescue poor Laurence, but they couldn't do that, either, not without a helicopter, and there was actually *none* available. You have *no* idea, my dears, what the world looks like out there. One would swear a *bomb* had been dropped, and along with all the visible damage, the villages are positively *littered* with the halt and the lame. They pushed me out of hospital the first minute they could, because they needed the bed, what with the injured pouring in from every part of the county.

'Well, I was feeling very much the fool. All those would-be-heroics, and no one could help Laurence after all. And then he turned up, not doing so badly, and told me all that had happened in my absence, and I saw what a *splendid* opportunity I had been given for publicity, so of course I notified the media – and here I am, like the proverbial bad penny.'

'And speaking on behalf of all lovers of the dance, I say, here's to your prompt recovery.' Pat raised her glass and we all followed suit.

Later Alan and I were getting ready for bed and doing all but the last-minute packing. We had managed a better connection with Jane and learned that the 'disaster' she had mentioned was our predicament at Branston Abbey, not some awful damage to our house. So I was trying to tie up the last loose ends of the Abbey problem.

I said, 'The one thing I didn't work out is what Julie was so afraid of.'

'Bates, obviously. She followed Dave and saw what happened, but not very clearly. She thought Bates pushed Dave into the river.'

'She said she didn't follow them.'

'She lied, love. She didn't want anyone to know what she knew. But while she was still suffering from hypothermia and somewhat confused, she said enough to the vicar to make him very uneasy. He came to me after Julie was "arrested" to tell me he didn't think she could have done it.'

'So you knew all along what happened!'

'Not "all along", only since her arrest. And I didn't "know" anything, only what a confused woman thought she had seen when under the influence of considerable alcohol.'

'But if you'd told me, I wouldn't have been so worried about helping John and Rose!'

'And if you'd told me what you were going to do, I'd have been able to fend you off.' He yawned and turned out the light. 'I think we're square. Anyway, if I'd told you, you wouldn't have been able to go home and tell everyone how you figured out that the butler did it.'

I threw my pillow at him.